Catching Rain

the sequel to

Mending Stone

Sharon Duerst

Praise for Catching Rain

"I had my coffee and started reading,
ate lunch while reading and didn't stop
until reaching the beautiful ending!
I laughed…I cried…I rejoiced in how Mia changed her life!
I loved this story!
It reminded me how important it is to take risks in life
and move toward what is wanted— even if not knowing
at all
where it will lead.
Following intuition can be life altering!
I feel the characters are friends, and I wonder what is next
in their lives!
I don't want to let them go!"
~Jet McCann

"I truly enjoyed it. I appreciate the characters so much."
~Karen Callin

"I loved the depth of the story, and the characters!
I couldn't put it down until I finished reading!
It was so good! Nothing left out! I loved the ending!!
I'm amazed at the places the story went.
I want to look up the attractions at the back of the book
and plan a Catching Rain Itinerary!"
~Karen Martell

"I could not put this book down! So easy to read…Really flowed. Great story line…Loved reading about the different locations."

~Katrena Meyer

"A great book!
The poetry is fascinating.
I love the travel, and especially being able to relate
to all the places in the Pacific Northwest.
I also love a great love story, and I needed tissue at the end!"

~Connie Van Sickle

"Catching Rain picks up where Mending Stone left off,
tied up loose ends with enough tragedy and heartache,
but ends beautifully—exactly where you would want it to!"

~Debbie Wiemeyer

"Love the story—the mystery unfolding about who Mia is…
Love the focus on intuition,
and attention to dreams and images…
Love the relationships…Love the locations…
many of my favorite places…the Northwest…
San Francisco…Mexico…
What a lovely story! I loved reading this book!"

~Maria Carlos

Praise for Mending Stone

"Mending Stone warmed my heart. It filled my spirit with uplifting whispers of the oft times mystical bond between mother and child, the reality of intuition, and the wisdom of listening to and following your heart."

~Sue Patton Thoele, author:
The Mindful Woman, and The Courage To Be Yourself,
among others

"Excellent. Fabulous. I will read it again! And I want to send a copy to several family members."

~Kathryn Olmstead

"I loved it! The story held me to the very end—and then, I cried."

~Anna Aram

"A spiritual journey pebbled with friends, family, and Native Americans, from the Pacific Northwest to Texas."

~Ginger Dehlinger, author: Brute Heart

"I finished Mending Stone in one day! I loved it! I can't wait for the sequel to see what else happens!"

~Jet McCann

"You are a talent!" *~Judy Jacobs Litchfield*

"Reading late into the night, I had to know: why were the two women brought together in such a haunting way? So many questions drew me from page to page to page! The ending was satisfying and sweet—but still I want more!"

~AnnaMariah Nau

"I couldn't put the book down!"

~Kathy Bingham

"A gem of a read. It was well written and very descriptive. It reinforced my sense that women should rely on their instincts. I can't wait to read more about Mia and Gerald in the next book."

~Kay DeBast

"A very real account of a woman struggling with grief and self-discovery. Vivid descriptions with true-to-life experiences. The poetry added a thoughtful angle to what was happening. I enjoyed the story within a story. I put the book aside with 36 pages left to read—I didn't want the story to end! A wonderful book! I can't wait for the next one."

~Simone Neall

"A captivating story—it took me to unknown places that now seem familiar."

~Karen Martell

More Praise for Mending Stone

"It is REALLY good. I couldn't wait to see what was going to happen! It reminds me of a Nicholas Sparks story. And everyone can relate to characters looking to find 'sweetness.'"

~Judy Bair

"I finally read your book, Sharon! You are an amazing writer!"

~Kim Olmstead

"Beautiful. Descriptive. And touching. A perfect read with love, death, mystery, thrills, and humor. A must read for anyone who loves the craft of writing and a spellbinding story."

~Joseph Duerst

"A gem of a read. It was well written and very descriptive. It reinforced my sense that women should rely on their instincts. I can't wait to read more about Mia and Gerald in the next book."

~Kay DeBast

"Sharon…Just finished your book, reading the last 1/3 in one sitting! I thoroughly enjoyed it, and can't wait for more!"

~Dianne Espy

"Very engaging! I really enjoyed it! An interesting adventure!"

~Bradley Lorang

"What a lovely read. A very spiritual book, with love crossing the lines of heritage and tradition. The author obviously dug deep into her heart to breathe life into her characters. I've hear there is a follow-up coming soon. Looking forward to it!"

~Kate Ayers, author: A Murder of Crows, and A Walk of Snipes

"Loved your book, read the first 50 pages (in the car) between The Dalles and the Oregon Coast. I can't believe this is your first book! It is so good! I know I will love the sequel, too!"

~Janet Clark Thomas

"Hi Sharon, I started your book this weekend and could not put it down and finished quickly. It was really good and you are very talented. Is there a sequel? It would be read! MOVE over Danielle Steel! WOW Sharon…"

~Katrena Meyer

"Part romance...Scenes with Gerald are full of sexual tension and intrigue; a reader can't help but fall for him...Landscapes are vivid...The mystery unfolds in snippets...Engaging story with developed characters and a sweet satisfying ending!"

~Gretchen Heberling

More Praise for Mending Stone

“Sharon, this is a haunting story that has triggered all manner of questions for me! I paid very little attention to my parents' stories when I was growing up and now they are not available to tell their tales. I found Mia's journey riveting, not just the sleuthing out her roots, but her reflections on her relationships and development of new ones. What a gifted storyteller you are. Thank you.”

~C. P.

“Great job! Can't wait for the sequel! This book brought back great memories of the area I'm from.”

~Connie Van Sickle

“I loved it! The story held me to the very end—and then, I cried.”

~Anna Aram

“Haunting. This book cast a spell over me and drew me through Mia's story like a magnet. Hers is a calling that we can relate to, but not many of us have the courage to pursue. Thanks to the author for such a compelling read.”

~Kate Bracy, award-winning author: That Crazy Little Thing

“Enjoyable. Thought provoking. I found myself asking, ‘What if…’”

~Shari Austin

“I'm reading your book and enjoying it. I have friends standing in line to read it.”

~Mollie Brusseau

“Nice little touches. Romance is definitely part of it...A slight overlay of fate...Nicely done...Wonderful descriptions...”

~Rodger Nichols-Haystack Broadcasting

“The descriptive vision brings us directly into the story. I love the interplay of storylines. We’re carried with excellent detail into the dramatic story of Rosa, the pace of her hard life. A fun book to read!”

~Diane Conroy

“I enjoyed reading this story of a woman learning what it means to have loved and lost, and to travel a path to understanding, healing, and strength. My favorite scene involves her finally claiming her power. And, I loved discovering the answers to the mystery of her family.”

~Maria Carlos

“Portraits of betrayal, friendship, and loss—with a satisfying outcome of hope.”

~Debbie Wiemeyer

“An enthralling read! Well researched, richly descriptive in a unique writing style fitting the story. I wanted to keep reading!”

~Lisa Anderson, independent reviewer

Catching Rain

a novel

Sharon Duerst

This novel is a work of fiction. Names, characters, incidents, and places (except those listed in *Attractions*) are either the product of the author's imagination or are used fictitiously. All characters are fictitious, and any similarity to people living or dead is purely coincidental.

Published by White Spring Publishing
21698 Rickard Road, Bend, OR 97702

Printed in the United States of America
ISBN: 978-0985537821 0985537821 (paperback)

Library of Congress Control Number: 2014914812

Cover design by Joseph J. Duerst

Cover Images:

"*raindrops on my car.*" by Till Krech (name of "*raindrops on my car.*" http://www.flickr.com/photos/extranoise/232823269/in/photostream/Modifications: multiple iterations on cover, opacity reduced, image cropped, proportions distorted, text and other images overlaid.

"*Just a little blue*" UBC Botanical Gardens" Image by Kenny Louie http://www.flickr.com/photos/kwl/8861889910/ Modifications: image cropped, text and other images overlaid.

Acknowledgements

Deepest gratitude to my dear husband, Jonathan, and our children, Gretchen and Joseph, who sustain and inspire me. My life and words are richer for the love and life we share.

To so many others who have contributed in large and small or inspiring and generous ways: Maggie Annschild, Kate Ayers, Elizabeth Berg, Gloria Bird, Rebecca Towner Bolin, Book Clubs: Meetup Moms of Central Oregon & P.M. Divas, Kate Bracy, Mollie Brusseau, Bunco Girls, Maria Carlos & Dusty Vonberg, Kathy Cascade, Carol Cassara, Central OR Writers Guild, Diane Conroy, Erica & Todd Davido, Kay & Paul DeBast, Ginger Dehlinger, LaDonna Denslinger, Beverly Donofrio, Vicky Dyrdahl, Dianne Espy, Sandy Fischer, Mathew Heberling, Stephanie King, Bradley & Debora Lorang, Janet Lorang, Michael Lorang, Timothy Lorang, Jet McCann, Karen Martel, Katrena Meyer, Linda Mills, Nancy Mills, Alys Milner, Simone Neall, Ingrid Preston, Sue Patton Thoele, David Thomas & Janet Clark Thomas, Diana Timmermans, Connie Van Sickle, Ellen Waterston, Ava Wilson, and some I may not have listed here and will sincerely regret failing to mention—my deepest thanks!

Great appreciation to AnnaMariah and David Nau for the oh so many awesome gifts they share!

Special thanks to Joseph J. Duerst for the beautiful cover, and to Gretchen Heberling for inspirations and consultations galore!

Thank you all—my shining lights!

Characters from Mending Stone also in Catching Rain

Mia Casinelli Maria Isabel Angelina Casinelli

Tim Edwards Mia's former husband

Valerie Young employee hired by Tim to work in the store owned in Portland

Gerald Native American in Oregon Mia could not forget

Victoria Maria Casinelli Wife of Angelo

Angelo Casinelli Husband to Victoria Maria

Angelina Casinelli Angelo's mother

Joyce Campbell Austin hospital volunteer and friend to Mia who traveled with her to Mexico

Blake Lodger at Las Mariposas Hotel in Oaxaca City. In early edition, this character was named Stefan

Rosa, Rosalia Mysterious woman Mia dreamed and wrote about—Mia dreamed her name Rosa, but it is actually Rosalia

Manuel, Mano Man Mia dreamed as husband to Rosa—Mia dreamed his name Manuel, but it is actually Mano

Guillermo Mano's cousin and husband to Victoria Maria

Jaime, Javier Man who rescued Rosa—Mia dreamed his name Jaime, but it is actually Javier

Significant Places in Mending Stone and Catching Rain

Portland, Oregon where Mia and Tim lived and owned a business 15 years

Rufus, Oregon small town on Columbia River Gorge where Mia's car broke down

Austin, Texas where Mia was raised

San Antonio, Texas where Mia was said to be born

Mexico City also known as *Distrito Federal*, or *D. F.*, capital city of Mexico, location of the Basilica of Our Lady of Guadalupe

Ciudad de Oaxaca, Oaxaca, Mexico

where Mia began the search following clues she thought were hidden in words on Victoria and Angelo's marriage license and the scrap of cloth found in an atlas on a map of Mexico

San Bartolomeo, Italy or Mexico

towns Mia searched for on maps and didn't find

San Bartolo Coyotepec town in Oaxaca where Mia found unique handcrafted black pottery

San Bartolome Quialana village in Qaxaca, Mia and Joyce found on a map

Catching Rain

a novel

Sharon Duerst

Looking Back More Than A Year To The Story Of Mending Stone

It rained 43 inches in Portland in 2006—seven inches more than the previous year which was even more than the year before that. Maybe all that rain precipitated Mia's desire to have a child. Maybe *it* was also responsible for her miscarriages. Winter rain seeped in after her latest loss. Though the spring of 2007 was drier, Mia still could not shake her dampened mood. Not until devastating dreams of a distraught woman forced her out from the cocoon of home. But was it already too late?

Sudden plans to rekindle romance with husband Tim led to a shocking discovery. Leaving their shop in shambles, Mia drove off into the night. Rain could not stop her. But the car did. Teetering on a ledge high above the Columbia River, she might have tumbled to certain death, but a gust of wind blew her back, arms stopped her fall. Heartbeats pounded in her ears, but her eyes would not open. She sank down, down into heavy dreams.

Waking the next morning in a stranger's bed, Mia searched, but failed to find a way out. The man offered more than temporary shelter. His eyes—deep brown and steady—warmed like coffee. Her story spilled out, as if she could not stop the flow of words or emotion, as if the coffee was truth serum.

Intense emotions plagued her. And at night, strange dreams tormented her sleep. Still she stayed—maybe waiting for car repairs, maybe waiting for something else.

Mia ran for release, ran the winding asphalt roads wrapping the hills like ribbons. Hot sun and wind moved her, and undulating fields of young wheat spoke of something. But what?

Withering relationships weighed heavy on her mind. After years of missed communications with parents Victoria and Angelo, Mia could not tell them of her failings or struggles. But where else could she turn? Without faith or hope or friends, where could she find something needed to shore up a shaky self?

Gerald's voice—slow and deep—was like a caress. His words sank into Mia like heat. And her eyes lingered on him, unable to look away as rivulets of water dripped from his long pony tail, down his broad back, and disappeared into the area of his cut-offs. Sun glistening red on his skin stirred something in her—something she could not, would not name.

Mia might have forgotten there was somewhere else she should be, someone else she should see, but an arranged meeting with Tim brought shocking news of family illness. With no time to explain when Gerald suddenly appeared, and no time to settle a spate of emotion, Mia left with Tim for Texas to see her parents.

Cryptic statements by Victoria elicited confusion as Mia waited helplessly for change, and for her recovery, but it was not to be. And Mia began questioning everything she thought was her life. A glimmer of hope was found in friendship with hospital volunteer, Joyce Campbell. But the strange dreams of the Mexican woman continued as Mia's life crumbled. Where could she go? What could she do?

Selection in a writing residency marked a way forward, and Mia was determined to build a new career, but had only inklings and emotion and no idea what would happen next.

Mending Stone, her residency manuscript, was submitted for review. Mia returned to Austin. Shocking revelations from Angelo soon pushed Mia into more changes. New activities and relationships could not quell a growing need in her, and a nagging voice inside could not be silenced.

Odd clues, a scrap of cloth, maps in a tattered old atlas pointed to some long-hidden secret—but what? Mia searched San Antonio and was pulled ever closer toward something—some distant but familiar presence.

By the water of an unknown Mexican beach, Mia found more than she ever believed possible, more than she could have imagined.

Rivulet

It was early. The sky was soft–faintly blue, pink, yellow. Colors worn by a million mornings. Already the air was warming with promise.

Mia pushed her feet down into the sand and patted it around her ankles. Bits of earth, sea glass, tiny sea creatures and shells made up the sand. A miniature community of color and texture. Light and dark. Simple and complex. Tossed and tumbled by wind and water—a tiny world drying in the warm Mexican sun.

She sighed, her eyes looking out to the water. Tide rushed the shore, and retreated, leaving scalloped lines of bubbling foam on the wet sand. Mia watched a shell being carried away by the water.

"I was carried away like that from Mexico. Maybe in someone's arms..."

A hand touched Mia's shoulder and she turned to look.

Joyce plopped down to the sand. "How are you doing?"

"I don't know."

"Yesterday was so amazing!"

Mia nodded. "Dumbfounding. I *believe* in intuition, magical happenings, and miracles. And I did think the clues would lead to something in Mother's past, some answer to the questions in my mind, but…"

"And wow! Did they!"

"I guess I hoped the adventure would somehow satisfy the longing in me, even if I found nothing. But I didn't know I could actually find someone! And Puerto Escondido wasn't even on our itinerary!"

"Love it here!" Joyce said patting a mound of sand beside her.

"Isn't it strange how each little thing was a piece of a puzzle and we were unwitting participants being led into putting it all together?"

Joyce laughed, "Welcome to the mystical universe!"

Eyes flashing with emotion, Mia said softly, "It was an answer to prayer I couldn't even voice."

"Led on a circuitous path to the mother you never knew you'd lost! Now *that's* the stuff made into movies!"

"I wrote *Mending Stone* based on dreams of the mysterious woman, but I thought it was only fiction and she was only imagination. I didn't know it was truth playing out in my mind—*my* truth!"

Joyce laughed. "All your little inklings and clues led right to where you needed to be for discovery!"

"I can't wrap my mind around it. Are my parents *really* from Mexico? I was raised Italian, but I'm not—not one bit?"

"May take time to assimilate," Joyce said softly. "How long will you stay?"

Mia's eyes were on the surf—waves rolling in to shore, sliding out again. "I don't know." She looked at Joyce and smiled, "I wish you weren't going yet."

"That makes two of us!" Joyce sighed. But, my new job waits—that's *my* big adventure! These weeks have been interesting! And it was good to see again the places Neil and I visited on our honeymoon so many years ago! I thank you greatly for such a generous graduation gift! Sure exceeds any gift I can ever send your way!"

Shaking her head, Mia answered, "Your enthusiasm and courage are contagious! You've helped me so much. And you deserve recognition for completing your advanced degree and developing a new vocation later in life! Such an awesome undertaking!"

"It *has* been trying at times," Joyce sighed.

"With all you had on your plate, still you were there for *me* through Mother's passing, my divorce, and when Papa remarried. It would've been *so* much harder without you."

Joyce nodded. "Same here, kiddo!"

"Kiddo? I'm only a decade younger."

"Right! But I'm fifty!"

"You're incredible no matter what age."

"Thank you!" Joyce laughed brushing back her reddish hair. "A girl can use all the good words she can get! Let's hope my new job works out. Keep some good thoughts for me."

"If you think that helps."

"Thoughts are like prayers! And just look at how your prayers were answered! The universe is full of possibility, and *you,* dear Mia, have amazing powers when you set your mind to something. You can tap into the creative energies of the universe and…"

Mia laughed, "You're kind of strange. But that's what I like about you, 'Sage.'"

Joyce glanced at her watch, then suddenly stood up. "I really have to go!"

"This whole crazy trip-without-a-plan was amazing! I loved sharing it with you, Joyce."

"Me, too, sweetie, me too. Is there anything you need done back in Austin?"

"No," Mia sighed getting to her feet. "Thanks for offering." She followed Joyce up the hillside trail to their lodging at the villas. "Oh, Joyce! Would you mind checking on my condo? I wasn't prepared to be gone so long. I'd ask if you would water my plants on the balcony, but they're probably dead by now."

"As much as you once loved your Christmas rose, those cuttings stolen from Tim weren't thriving in Austin anyway."

Mia paused while unhitching her condo key from a ring, and sighed, "I know. And it's better to let go of all the little pieces of *that* painful past."

Joyce accepted the key, and carried a suitcase out to the courtyard. They hugged good-bye while a taxi waited outside the iron entrance gates to the villas. Joyce walked toward it, then turned suddenly, and came back. Unclasping her necklace, she pressed the string of shimmering beads into Mia's hand. "I had this made especially for *you* by Bold Bodacious Jewelry, but the stones just begged to be worn! I couldn't resist their energy!"

Laughing, Mia stared down at the stones. "They're beautiful! Thank you so much!"

Joyce was hurrying toward the gates. She turned and yelled, "Rainbow moonstones, they'll assist in your search!"

"I already found what I was looking for," Mia called.

"Your story...More about you," Joyce hollered while getting into the car.

"You mean *Mending Stone*?"

Joyce only smiled and waved out the window as the car was pulling away.

Mia stared down at the sparkling stones in her hand. Smooth. Creamy white. Like something from a dream, something...Heavenly. She fastened them around her neck, and wandered back down to the beach.

Her feet scooted across the dry sand, making loud squeaky noises and she was giggling as she sat down.

Bright sun warmed the stones at her neck.

"Smooth like satin…" she murmured, stroking the beads. "Smooth like skin…" Her mind filled with images of Gerald. Closing her eyes, she sighed, "Ohhh, Gerald."

How you rush my heart
Hands reaching my deepest retreat
Breath warming like sun on my skin
Voice stirring like music

Sometime later, Mia walked from the villas up the road: dust to gravel, gravel to pavement. She crossed the highway and continued on into the business district. At an internet shop she sent a message to Gerald. She sighed, and walked up the street, her eyes scanning the shiny glass windows for some sign, something to settle the disquiet in her. At *el Mercado* (the market), her eyes lingered on colors and textures of the wares and food. Eventually she made several purchases, and headed back toward the villa. But something niggled at her brain and her heart was hurting.

She stopped at a phone booth and placed a call. "Gerald, it's Mia. How are you? I sent you an email..."

"Just got it."

"Oh! Are you in The Dalles?"

"Yep. Came over to see Gram…"

"Tell Charlotte hello for me."

He replied quietly, "At the hospital. Gram had a stroke."

"OH, NO! Is she showing signs of recovery?"

"Not much. Hope she will."

"Does she know where she is?" Mia choked back tears. "I'm sorry. It must be so hard to see her in such a state."

"Gram knows I'm there, but isn't speaking or opening her eyes. Maybe conserving energy. Time might make a difference."

"I hope so," Mia sighed.

"Y'r news was surprising. How'd y' and Joyce end up at the beach?"

"We searched all around Oaxaca City. Signs pointed to something, but I couldn't guess what. And I was tired. We thought walking in warm sand, waves striking the shore, and wind in our hair would be a pleasant end to the trip. But when we reached Puerto Escondido, I felt something—a strange pull, things 'speaking' to me. We saw angels and more angels. When we happened down a road to an unknown beach on a little bay, I couldn't resist the water. I felt as if I'd waited all my life to be in that place. An old man with flowing hair sat down nearby and played guitar. Amazing tones came from that old instrument. I was captivated! I closed my eyes—only a moment it seemed. When I looked again, the sun was going down and the man was walking away—glowing in strange light. And just like your gram said, 'By water, wind whisper name…' I heard my name called.

I turned; something caught my eye. I walked toward the trees. A sign—white with a painted rose and the name ***Angelita***—hung from the rafters of a hut."

"Cool."

"At the shop, a woman was sitting and sewing. She looked up and smiled with such a sweet familiar face. She said the bay was named Puerto Angelito and she thought it was a sign her daughter, Angelita, would come someday! When I pulled the scrap with the name '***Angelita***' from my pocket, the woman gasped! I thought the clues were leading me to Mexico in search of my real father. But I knew *she* is my mother!"

"What happened to *him*?"

"I don't know yet. Isn't it strange, and thrilling? Who am I? Is *this*—not Italy—my home country? For *real*? Is this the answer to who I am?"

Gerald replied in measured words, "Takes time to sink roots."

Hearing the slow caress of his voice, she shifted from one foot to another. "I'm not sure I want to sink *roots*. But I might stay here a while…"

The phone crackled loudly. Mia stared at the phone. "Gerald?" She redialed. The call would not go through.

She trudged toward the villas, took the fork in the road down to Puerto Angelito. Under the trees at the base of the hill, she searched for the painted white sign. Tears stung her eyes. "Still here. Still real," she whispered.

Near the shop, Javier, the man in Rosalia's life, was cooking over a fire, his cheeks rosy with heat, long dark hair pulled back in a wrap of leather.

Rosalia looked up from sewing and her eyes glistened as Mia approached.

They embraced, sat down smiling, and Rosalia resumed sewing while Mia looked on. They said little. After a time, Javier served up plates of warm tortillas stuffed with thinly sliced chicken layered with soft Oaxacan cheese and grilled peppers. They sat on a wooden bench at a small table.

"How great to work and live here, Jaime…I'm sorry, Javier. I wrote a story—*Mending Stone*—about a woman and her men named Manuel and Jaime. They lived in Northern Mexico."

Rosalia pointed to the back portion of the hut. "Live here only short time. Javier make house." She pointed west.

"Building a house? Over by Carrizalillo Beach?"

Rosalia nodded, pointing again in the direction of the next little bay where Mia was staying at the villas.

"Do you have family nearby?"

"*My* family," Javier responded, "Queretaro. Big town. Three hours north of Distrito Federal, *D. F.*"

"Ohhh, north of Mexico City." Mia sighed, "In the story I dreamed, Jaime lived near Durango."

Rosalia gasped. "Daughter hear words! So much I say!"

"Was it you speaking in my mind? In my dreams? Where is *your* family—*my* family?"

"Many years no see," Rosalia's head moved slowly side to side, as if it was so heavy with memory and pain she could not say more.

"I came to Mexico in search of my father. Do you know where he is?"

Rosalia shook her head. "Long time no see Mano. Maybe something happen. Sad. Everything go. Pray *my* life go! But *La Virgen* no listen!" Rosalia smiled at Javier. "*Madre* know better! She send Javier! Make good care, and ask only I sew something pretty for table." Rosalia looked down at her hands. "Smart man.

Know work make better. Each day offer sew for life better. Understand?"

"Sewing as offering? Like penance?"

"Make something of life."

"Yes. Grace," Mia whispered.

"Maybe *La Virgen* think I good." Looking up at Mia, Rosalia whispered, "Maybe *She* bring daughter."

Mia nodded, eyes glistening brightly. "I prayed Mary would help me find what I was missing, an answer to the longing of my heart. I hoped for some sweetness to take away my heartache."

"Like sweet?" Javier asked suddenly hopping up from the bench to retrieve a plate of sliced strawberries with white cheese and tortillas.

"Ohhh, delicious!" Mia said sampling a wrap.

After chatting a while longer, Mia returned to her villa. Later, with the sound of the ocean tide rushing the shore, she slept, and dreamed.

Every dream I dreamed is true
My heart cries for sweetness
Now found
Surely... I am home...

Sound on glass woke her in the morning. Tap, tap. Tap, tap, tap tap. Tap tap tap. She listened to words in her mind.

Wind blows
erratic
like my heart

More tapping. Mia went downstairs. She opened the door to bright sunlight and Rosalia rushing in. Cradling her head and wincing with pain, Mia said hello.

"I fix," Rosalia said smiling and pointing to Mia's head, then started water heating and spooned coffee grounds into a filter. "Bahias de Huatulco. *Fincas cafetaleras* (coffee farms)."

Mia nodded dully. "Yes, I read Huatulco's known for its coffee and gorgeous scenery."

Rosalia added sugar and cream to the freshly dripped coffee, stirred, and brought a cup to Mia.

Relaxing on the canvas cushions of the wicker love seat and sofa, they sipped the strong coffee.

"I think the pain is beginning to lift. Thank you..." Mia said glancing at her mother.

"*Madre*?" Rosalia offered.

Mia's brow furrowed. "I called your sister, 'Mother.' Everything about her was reserved. Even her name—Victoria Maria—was formal. I thought the woman I dreamed was named Rosa. And your name, Rosalia, is sweet. Even though I've only just met you in person a few days ago, you are as familiar to me as the woman I dreamed. Already, I think of you as 'Mama.'"

Beaming, Rosalia nodded. "Get dressed. And shop with Mama?"

Mia smiled, and gulped down her remaining coffee. After changing clothes, she walked side by side with Rosalia up the dusty road. As they approached the business district, she suddenly asked, "You're not working at your shop today?"

"Take time with daughter!"

"Ohhh," Mia sighed. "So generous!"

"Maria work?" Rosalia asked, but when Mia did not answer readily, Rosalia said, "When a girl, I call sister Maria."

"No, Mother didn't work outside the home, but she did take care of Papa and me and the house, and she played golf and helped Grandmother Angelina and did a lot of gardening."

Rosalia nodded. "Different in America. Maria and husband have much money?"

"Yes," Mia answered gently. "More than enough."

Rosalia smiled, "Good! What Maria want! Maria say marry for riches. Have love? Maria happy?"

"Maybe…" But Mia's look was doubtful. "She did seem to suffer some secret torment, something weighing on her, something not about the life she was living."

Just reaching *el Mercado* (the market), they went inside. Vendors along every aisle smiled in greeting as they shopped.

"*Mi hija*! My daughter come after many years! *Un milagro* (A miracle)!" Rosalia excitedly related to anyone who listened. And after hearing how Mia had been led by a scrap of cloth and other clues to Rosalia's shop at Puerto Angelito, the vendors/friends offered hugs, warm wishes, even spontaneous gifts: colorful produce, linens, decorative housewares, and bunches of flowers.

Following the route back to the villas Mia and Joyce had walked only a few days before, Mia and her mother passed by the old fire engine with gleaming chrome and bright paint like fire.

Mia shook off a disturbing image burning in her mind.

"How I cry for you!" Rosalia said suddenly, eyes also on the fire engine. "Fire burn fast. Hot. Pray baby safe, but no find! Next time fire come for me, think even Mano gone. I pray fire take me. But something save and push out. I look back, eyes play trick—see Mano burn in night!"

"I dreamed that," Mia gasped. "I wrote it in my novel, *Mending Stone*."

As they neared the bottom of the hill at Puerto Angelito, Rosalia hurried toward Javier who was wielding a giant machete and splitting coconuts on a stump near the shop.

He grinned and pointed to a line of clean silver bodies on a board at his feet. "Make fish!"

They laughed and showed him the assortment of items given at the market.

"Blessed so much!" Javier grinned.

"Yes, so much kindness here…It's amazing," Mia said.

Rosalia sat and began stitching an intricate design of flowers and winding vines on a length of fabric.

"That's beautiful work."

"Maria sew?"

"What Mother embroidered was done well, but I don't know if she enjoyed doing it. When I was little, she machine stitched all my clothes." Mia's brown eyes clouded. "I'm not sure why she did that. We had money for anything we wanted or needed. She didn't need to scrimp on hand made clothes."

"Sister's husband work?"

"Papa worked in the family—*his* family—grocery. He was much older than Mother and retired when I was little. Still, somehow I learned to work long and hard."

"What work?"

"I worked many years with my husband, Tim, in a shop we owned. We sold jewelry and pretty things for the home. Now I'm a hope-to-be published writer."

"What write?"

"The story of the woman I dreamed lived in Mexico—the tragedy and hardship of her life."

Rosalia's eyes grew wide. "Maria say what happen?"

Mia shook her head. "What *did* happen?"

Rosalia did not answer, only gave a troubled look.

"Mother *never* spoke of herself, or her family, or past."

Nodding gravely, Rosalia replied quietly, "Better Maria learn keep quiet."

"I used to feel angry with her: so much she didn't express! After she passed, I realized she had been guarded for some reason. And I remembered things she hinted at. I thought she left clues for me to follow. Still, it's a miracle I found you."

Rosalia's head nodded as she sewed.

Javier busied himself at the back of the shop, but every so often stole a look at them.

Quiet words came from Rosalia, "Maria say no like work of family. Say maybe go far, marry for riches." Lines of hardship showing on her face, Rosalia pierced the fabric and pulled the needle in quick movements.

Leaning forward as if reeled in by the thread, Mia listened.

"Maria say baby spoil looks. And sister say want only handsome husband."

"So like Mother. So self-absorbed. So selfish."

Rosalia's hands stilled, but her head moved side to side. "Isabel, our mother, suffer much with baby. No want more. She keep husband from bed. Father angry, yell to mother. But Maria stand to him, 'Mother suffer enough.' He no listen. He say women make trouble, daughter shame speak like this. Mother cry, but Maria…" Rosalia shook her head, "no tears."

"Sounds so hard, frightening."

"Is life only," Rosalia replied and shrugged. "Maria different: strong. Something in mind like stone. And Maria pretty. Everywhere get much attention. And Maria like boy Father no like. He say no see this boy. Maria listen to boy only.

Maybe Guillermo say, 'Leave village. Leave family.'" Rosalia shrugged. "One day, no Maria."

"Mother said her home country was Italy, that she did what she had to do to leave."

"How I cry, 'What happen to Maria?' Maybe some devil take in night. Maybe sister go with Guillermo. I pray Maria come. Hear nothing; family talk little of sister." Rosalia looked up with sorrowful eyes. "But I sew. And I change." She smiled shyly. "And one day, at market with family, I see Mano."

"Where does your family live?"

Rosalia pointed north toward the mountains separating the coastal area from the interior valleys of Oaxaca. "Other markets, I look again and again for Mano. One day at market of Tlacolula, *Domingo,* Sunday, yes? Many people. Grandmother say keep eyes on work. But I think only of Mano and many mistake I make! And Mano come! *Abuelita*—'Little Grandmother' Inez—no like look Mano give to me. But I know this look and I like!"

Mia laughed.

"Mano come to market of my village. *Martes*."

"Tuesday?"

Rosalia nodded.

"I'm learning some Spanish! How did you and Javier learn to speak English so well?"

"Javier travel from mountain to city for sale many things. Learn. And many tourist, say much here."

"Javier's an interesting man." Mia glanced over at him and smiled, but his attention seemed to be occupied by something other than their conversation.

"Market of my village, no tourist," Rosalia continued. "Women make much talk, teach, work, laugh."

"What was the name of your village?"

"San Bartolome Quialana."

"*San Bartolome Quialana*?" Mia asked excitedly.

Rosalia nodded.

"Joyce and I found it on a map!"

"House of family: parents, grandmother…"

"And Mano," Mia gulped, "where was he from?"

Glancing to Javier who was captivated by a bug crawling at his feet, Rosalia replied quietly, "San Bartolo Coyotepec."

"Mother collected the black pottery made there! I met an old couple…maybe relatives of Mano." Mia barely whispered, her eyes on Rosalia's hands making fast even stitches.

They soon ate the fish Javier had cooked with coconut milk and peppers over a hot fire. Mia enjoyed the flavors. But later in the night, as she tried to sleep, her stomach and throat burned with fire. "The spices used here are so different from Italian spices: oregano, marjoram, basil, rosemary and thyme," she whined. "So much is new." Other differences flooded in and weighed heavy on her mind. Hints of prejudice settled over her like volcano ash—abrasive, impossible to brush away. When finally she slept, Mia's mind filled with terrifying images.

> *A hand covered her mouth. She struggled to get free, but he brought her down. His unshaven face rubbed against her, mouth pressing hard, darting tongue pushing for an opening. She bit his lip. He pulled back enough to strike her face with his fist again and again until she no longer squirmed beneath him. When finished, he said, "Make no baby," and pulled out a knife...*

"OH, MY GOD!" Mia exclaimed. "Why do I dream such things?" Attempting to shower away the horror, she stood in the stream, turning it hotter and hotter until her breathing calmed.

She dressed, hurried to the hotel office, and begged to make a call.

"Gerald, I…" her voice broke. "I had another nightmare. It was terrible. Horrifying."

"Just a dream."

"Again you say it is just a dream?" Her voice was elevated, sharp.

"Mia."

"Don't be placating! My dreams MEAN something. They led me here to my real mother after all these years. But why would I dream such horror? Why now?"

"Maybe telling y' something."

She sighed, "I don't know what to do here."

"Sorry my exhibition prevented coming. But I can listen. I'm here for y'."

"Yes! You're there!" she whined. "I *wish* you could come *here*."

"Could've next week if it weren't for Gram."

"I know. I'm sorry. I sound like a brat. I know you have your photography show to prepare. It's important. And of course, I know Charlotte needs you there. I pray she improves."

"Thank you," he said, voice like honey.

"I miss you," Mia said quietly, "San Antonio was…" She paused, "Like a dream. But it seems so long ago. So much has happened..."

"It *was* good."

"Yes," she breathed. "But everything seems changed for me now. I don't know how, or *when*, I'll figure out my future."

He was quiet a moment, and then he said, “Make it how y’ want.”

“If I *knew* what I want!” she snapped.

He made no response.

“I’m sorry. I’m on edge. I don’t know what’s the matter with me. I don’t feel well. My stomach’s upset and…”

“Sorry. Wish there was something to do for y’.”

Bennett, the office manager chimed in, “Ma’am, it’s a business phone.”

“I’m sorry. I have to go, Ger.”

“Eat. Write more emails. Take care of y’rself.”

The softness in his last line reached her like an embrace. Mia swallowed hard, and said a quiet good-bye. Her hand set down the phone as if too heavy to hold.

Back at her lodging, she plopped onto the bed. Words sprang to her mind.

Ay…so much pain…

Mia hurried out the door and down the trail to the beach. A breeze fluttered her hair.

She walked to a small stream draining from the hillside—like a rivulet streaming from Gerald’s dark ponytail at the Deschutes River in Oregon last summer—sweet moments and solitude—after finding Tim with Valerie. But there was no going back to that simple, sustaining, and rural snatch of life. It was Gerald’s, not hers.

Dropping to the ground, Mia scooped up a handful of sand. She examined earthen particles, tiny shells, bits of glass worn smooth. Life was like that—time wearing smooth the hurts, the sharp edges.

Eventually, she went back to the villa, and then over to the shop where Javier was chopping branches nearby.

"Good see, daughter!" Rosalia exclaimed hopping up from her sewing stool.

"Good to see you, too, Mama."

"I make coffee," Rosalia said beginning to heat water in an old pot and setting out cups.

Mia glanced at the stitching on the shirt Rosalia had been sewing. "Your work is so fine."

"Grandmother say work keep trouble away. Each day work and work. I no want trouble," Rosalia said handing Mia a cup of strong white and sweet coffee.

"Only working and working is not much of a life."

Rosalia shrugged, resuming sewing, making fast stitches forming green leaves. "Make money for life." She glanced around, and seeing Javier at some distance she said, "Women of village teach stitches. Secrets. Make wishes true."

"Stitching wishes onto the fabric?" Mia rubbed chill bumps from her arms. "Like magic? Did you learn it? Did *you* stitch the scrap of cloth I found with the flower and the name ***Angelita***?"

Rosalia nodded. "I sew for baby—daughter. You!"

"It seems you cared for me…that you…wanted me and loved me. But what happened? How were we separated? Why did Mother raise me?"

"A tragedy," Rosalia breathed.

Mia waited.

Her mother's hands stilled, then covered her face. Rosalia's hands dropped to her lap, then clenched into fists. Her face masked with hatred as she spat the word, "Devil…"

"What devil? Who was he?"

"Devil take…me..." Rosalia tensed like burned wire—stiff and pale. Clutching her chest, eyes rolling back, she collapsed.

"Mama!" Mia checked Rosalia's pulse, started CPR. "Get help!" she shouted to Javier between compressions.

He took off running.

Words fell from Mia's mouth, "*Virgen*, keep Mama safe! I've only just found her! Please, help!"

The ambulance whisked up to the modern hospital in Puerto Escondido. Some exterior masonry walls were straight, others curved. Each was painted differently: red, bright blue, deep tan, white. Decorative metal work hung jauntily from the roof. Green plants and grass growing along the drive were manicured.

The gurney rolled through doors, across shiny floor tiles—dark red like blood.

Mia shuddered.

As doctors and nurses assessed Rosalia's condition, Mia paced, her steps clacking up and down the hallway to the rhythm of whispered prayers. "God! Please don't take Mama! I can't lose another mother. It's not fair! She should be happy. I should be happy. We should be happy together! We should have years and years ahead."

Medical staff determined Rosalia must have life-saving surgery.

Mia fell heavily into a chair, and waited. Javier sat on the edge of his seat, his dark eyes on the floor. Hours passed. At last, word came via a plump nurse in oversized scrubs, paper booties over her shoes. "*Familia de Rosalia* (Family of Rosalia)?"

They rose from their seats. "Yes," Mia answered.

"Rosalia rest now. Doctor see soon."

They exhaled, nodded. Their measured steps paced the hallway. Waiting. More waiting.

An hour later, a doctor emerged through swinging metal doors. “Relatives of Rosalia?”

Mia stared at the man’s lean and tanned face, silvery-grey well-cut hair, muscular forearms, neatly trimmed nails on tapered fingers. She found a voice, “Her daughter, Mia.”

“Dr. Grimaldi.” He shook her hand.

She introduced Javier.

“Rosalia’s husband?”

“How is she? What was it?” Mia asked quickly.

“Aortic valve stenosis. She’ll have quite a bit of scarring from the incision. We replaced the valve. She seems to be in good health overall, despite evidence of previous damage to the heart. We’ll do more tests just to be sure we don’t run into something else surprising.” Dr. Grimaldi looked from one face to another. “Questions?”

Mia stared at him, shaking her head, finally able to mouth, “Thank you.”

Dr. Grimaldi nodded, and walked away.

Javier’s face was strained. “Okay?”

Mia replied gently, “Hopefully she will heal. Has she said anything about a previous heart attack?”

He nodded. “Heart break. Devil take from Rosalia.”

“Who was this devil? What did he do? Did police arrest and charge him?”

“Mexico,” he shrugged. “Family problem.”

“FAMILY?” Mia forced down a shudder.

Just then, a nurse was walking toward them, “See Rosalia?”

They started toward the room.

The nurse put up an arm to stop Javier. "Family only."

Mia pleaded his case.

The nurse went to the desk, scribbled something on a chart and did not look up as they continued on.

Hooked up to monitors, oxygen, and I.V.s, Rosalia was only a small bump under the covers in the ICU.

Mia pulled straight chairs up to the bedside.

Javier sat with his eyes closed, hands clasped together in prayer, smooth face looking long with intense prayers on his lips.

They kept vigil through the night, the next day, and on into the night again. Rosalia had not roused. Mia stroked her arm and pleaded, "Mama, don't leave us. Perhaps it is beautiful where you are floating. Perhaps you want to see your loved ones already passed. Perhaps you are tired of this life and working so hard at sewing. But stay here! We've only just found each other! Please hang on for me! We have so much more to share. So many years ahead…" A lament played in her mind.

Mother
I am lost
so lost
I cry for you…

Sounds escaped from Rosalia. Caught in a dream of suffering, she moaned with anguish.

Hands held her down. She screamed, fought and *scratched. Her mouth bloodied by a fist, she spat, and bit, but another blow struck her hard. He tore into her with his hot blade.*

"Leave!" Maria yelled, pounding him. A fist caught her. She fell back.

He pounced on her. There was scuffling, then brutal grunts and satisfied gasps before he left them alone.

As Maria stanched Rosalia's blood, tears flowed from her eyes and she scolded, "I say no safe here! Now must plan something before Mano come back."

Stroking Rosalia's arm, Mia studied the blue veins branching like waterways. She conjured a calming vision of Rosalia floating on satin water of an indigo pool. Words played in Mia's mind.

Save me…

Mia whispered, "Come back to us, Mama." She prayed silently and long.

Rosalia stirred a little. Her eyelids fluttered.

The nurse was called, and then the doctor.

Dr. Grimaldi put stethoscope to Rosalia's chest and confirmed a weak heartbeat in normal rhythm. "Still early, but this is encouraging," he said pocketing the device.

"Yes, yes!" Javier laughed. He leaned down and gently kissed Rosalia's hand. "Forever stay here!"

Stepping out of the room alongside Dr. Grimaldi, Mia drew a breath and asked quietly, "When will we know she'll be okay?"

His kindly brown eyes took in her face, her tousled hair. "A few days will give a better idea. If she comes fully awake."

"Then what?'

"We'll see."

Nodding, Mia smiled weakly, but her knees began to give way.

Grimaldi's arms caught and carried her to an empty gurney parked along the wall.

Mia tried to sit up immediately; a woozy head forced her to settle back again.

"We should take a look at you."

"I'm alright. I…" she stammered, "I haven't eaten. And I forgot to drink anything." Mia covered her mouth with her hand, and burped.

"Having a bit of dyspepsia lately?"

"Some." She glanced at him. "Everything is different. I…I've been excited and upset. My life—what I thought was my life—is turned upside down. And the food is different than what I normally eat, how I was raised."

Grimaldi surveyed her coloring, palpated her wrist, glanced at her ring-less fingers. "Spices south of the border can be overpowering to novice digestion."

Mia blushed. "I was raised in Texas, mostly on Italian cooking."

Dr. Grimaldi's smile showed confidence as he leaned in close and put a hand to Mia's forehead. "I learned a lot of good Italian cooking at Mother's knee." He signaled a nurse to bring over a paper cup of water.

Mia drank it down under his look.

"Better?"

She nodded, swinging her bare legs off the edge of the gurney.

Grimaldi's hand under her elbow assisted her to standing. "A solid meal might bring you to even keel."

Mia smiled uneasily. “Maybe. I haven’t been very hungry…OH! Excuse me!” She bolted down the hallway, her footsteps clacking loudly on the shiny tiled floor.

Frantically pushing the door open, she rushed into the lavatory.

Gorge

Mia rested her hands on the cool rim of the porcelain sink and drew slow breaths. Her legs were shaking. "I need something to shore me up."

Her mind flew to the windy gorge of the Columbia River, and Gerald. "*He* steadied my shaky composure. *He* cared for me." Her mind drifted to the tall pine standing in his yard—the peaceful praying pine whispering with wind. Mia sighed loudly. "It's *his* life, not mine. My life was Portland. Then I thought Austin. But now I'm here."

She glanced into the mirror. "*This* is where I need to be right now." Mia splashed cool water on her face again and again.

Gathering her wits, she returned to her mother's hospital room. Rosalia and Javier were sleeping. Mia forced down a lump in her throat. "Just like when Mother was dying with Papa at her bedside in Austin."

Mia left the hospital and went to *el Mercado.* The flower aisle drew her over to breathe in the scents and colors of the many varieties of blooms. She selected a tin angel vessel with a reservoir on back, and filled it with sweet smelling coneflowers and yellow dahlias. "So pretty!"

She hurried back to the hospital and entering Rosalia's room with the flower arrangement in hand, nearly ran into Dr. Grimaldi exiting. Her eyes jumped nervously to Rosalia who was sitting up in the bed. "How are you, Mama?"

"*Estoy bien* (I am fine)," Rosalia answered attempting a smile, but dark circles under her eyes said more.

Mia set the flowers on the bedside table, and went out to the hallway to speak to Dr. Grimaldi. Steadying her shaking hands on the wall behind her, she asked, "How is Mama doing really?"

"She's quite weak."

"But she'll recover, right?"

"We are cautiously optimistic."

"How long will she need to stay here?"

"A week perhaps," Dr. Grimaldi replied, his voice calm, reassuring. "She'll tire easily. Tedious or strenuous tasks must be avoided."

"Oh, yes…" Mia moved over to a chair. She gripped the cool metal arms and sank down with a loud sigh.

"Still haven't eaten?"

"I went to the market, but the food was not appealing."

"Sit tight." Dr. Grimaldi left, and returned several minutes later with a glass of milk, sliced bagel, and dish of yogurt. He set the tray on her lap.

"Thank you." Her face flushed.

"I have rounds. I'll check in on you all a bit later."

She nodded. "Sorry to keep you. And thank you for this."

He smiled, and strode down the hall.

Mia ate; her stomach began to settle. She set the tray aside, and closed her eyes. Words and images appeared.

Come back...

She rushed back into the room and waited for Rosalia's recovery.

Ten days later, after setbacks, and more rest, Rosalia was discharged from the hospital.

They rode in a taxi to the hotel where Mia and Javier helped Rosalia to the lodging next to Mia's and got her settled.

"Is much, I thank you," Rosalia exclaimed.

"I'd give anything for you," Mia replied, fussing over fresh flowers in the angel vase she had placed at the bedside.

Smiling weakly, Rosalia nodded.

"Rest now."

Javier glanced at the other small bed.

Mia said warmly, "*Both* of you rest. If you need anything, ring." She handed him a bell on a handle.

He gave it a shake, and grinned.

"That should work!" Mia laughed.

Outside their rooms, she relaxed in a chair beneath the overhanging roof. Her eyes looked out to the blue-green water rolling into the bay below. Waves pushed toward the beach: swelling, rising, falling. Mia sighed, "I'm water looking for shore." Words tugged at her mind.

Oh my love
tumbles down
headlong into the bramble
I am tossed and torn and oh, so forlorn
without you

Mia said quietly, "I'm searching for shore. Which shore? How will I know when I am home?"

The bell rang. She rushed into Rosalia's room. "Are you okay?"

Rosalia was giggling, but Javier's look was contrite on seeing Mia's worried expression. "Only try," he said.

"Can I do something for you while I'm here?"

Rosalia opened her arms.

Mia sat on the edge of the bed next to her mother and was pulled close.

Every dream is you...

Startled, Mia pulled back and looked at Rosalia. "Did you say something?"

"Only think."

"I heard you!"

"So many times I pray daughter hear!"

"I've always had a good imagination. When I was a child, I made up stories seeming so real to me, the people in my mind were like close friends—or family."

Javier eyes lit with interest. "Tell story?"

"Let me think of one." She sat quietly a few moments, and then began...

> "Once there was a little girl—a princess—
> who lived in a sunny place. She had many fine
> things. And she was loved so very much. But
> even when wanting to be happy, she could not be.
> Something ached in her. She was stiff and sore
> with longing.

Opening arms to the heavens, the girl said, 'Fill me with softness.' Fluffy clouds raced across the blue sky, and she was cheered.

But when night crept in with darkness, she cried, 'I can't see! I need light.' One by one, stars began glittering, filling the sky with millions of sparkles. 'Do you shine for me?' she asked of the brilliant constellations.

But there was no answer, only stillness. And she was lonely in that stillness. 'I need to hear you!' the girl pleaded, but heard nothing.

She cried herself to sleep, and dreamed: clouds thinning and dropping to the horizon, frothing waves rushing ashore like rhythm of a heartbeat. Loneliness subsided.

But when she woke, the girl forgot the dream, and longing returned.

Once, the girl visited a beach at dusk. She lay in the sand and stretched out her arms. 'Come to me!' she begged. A mother-moon looked down on her. The girl drifted to sleep under the blanketing sky and waves lapped the shore like a comforting heartbeat. In early morning, she stretched, her hand brushing against something in the sand—a shell with blushing hue like the faint sky.

A man with flowing white hair was walking up the beach. He paused, and said, 'Sunrise tellin' y' somethin'. Listen close.'

The girl put the shell to her ear. The sound of a heartbeat rushed to her ears. She clutched the shell to her chest, and smiled."

Javier yawned, "Thank you." But Rosalia was already sleeping.

Mia tiptoed outside. She paused at the cliff's edge, then hurried down the path to the beach and into the surf.

"Ahhh," she sighed, turning over to swim on her back with face to the sun. "What do I do now? I can't keep floating through time with no goals."

Cook.

Startled by the word voiced in her mind, Mia swam to shore. Rosalia and Javier were still sleeping, she showered, dressed, wrote out a shopping list, and departed for the market.

Up and down the aisles of *el Mercado*, she shopped for ingredients: a smoked pork leg, plantains, nutmeg, ginger, sugar, oranges, lime, tomatoes, tomatillos, onion, and several peppers. At a small store, Mia showed the shopkeeper what she'd purchased and tried to explain what she planned to make.

The shopkeeper brought forth several samples of *mezcal*—liquor made from the agave, or maguey plant.

Sipping, Mia responded, "Too bitter." Several others were sweeter. "Oooo," she cooed at a flavor like spiced rum, bought it, and went away smiling.

She baked the pork leg in fresh salsa, cooked rice with the plantains seasoned with nutmeg, ginger, citrus, and *mezcal*. The enticing aroma played with her mind: conjuring images of rainy Portland evenings when she had often experimented with flavor profiles and ingredient combinations, meals eaten with only wine and dishes for company. Mia forced down a lump in her throat, and whispered, "Now is better. So much better." She served up plates and brought them to the other room for Javier and Rosalia who grinned while eating.

"I love to cook for people. I'm blessed to be able to share this meal with you: my family. For so long, I've wanted to share my passions with someone."

You in my heart
You in my mind
I want to feel you
like cool satin on my skin
in rising heat

Mia brushed back a lock of hair.

"Daughter make delicious life," Rosalia replied, eyes soft with emotion.

Mia hopped up, and fetched dishes of *flan* topped with lit candles. "Both of you make a wish, then blow!"

Rosalia and Javier smiled and blew out the flames.

"Why this?"

"Birthdays! *Cumpleanos*? I don't know when they are, but I thought we should celebrate!"

"Ahhh," Rosalia nodded. "Noviembre. 1951."

"When was I born?"

Rosalia sighed. "Deciembre. 1967."

Mia's brow furrowed. "1967? That explains why in the picture dated December 1968, I was already a toddler. My parents said my *birthdate* was December 23, *1968*. But I have no birth certificate. That was the date of my Baptism." She groaned loudly, "I'm not 39! I'm forty!"

Rosalia shrugged and took a bite of dessert.

"Only *sixteen* when I was born? Married so young!"

Color crept over Rosalia's cheeks, her face tensed. "Marry Mano in heart only. Sin. Maybe sin bring danger..."

Rosalia's eyes clouded and hands clutched to her chest. Then she fainted.

The ambulance whisked up to the Puerto Escondido hospital emergency room. Rosalia was wheeled quickly inside. Javier and Mia walked on wooden legs into the waiting room, eased down to upholstered chairs. They watched time pass with ticks of black hands on a white clock hanging on the wall.

Javier's palms pressed together, his lips mouthed silent prayers. His dark brown eyes looked up as if seeing hope there.

Mia gathered in mind the details of every day since coming to Mexico. She stared at the lines on her palms. "My life is changed. Forever changed. *I'm* different than I ever thought." She examined her skin. "Not dark, not white. Do I belong? Am I like these people in more ways than blood? Do I fit here? Or anywhere? And, if I lose Mama…"

Her eyes were drawn to a row of windows where a white moth with faint markings darted back and forth across the glass. "Are you good luck, tiny angel?" she whispered. "I could use some luck."

Fluttering white wings
like angel clouds
don't steal my sun

Words sprang into Mia's mouth. "Please, God. Don't take this mother from me! Keep her safe! We need time. Please! *Virgen*, do you listen? I'm thankful for all I've been given. I don't deserve more. I know I'm selfish. I've done little for anyone but myself. I have been trying harder lately though to be good. Please, Blessed Mother. If not for me, save Rosalia for the life she can live now. She deserves so much happiness after so much suffering through the years. She may have lost faith once, but she worked hard. She tried to believe. Isn't that enough?"

The white figure of Dr. Grimaldi came toward her.

Mia glanced up with a look of dread.

"Rosalia is stable. For now. We'll keep her a few days for observation. She's resting comfortably. That is what she needs to do now," he said.

Mia nodded dully.

"However, when it is time for discharge, I recommend a diversion. A trip somewhere meaningful, beautiful, restorative."

Mia glanced at Javier. "Okay."

"A caution: any fainting, palpitations, pain, shortness of breath, slurred speech—get her to medical care immediately."

"Understood. Thank you."

"My duty and privilege to serve." Dr. Grimaldi smiled, teeth gleaming in a shaft of light from the window.

"See now?" Javier asked.

"Quietly."

"Yes, yes," he edged toward Rosalia's room.

Mia watched Dr. Grimaldi walk away with long strides in quiet shoes on the shiny tile floor. Words flooded into her mind.

Oh fairy
how you flit and flirt
on light wings

After spending the night at Rosalia's hospital bedside, Mia walked back to the villas. She freshened up, then did shopping for food. Walking back, loaded down with packages, Mia stepped off the curb awkwardly. She stumbled, dropping one bag which spilled into the street. Mia bent down and rubbed her ankle, then scrambled for the scattered items.

A man on a bicycle screeched on his brake. "Are you okay?"

"I think so," she said, cheeks flushing.

The man set his bike aside, ushered her safely to the curb, then retrieved the remaining items. He shed his gloves, mirrored sport glasses, then his helmet.

"Oh, Dr. Grimaldi! I didn't recognize you with all the gear."

He held out his hand, "Lanzo—when I'm not working at the hospital, Ms. Casinelli."

She smiled back at him. "Mia."

"May I carry something?" He pointed to the flat rack on the back of his bike. "Could hold most, if not all."

"Oh, that would be great! These bags were getting heavier by the minute."

He placed the large plastic bags beneath the spring of the bike rack. Some plastic hung over, but a light weight wheel cover prevented contact with the spokes.

"Lead the way," Lanzo said donning his helmet and gloves, tucking the glasses into his pocket.

They crossed the street, Mia picking her way while watching for hazards, he watching her gait.

"I hope I won't make you late," she gushed.

"My morning off. Usually ride twenty miles or more. A bit shorter won't hurt."

"That seems really far, but I haven't done much biking."

"I enjoy covering that much ground quickly. Keeps me fit and clear headed for work."

"I imagine it could be taxing."

"Not so much in Puerto Escondido. Tourist type injuries, run of the mill illnesses mostly."

"Oh. I thought you worked only as a cardiologist."

"It's my specialty. But we pretty much take whatever comes on shift. It's generally much slower paced here than stateside."

"You've practiced in the U.S.?"

"Yes. Texas. Do I detect an accent?"

"I was born in…" Mia stopped abruptly, and glanced at him with a pained look. "I was *raised* in Austin and recently moved back there."

"I visited there once on a weekend trip while training at UT's Southwestern Medical, in Dallas."

Mia nodded.

"A very intense program. Three years with little time for sightseeing."

Again she nodded. They crossed from the paved road to gravel and then dirt. Breezes moving inland from the water played at tall grasses lining the rutted path. She breathed deeply, and let out a sigh.

"Tired?"

"I was up most of the night at the hospital."

Lanzo's expression changed to the measured reserve of Dr. Grimaldi. "Early days can be troublesome, nerve wracking for loved ones. Rosalia seems stable at this point."

"I bought all this food to cook her something really good. Not that the food at the hospital isn't," she added quickly.

He laughed, "No offence taken. I appreciate your desire to do something out of the ordinary."

"We have no ordinary. We barely know each other."

He studied Mia closely. "You seem to get on well."

"Oh, yes. But we've only just met. In person, that is."

"Sounds like quite a story I'd enjoy hearing later," Lanzo said, stopping outside the iron entrance gates in the high wall surrounding the villas. "May I see you to your door?"

"This is fine. Thank you so much. It was a great help." Mia smiled up at him.

He handed her the sacks. "Ankle not bothering you now?"

Mia flushed. "Only a little sore."

"Give it a rest. Take a taxi over to the hospital later."

"Yes, I will. Thank you. Perhaps I'll see you there."

"Possibly." He cinched the helmet strap, donned the sunglasses. His lean muscular leg of Lycra swung over the seat and settled his foot into the pedal. The bike moved forward, made a turn back, and he smiled, waving a hand. Then his helmeted head righted, and he pedaled away.

Stream

Mia baked tortilla slices until crisp like chips. She prepared eggplant: peeling and slicing rounds she dredged through oil, salt and black pepper before coating with flour. In a fry pan of bubbling oil, the slices were browned on each side, then transferred to a baking sheet. Freshly prepared salsa was spread over top, then a layer of cheese and another layer of browned eggplant and more cheese. "Blending elements of two cultures in cooking, just like in me," she remarked while placing the casserole—an adaptation of an old Italian recipe—into the oven. Words and stirring images popped into her mind.

Red-brown
oh so appealing
I hunger
warmth spreading through me
in anticipation
my lips taking you in

Wiping perspiration from her neck, Mia sighed, "No time for sentimentality!" But her mind kept going where she could not.

> Gerald would lean in behind her, lips brushing her hairline. She'd turn, meeting his mouth, arms circling his neck. He'd lift her up, pulling her close. Refusing to let lips and limbs part, he'd move toward the wall, bracing his hands there, a leg supporting her weight. His lips would move to her shoulder. Her fingers would pull the band from his dark ponytail. Her hands would rake through his smooth strands…

"Ohhh, my goodness! Stop!" Mia exclaimed. Bothered and warm, she dashed to the shower and stood in a cooling stream. Thoughts of Gerald evaporated.

She went by taxi to the hospital. Rosalia and Javier awoke as she came into the room. "Are you hungry?" Mia asked, removing towels around the casserole. Savory aromas rushed out. "I modified an Italian dish by varying the spices and cheeses."

They smiled.

Portions of casserole were served to plates she'd brought, and Mia added baked tortilla chips.

"Need something more," Javier said, eyeing the plates. He made motions of hand to mouth. "Need eat."

Mia chuckled, "Ohhh, utensils! I'll get some at the cafeteria." Her heels clicked down the tiled hallway and returned a few minutes later to laughter in the room.

Dr. Grimaldi turned and smiled at her. "Now *this* is a celebration!"

She looked from face to face. "What celebration?"

“Tomorrow go home,” Rosalia and Javier chimed.

Dr. Grimaldi sampled a few bites of the casserole. “Delicious! I’ll add this to my meatless recipes.”

Mia smiled. “There’s not a lot of cheese either. Might be really healthy.”

When finished eating, Dr. Grimaldi said to Mia, “May I have a word with you?”

She followed him out to the hall.

“We’ll discharge Rosalia to your care. After several days’ supervision with no further problems, she can go to her home as she feels able.”

“Great,” Mia breathed.

“How’s the ankle?”

“Just fine.” She smiled up at him.

“May I interest you in supper out later?”

“That’d be very nice.”

“Meet here after my shift?”

“Alright.”

Dr. Grimaldi drove Mia to a restaurant at the beach Playa Zicatela. A bright moon was shining in clear evening sky. Distracted, watching waves rolling to shore, Mia hadn’t even opened her menu yet when the waiter arrived.

Lanzo ordered Margaritas and appetizers.

Mia took a sip from the generous glass lined with salt, and smiled. “I’m glad there’s no alcohol.”

He nodded. “I seldom drink. Doesn’t fit with the occupation.”

Savoring sweetness in her mouth, Mia sighed, “Mmmm. LOVE mango and peach!” She sampled spicy fish on crusty tortillas, *carne asada* (grilled steak) with avocado and roasted tomatoes served on tortillas, but gulped down some water after trying one of the side salsas. "Oooo. The spices are a bit intense. I'd better stick to the fruity salsa so I don't have indigestion all night!"

Lanzo nodded, "Tell the story about you and Rosalia."

They continued to eat and sip their drinks while Mia talked. "I was raised in Austin by my parents, Victoria Maria and Angelo Casinelli. Mother wasn't even twenty when she and Papa met at a festival in La Villita (little village), the original neighborhood in San Antonio. They were instantly drawn to each other and married the next day! Grandfather owned a market there, but when he passed away the business was soon sold. My parents and Grandmother Angelina moved to Austin. I was raised in Italian and Catholic traditions. We had a very nice life. But I was lonely—a lonely only child longing for something I didn't have. When I met Tim…"

"He had the *something* you were looking for?"

Her face colored. But she shook her head. "We married and moved to Portland. I threw myself into our business. But as time went on, I felt a stirring, a return of longing. I thought it was a baby I needed." Mia sighed, "I lost several early in the pregnancies and one a bit further along. It was devastating. And combined with that heartache, emotionally wrenching dreams of a woman plagued me. I heard her words in my mind, *knew* her suffering."

"Interesting."

"In the midst of loss—Mother dying, divorce, end of my retail career with Tim—the dreams continued. I became more aware of other odd things."

"The power of change: we can be transformed, if we allow new possibilities to be considered?"

"I listened to the woman. I followed clever clues I thought Mother left for me. I searched for answers to questions about Mother's life, a missing father. I *found* Rosalia—Mother's younger sister—the mother I never knew I'd lost."

"Good story."

She finished the last drips of sweet drink. "Tell me about your life."

Lanzo said he'd grown up in Philadelphia, had two brothers and an older sister. After junior college, he went to university in Indiana, medical school in Texas.

"Did you always know you wanted to be a doctor?"

He laughed and remarked wryly, "Would have been easier if I had. I first wanted to be a musician. A violinist."

"That's unusual. You seem so athletic, I'd think the hours spent indoors practicing would be difficult."

"Exactly."

"What led you to Indiana?"

"Besides an excellent program with world renowned musicians?"

She grimaced.

"A girl actually. We married young. Had two daughters. Attending medical school while raising small children not recommended for marital or family bliss, however."

"I wanted to have a daughter or two," Mia sighed, eyes blinking as she glanced up at stars appearing in the sky.

"I didn't take much time with my girls when they were small, but I do enjoy them now whenever we get together."

"So, are you divorced?"

"Yes, and no." His eyes leveled with Mia's. "My wife, Nancy, was stressed. We both were, but she bore the heavy load of holding home together. She suffered recurring, unexplained bouts of discomfort; we didn't suspect cancer. Not until it was already advanced."

"Cancer is terrible!" Mia stated.

"Nancy fought valiantly through surgeries and chemo. And we had several years of what we tried to make seem like normal life. The girls were in middle school. We pretended everything was fine, and even as Nancy struggled, she tried to hide how she was really feeling. She didn't want more surgery, more chemo or treatments. It was difficult to face the decision and finally accept the inevitable decline and watch her slipping away."

"I'm sorry," Mia said quietly. "I lost Mother to cancer just last year. It's been so hard to get over, even though we weren't close. Maybe not being close made it harder—all that regret. And then Papa remarried only a few months later. I was shocked he could recover from the loss so quickly and move on! But he's in his 70's, why wait?" Mia let out a long sigh. "Now, it is all fine: I like Maggie and they seem well matched and happy."

Lanzo was nodding. "I married Eileen soon after Nancy passed. A friend of the family, Eileen already knew the girls. And Nancy had mentioned she'd be happy if we were to get together after her death." He shrugged. "Perhaps Nancy was happy, not us! OH, NO! Two taciturn and rebellious teenagers put extra strain on the marriage," Lanzo chuckled. "The drama would've been funny if it hadn't been so difficult!"

Eyes glistening, Mia said, "I was a taciturn teen. Now I realize, I was feeling something amiss even back then."

Finishing supper, they took a stroll on the beach. Mia carried her sandals and walked barefoot in the warm sand, her eyes scanning the water. "Did you see that splash?"

"Dolphins."

Watching more splashes, she smiled. “So magical!”

“Could be.”

“Are you a skeptic?”

“I believe in what I see. Thoughts of the unexplainable I leave to others.”

“What about mystery.”

“I acknowledge mystery; I just don’t feel compelled to explain it or seek answers outside of science.”

“Probably you’ve seen a few amazing healings. Do miracles fit into your sphere of mysterious?”

“My ego would like to think healing is a result of successful medical intervention and patient will.”

Mia smiled at him and shrugged. “Could be.”

“Now who’s a skeptic?”

She laughed.

They soon walked back to Dr. Grimald’s green sedan. He opened the door for her, and leaned down for a quick kiss. “Thank you for a delicious evening.”

She ducked into the car.

He closed the door, smiling through the glass at her.

She nodded with a half-smile.

Lanzo drove to the villas. His eyes lingered on her as he turned off the key.

Mia’s hand unlatched her seat belt. “Thank you for taking me out. It was a lovely evening.”

They exited his car, walked the short distance through the courtyard and down the concrete walkway to her room.

She unlocked the door, and they stepped inside. “I really appreciate the dinner and conversation.”

“It was more than just conversation.” He reached for her.

“Yes,” she said quietly. “It was helpful somehow.”

His hands were torches on her bare arms.

"When do you need to be at the hospital?"

He leaned down and met her lips.

Joyce was transferring wet clothes from washing machine to dryer when the phone rang. She picked it up after four rings.

"It's MIA!"

"I hear you," Joyce laughed. "How's it going down there in Mexico?"

Details about Rosalia's heart condition spilled out. "It was terrifying! I was so afraid I'd lose her before having time together. The valve replacement went well it seems, and she'll probably be okay. She's weak. Needs rest, less work. I hope to take her on a trip to see family. Lanzo—Dr. Grimaldi—says a diversion would be good. Maybe he can help me convince her."

"What's that I hear behind your words? Something going on with the doctor? Something HOT?"

Mia laughed, but changed the subject. "How are things with you, and the kids?"

"Good actually. I'm doing laundry and packing for an adventure with Tony out-of-state."

"Which one?"

"Oklahoma. Never been." Joyce glanced out the window to her flowerboxes brimming with Texas petunias. "Seems so far away."

"*I'm* far away!"

"Keep me posted on the latest. Take down the number of my new cell. Get one and we can text!"

"I don't know about that. Maybe I could learn."

"*Lanzo* interested in schooling you on anything?" Joyce asked suggestively. "What about Gerald?"

"I don't know," Mia sighed. "I'm different than I thought. Maybe I feel different now about *everything* in my life, and *everyone*, too."

There was a long silence. Finally Joyce said, "Listen to what is in you. Ask for what you truly want. The you that you are, and have always been, is not different. Only your *idea* of yourself is changed. *Location* is changed. *Family* is changed. *You* are still you."

"Thank you, Joyce," Mia barely whispered.

"Just think on these things."

"I will, Sage. I promise."

"Be easy on yourself. Allow a range of emotions. Allow a wide swath of possibilities."

Mia laughed. "Thanks for the insights."

"Hope those moonstones will be working to bring clarity and calm, alignment with the Goddess energy, connection to spirit."

"I could use some of all that!"

Rosalia looked out the window as the taxi pulled away from the hospital. "Many years live small place in desert. Now big town and ocean make smile."

Mia nodded, "Yes, LOVE the water! And I feel so blessed to be here *and* have *you* to share it!"

"Much thanks! Every day I pray, '*Gracias a la Virgen*.'"

The taxi stopped outside the gates at the villas. Rosalia exited the car without help, and walked straight and strong down the concrete walkway toward the rooms rented before the hospital stay.

"This way, Mama! I rented a larger unit for us all to share: two bedrooms and a bigger kitchen."

"Is much more money?"

Mia shook her head while unlocking the door. "Less actually. And more practical: Javier and I can cook. And when he is away working, I can look after you easier than with two units."

Any objection melted away as they stepped inside. Rosalia sank heavily to the cushioned sofa. After resting a bit, she was helped to the bedroom. Settled into a bed with pillows propped behind her, she sighed, and soon drifted to sleep.

After a few more days recuperation, Rosalia went to her shop at the beach. Though a bit tired, she began sewing and showed Mia some special stitches: secrets handed down by the women of her village.

Mia struggled to duplicate the stitches, but when calm settled on her like a hoop of patience, her stitching improved. "How old were you when you started sewing?"

"Only a girl. At market, women, Mother, Grandmother work, sell, talk, show stitches. Maria stitch good, but after sister go, I do more work. With much practice, soon stitch better than sister," Rosalia giggled. "Then see Mano and friends! 'No look. Sew,' Mother and Grandmother say. But I see Mano and heart go!" Rosalia's cheeks colored. "I feel something…"

Mia sighed, "I know how that is. Some men have special charisma."

"Mano make special words. Special kisses. I think of Mano and make many stitches wrong! Women say much of this: too young for love."

"If they opposed him, how did you get together?"

"How I like look of Mano! I like sweet words Mano say. Family say no listen. Say no good come of this. I hide with Mano at *ahuehuete*. Special place. Special time of love. And Mano say: make woman, *his* woman. I want Mano so much! But family no like boy from another village. Family say girl with man from other village break heart of family."

"Yes…" Mia sighed. "I left my parents and grandmother when I got married."

"But I want Mano so much! And I want own life!"

Again Mia nodded. "I was not as young as you were when I left home. But I wanted the same thing: to make my own life, in my own way."

"I think easy go, and Mano good at loving! He make smile…" Rosalia sighed, "But Mano no good at work. Everywhere he say no work for him…" A frown creased her forehead, her breathing labored.

"Don't say more, Mama. I don't want you to be upset." Mia watched her mother's hands sewing. "It's not good for your heart."

Rosalia's hands stilled, her eyes looked up. "I pray *La Virgen* listen."

"She does," Mia said with confidence. "I know she does. She answered my prayers—some of them at least."

"I say I want to live. Help me live. And I dream *La Virgen listen*! *Madre* say no worry, heart heal."

"When was that?"

"Last night. Today…" Rosalia shrugged…"better."

"You have amazing faith, quiet strength and confidence. Mother was strong, too, but in a different way. She tried to always be in control. And she ruled our home. Papa would do whatever she wanted, but he is a good man."

"Mano good man."

"Loving a *bad* man would be terrible. *Mending Stone*, is about love and pain, hardship and loss, the power of prayer and hope. You've had all of it."

"No love without pain."

Sighing loudly, Mia remarked, "I don't want pain. No more pain."

"Some men pain to live. Other men, pain when go."

"Tim and I were efficient business partners, and our marriage was efficient, too," Mia sighed.

"Husband love good?"

Mia glanced up from her stitching. "Good *enough* I thought." Then she added low and quiet, "Now I know better."

Rosalia only nodded, needle piercing the cloth with quick stabs and pulls.

Ocean

Rusted dents in the sides of the long Ford van and cracks in the windshield caused them to inquire if it was the correct vehicle to take to the central valley.

"Must be safe enough," Mia commented, but her look was dubious. "Better than flying: time to see the landscape. I actually love mountains. Wish we'd see some dressed in white..."

Rosalia nodded, but her hand gripped Mia's tightly.

Doors were opened. Passengers boarded. The driver donned large sunglasses, and drove out of the station. Mia and Rosalia were sitting side by side on the bench seat and glanced out the window as Puerto Escondido disappeared behind.

The winding road narrowed to two small lanes. There was no emergency lane. Steep hillsides or ravines on either side of the road made pull outs impossible. Chunks of pavement had broken from some edges and frequent new and patched potholes dotted the concrete. Oncoming vehicles—mostly other transport vans—passed by every twenty or thirty minutes, but there was little traffic coming or going. Gripping the mouthpiece of some type radio with one hand, the driver continually talked into it while his other hand steered around road hazards.

Dotting a narrow corridor beside the road, small residences had tilled gardens and small fields. A few times the van was forced to veer around goats staked on short ropes to eat tall grass beside the road. One goat with bulging belly slept in the road, and was nearly crushed beneath the van's wheels, but he did not budge.

After traveling several hours, the van pulled to a stop at a store/restaurant perched on the side of a steep and shady hillside. The driver advised all passengers to get out and stretch before travelling the next leg of the trip.

Mia walked to the edge of the road and peered into a deep ravine. Damp and dark tropical vegetation covered the hillside. Moss grew on stilted lumber supporting the building hanging out over the plunging earth. Walking back around to the front of the building, she passed a wooden platform where a greying brown and white dog slept with head resting on outstretched paws beside discarded plastic jugs, wet cardboard boxes, and rusting metal crates. Mia snapped pictures of the dog and a *BIMBO* sign posted on a tree. Aging side by side, they stirred something in her.

Inside the store, Mia bought a package of small cakes they quickly ate.

Her mother smiled and wiped crumbs from her lips as they loaded back in the van.

"I'd love to eat another, but I'm getting a little plump around the middle!" Mia remarked.

Rosalia wrapped an arm around her and squeezed. "I like daughter soft."

"Good thing," Mia chuckled.

Many minutes later, the van descended from the forest to the central valley of Oaxaca. Mia watched out the windows with anticipation and rubbed her legs as if rubbing away soreness.

"Sewing good for this. Make plan. Work: one stitch, two stitch. Breathe stitches. Day, week, year…Time pass quick." Then Rosalia tapped her chest, and sighed, "Only here make slow."

Mia nodded and smiled, "Good advice, *stitching calm*. That's not how I worked at the shop Tim and I owned, or at home. I worked at top speed, my mind constantly spinning, 'What's next? What's next?' And there never seemed to be a moment to breathe, or relax."

"Learn," her mother said softly. "Breathe. Like make love: slow. Make life slow and good."

"You're so optimistic," Mia whispered.

Rosalia shrugged, "Life good."

"How could you simply put your hardship behind and forget the suffering?"

"No simple! *Never* forget." Rosalia pointed to her eyes. "Look only ahead. Bad memory fade behind." She pointed to her heart. "Save good here."

Mia nodded, and said softly, "Wise. Just like I always wanted to hear from a mother."

As the van reached San Bartolo Coyotepec, their eyes eagerly searched the streets, houses, and buildings. Rosalia pointed to a white cathedral with red-roofed spires and a flower shaped window atop giant wooden doors. "See this before!"

"It was a clue I thought Mother left for me to decipher. She said my Tudor house with a curved door and etched rose design in glass was like her village church. Joyce and I came here: giant black ceramic urns beside the gate are like the pottery Mother collected; and the flower window above the door *does* look like flowers that were etched in my glass door. I wondered if this was her town, or one she meant for me to find."

"Make pledge with Mano: love always." Rosalia said quietly, eyes downcast. "Only marry we make."

"It's a beautiful church. But why here?"

"Cathedral of family of Mano."

"Oh, my gosh! I might have met relatives of my father when I came here with Joyce and our friend Blake. I'm not sure where the old couple lived. Maybe it was nearby. We wandered around so much…" Mia stared out the window for a recognizable street.

"Much change since I see," Rosalia offered with a shrug.

The van left the town. They watched out the windows as interesting landscape stretched across the valley floor. About twenty miles from San Bartolo Coyotepec, rural plots clumped tighter together as the outskirts of Oaxaca City were reached.

In the city, the van entered a doorway to a large indoor station. Mia and Rosalia's luggage was transferred to a waiting taxi, and they were soon away down the narrow cobblestone streets of the historic district.

Mia smiled at the iron entrance gates of Hotel Las Mariposas where she and Joyce had stayed before going on to Puerto Escondido. A painted sign with signature butterfly design offered familiar welcome. The driver set their luggage beside a large reception desk in an open-air lobby where they were checked in by the smiling owner, who then escorted them to their room beyond the bubbling courtyard fountain.

"Pretty," Rosalia sighed, dropping her bag and plopping down onto one of the double beds in the ochre colored room.

"Let's have a rest," Mia said latching the screen door, leaving the curtained French door ajar. She switched on a standing fan, and lay down on her bed. Looking up through a square of glass block in the ceiling, she caught the glimmer of a first star in the dusky sky. "Maybe it *is* a planet. Maybe wishes made on planets do not come true—that's what I believed before. But now maybe I'm beginning to believe *any* heartfelt wishes can come true. Maybe *every* wish can come true?" Mia yawned, and the whir of the fan muffling traffic sounds from the cobblestone street lulled her to sleep.

Early morning activity outside in the courtyard woke them from a long slumber. Once dressed, they went for coffee and cereal and yogurt, and joined other lodgers breakfasting at long plastic tables. Chatting, Mia described her last stay here and the sightseeing tours she took with Joyce and Blake to Monte Alban, Mitla, Santa Maria del Tule, and San Bartolo Coyotepec. "Coyotepec means something like 'hill of the coyote.' And San Bartolo's patron saint is Bartholomew." She laughed, "That is about all I remember of the history lesson from our guide, Claudia. It was informative, but I was distracted by the wind fluttering leaves in the trees, and the grasses rustling, and something else—maybe the ancient stones whispering or the many who were there before me. At Monte Alban, I looked out over the valley to the mountains beyond. I felt the pull of a distant tide. I could almost hear the ocean calling to me. It was so powerful."

"How poetic!" remarked their new acquaintance Barbara. "You MUST be a writer! If you're not, you should be!"

Mia blushed. "Thank you. Yes, I am a writer. I'm anticipating the publication of my first novel. Hopefully coming out this year."

"I'll read it!"

"Oh, my gosh. Thank you! That's very encouraging," Mia smiled, her eyes taking in other nodding heads around the table, including her mother's.

The day was warming, golden light warming the cobblestone streets and stucco and brick of houses and buildings of the historic district. Creamy patina of aged walls of Templo Santo Domingo de Guzman shimmered in the morning sun.

Mia grasped Rosalia's hand as they stepped through the aged wooden doors. "I wanted to bring you to see this," she whispered. "I felt something here, something real. I prayed for love to fill me; I prayed for an end to longing. I prayed to be led to my heart's greatest desire."

Rosalia's eyes filled with tears, her hand gripping Mia's ever more tightly as they marveled over ornate carvings and statues with sparkling gold and color shining on ceiling and walls, every inch covered in ornamentation.

They knelt in the chapel of Nuestra Señora del Rosario. Resplendent in a glowing ivory gown covered in jewels, Mother Mary held baby Jesus in one hand, a rosary in the other.

"This is where I prayed, pouring out my heart to the Blessed Mother. She heard my plea! *She* listened! *She* answered!" Mia studied Mary's sweetly smiling face. Familiar words flowed into her mind, "Hail Mary, Full of Grace…"

Rosalia, too, prayed with murmuring lips. After a long time, she sat back and rested against the pew. "Is good I come inside with daughter. Only see outside before."

"Why?"

"*Catedral* (cathedral) of city. Family no like big city. Outside make pledge with Mano," Rosalia breathed. "Pray for safe. Think pray make good luck."

"Probably it does."

But Rosalia wore a grimace and shook her head while saying shakily, "So young, think prayers keep devil away."

"I'm not sure what keeps away evil. I like to think prayer can," she whispered. "Maybe prayer only brings strength to cope with what else comes…"

They wandered into the gift shop, perused a rack of postcards and other pretty items for sale. Mia purchased a necklace: clear glass pendant with pink rose inside. She fastened the golden chain around Rosalia's neck, and kissed her mother on the cheek. "For you, Mama. Rose is your symbol—a secret center, and source of strength."

Rosalia pressed the cool glass against her skin and smiled. "Like hands on heart."

Outside, they followed other pedestrians down the sidewalks. Five blocks away at the *zocalo* (main plaza of the city), they rested on an iron bench in the shade of a giant laurel tree and watched patrons visiting shops lining the courtyard.

Attracted by sounds of cascading water, they soon went to examine a carved stone fountain with fanciful figures perched beside massive green stone bowls with high tiers running over with water. "Now I see why this was nicknamed the city of green stone," Mia sighed. "So appealing I want to run my hands over every satiny inch! Ohhh, wouldn't a bathtub made of this be heavenly!"

Rosalia laughed. "Daughter dream of water and more water!"

"Yesss," Mia sighed."

Nearby, a waiter in formal attire bid them come inside a stately restaurant for *comida,* the afternoon meal. His smiling mouth with full lips was so welcoming they could not resist.

"Javier like this man. Heart sad now."

"I'm sure you miss him. I know a man with similar smooth and radiant skin, full mouth, sparkling brown eyes that melt me." Mia waved her napkin like a fan, and laughed.

"Good man? Maybe come to Mexico?"

"Ohhh," she sighed. "I wish he could. But Gerald is caring for his grandmother who is very sick. I haven't been able to reach him lately to see how she's doing. I keep sending emails, but he hasn't responded."

Rosalia shrugged. "Some man go, say nothing."

"I don't know what I want to do about him. Maybe our timing is off. Maybe it's just me too late again for things I want in my life."

"Food come! Not too late to eat!"

Mia laughed and took a bite. "I *do* love these vegetables with the *queso*! LOVE cheese! And I like these tortillas so thick they seem like bread. LOVE bread!"

After lunching, they browsed at the market until Rosalia's energy lagged. Mia secured a taxi to take them back to their lodging.

Leaning her head against the seat, Rosalia watched buildings passing by.

"Does it look different?"

Rosalia shrugged. "Forty years. Maybe mind forget. "

"How long did you stay in the city?"

"Few months."

"I can't imagine leaving home and being on your own at fifteen! Even Mano at nineteen. Were you frightened?"

Rosalia replied quietly, "Miss village! Miss family! Every day much see. Try forget home. But I cry. Mano try make smile."

"He was a good man to cheer you."

Rosalia nodded. "Another good man, Javier make smile. But here," she patted her chest, "love Mano always."

"Love lives on," Mia responded wistfully. "Even with separation of time and distance." A detour forced the taxi off course, and when Mia glanced out the window at a passing cemetery, she said to the driver, "Oh! Could you stop and wait here a few minutes?"

He pulled over to the curb, and they got out.

"Mama, I want to show you something I saw when I came here with Joyce and Blake. The most stunning thing..."

Through the iron gates in high concrete walls, Mia led the way down earthen paths to a headstone—a life-size relief of a young woman weeping with face in her hands as if every heartbreak was heaped on her small shoulders. "She looks as young and homesick as you must have been when you came with Mano to this city," Mia said softly.

"*Ay*! Is true! I cry like this!"

"And you were not much older when you lost me…"

Rosalia nodded, blinking back tears.

"She's as no more beautiful than you."

Hands to coloring cheeks, Rosalia replied, "Javier, man of country, know herbs for skin. Maybe keep soft."

"I could use some of those herbs for my aging skin!"

Rosalia patted Mia's cheek with tenderness.

"Mother used many lotions and potions and always kept out of the sun. And I do, too. Though lately, my skin seems different. I *feel* different. Something is changing in me…"

"Look pretty. Daughter like both mothers!"

They were quiet on the ride to Las Mariposas. After a rest, and a delicious evening meal, they fell into beds, and slept.

But Mia traveled the night in dreams and cries were in her throat.

Mama…Mama…

Waking in the morning, she whined, "OH, my GOSH! We overslept! And I dreamed such disturbing things!"

Rosalia sat up in bed.

"Why do I *still* have such dreams?"

Her mother shrugged.

Mia drew a deep breath, then threw off her bedcovers. "We need to hurry and get ready."

"Bus come here?" Rosalia asked with raised eyebrow.

"We *could* go by bus or van. But the private car I booked will be much more enjoyable; we can stop whenever and wherever we want."

Rosalia shook her head. "Too much money. Take bus."

"Comfort is worth the expense. And I have enough money," Mia smiled with a look of pride and confidence. "That is the joy of having plenty—using it for pleasure and adventure! And sharing it with people I love!"

They dressed, ate, and were soon heading down the highway in the car toward Santa Maria del Tule where Mia insisted they stop at the ancient tree standing fifteen stories high and dwarfing the church beside it.

"*Ahuehuete*!" Rosalia pronounced.

"Yes. Isn't she wondrous? A mother tree more than 2000 years old!"

They stared up into entwined branches like twisted strands of hair tossed by the breeze.

"*Abuela grande* (tall grandmother)," Rosalia quipped.

"It takes more than thirty arms stretching fingertip to fingertip to circle her trunk," Mia said repeating facts Joyce related when they'd visited before. A leaf fluttered down. She caught it in her hand. "Lost your hold little one? Loosened from your roots? Drifting and alone?"

"What this?"

"Ohhh," Mia sighed. "I was only musing." She did not say what else came to mind: an image of Gerald in his yard, his tree with rough bark—honey locust with creamy white flowers he said smelled heavenly when blooming in summer.

"This good tree. Like *ahuehuete* of village."

"Will you show it to me when we're in San Bartolome Quialana?"

Rosalia nodded, but in the car again, she looked out expectantly as the miles to Tlacolula flew by.

Entering town and nearing a cathedral, Mia said suddenly, "Let's stop and go inside! I've read there are many unusual statues."

Rosalia shivered. "Dead saints."

"Aren't all saints dead?"

"These how die! Even one head below!"

"Oh, how gruesome! But I read there are also angels, and a silver picket fence. *Those* sound lovely."

Still Rosalia objected with shaking head. "See market?"

"If you like. But tomorrow is the big market day."

Rosalia shrugged.

The car stopped on a nearly deserted street.

"Market *de Domingo* (of Sunday) like this quiet. Then bus come. Bring color, much fruit, vegetable, flower. Even turkey, chicken."

Mia laughed, "Live?"

Nodding and laughing, Rosalia responded, "Some run. Everywhere people, food, animals!"

"If we stay only tonight in San Bartolome Quialana, we could stop here again tomorrow on our way back."

Rosalia shot Mia a look, but said nothing as they walked the quiet street.

"Are you worried about going back to San Bartolome Quialana after so many years—what you will find?"

But Rosalia only glanced around and quietly got back into the car.

Veering left, right, left again around a one-way street several blocks in length, the car traveled quickly. Across a dusty flat of land, it veered left at another junction and sped toward the Sierra Madre del Sur mountain range. Trees and green vegetation in the shadow of the peaks rose from the flat earth.

A village huddled at the base of the mountains. Only outlines of buildings appeared, then colors, people. As the car crept into town, villagers paused in their pursuits to gawk.

Mia studied the style of their dress: women wore bright aprons and satin dresses or colorfully embroidered tops and patterned skirts. Flower-print scarves covered the heads of women, and lengths of ribbon wound around the braids of girls. Men wore light pants and button-up shirts in cotton, usually plaid. It was warm, at least 85 degrees, but no one was scantily clothed.

"Where do we go?" Mia asked quietly.

Rosalia scanned the road ahead. After several more blocks, she pointed.

The driver turned the car down a street leading toward the far edge of town. Concrete, clay, and brick walls separated residential compounds from the street and neighboring houses.

Face a mask of anticipation, Rosalia suddenly rasped, "Stop."

They got out. Rosalia walked on wobbly legs toward a gate. She righted her shoulders and drew herself up, then pulled a rope dangling from a stick. A bell on the other side of the high wall rang.

They peeked through cracks in the wooden gate to see a young man approaching across a dusty courtyard. He addressed them in the language of the village: *Zapotecas*.

Rosalia remained quiet.

He looked to Mia. "Spanish or English?"

"What?" Mia laughed. "English for me; my mother speaks better Spanish than English."

"Is good," he replied.

Rosalia's voice shook on inquiry to the residing family.

The young man answered.

She uttered a few words in barely a whisper.

His hand unlatched and opened the gate.

Rosalia gripped Mia's arm as they walked into a central courtyard surrounded by single-story structures. From one larger house, a woman in a print dress of blue flowers, head covered in traditional scarf came out. Her keen eyes studied them as the she conferred with the man, and then her hand went to her mouth. She moved quickly to embrace them.

"Who is this?" Mia asked, arms hugged to her sides by the woman.

"*Tia* Patrice (Aunt Patrice)!" Rosalia laughed, tears springing into her eyes. "*Ay, Dios*! I think I never see again!"

Patrice kept a tight arm around each of them, while turning and calling loudly. People straggled out from house doors and were introduced. "Isidoro, Katia, Spiro, Silvia, my sons

Otilio and Victor, Victor's wife Ofelia. And Juan," she added as a small boy came running. "Grandson."

"Would you like to come inside for shade? Something to drink?" Victor offered.

"Yes, thank you," Rosalia and Mia managed with smiles, and followed the group into the largest house.

The walls of the main room were painted bright lime green. The floor was old and cracked terracotta tile. A large table at the center was surrounded with an assortment of chairs, mostly plastic, but some wooden.

Patrice instructed Victor to pull out one chair with upholstered seat for Rosalia who sank to the cushion with grateful praise. Drinks were poured and people scurried about bringing food from behind a partition separating the kitchen from the large dining/living area. Finally, all gathered around the table.

Rosalia said, "Forty years since I see *Tia* Patrice. Live then in Tlacolula de Matamoros."

"Here five years. I come back San Bartolome Quialana when…" Patrice paused.

"When what?"

"Isabel sick. *Lo siento, su madre esta muerto* (I am sorry, your mother is dead)."

Rosalia tapped the center of her chest. "I hear nothing of family. I pray *La Virgen* keep safe. But here, I know this."

Eyes around the table blinked back tears.

"I pray mother know daughter safe and think of her."

"Hear once news of baby," Patrice ventured.

Rosalia smiled, and nodded toward Mia.

All eyes turned.

Mia stared back.

"Hear nothing of Maria."

"Sister, Maria, go to *los Estados Unidos*!"

"Ahhh!" breathed the crowd.

"Yes," Mia interjected. "She married in San Antonio and moved to Austin, Texas. Only a few months ago, she died."

"Ohhh," sighed the group, offering condolences.

"Much of family gone. *Su padre* (your father) is now gone many years."

Rosalia nodded.

Patrice offered, "Drink much."

Uneasy looks were exchanged.

"I know this," Rosalia acknowledged quietly.

The crowd seemed to relax, and after a short prayer, they began eating and continued talking. Loud chatter of younger family members was interspersed with laughter.

Mia asked many questions in attempts to piece together information about their lives and relationships. And she answered many inquiries about the United States.

After nearly two hours of eating and talking, Rosalia began to sag in her chair.

"*Tia* Patrice, my mother tires. She has a weak heart."

Patrice offered an adjoining room. "Have a rest."

Several people jumped up and assisted Rosalia into the room where she reclined on a lumpy but soft bed against the wall. Window shades were pulled; afternoon sun through old canvas cast a golden glow on dusty-pink colored walls.

"Thank you, *Tia* Patrice," Mia said. "I think the trip wore her out. Maybe, too, Mama was worried what we might find when coming here."

Patrice examined Mia closely. "Why come now from U.S.? And why Rosalia come only now? So many years pass with no word..."

"A long series of events led us to find each other. Something nagged and pulled me. All my life, an empty place was inside. My heart hurt. I dreamed of a woman, heard her voice calling, telling me a story. After Mother—Rosalia's sister, Maria—died, I found an embroidered scrap of cloth and clues seeming to point to Mexico. And I learned Papa—the man who raised me—is not my father. I came in search of a father I never knew was missing and found Rosalia—the mother I never knew I had!"

"*Un milagro*!"

"Yes," Mia laughed. "A wonderful lucky miracle."

"Prayer, work, hope make much happen," Patrice answered cryptically, her eyes sparkling with intensity.

"I'm discovering life is so much more mystery than I ever suspected."

Patrice nodded, a smile lingering on her face. She tiptoed over to the bedroom doorway and peered in at Rosalia who was sleeping and snoring lightly. Patrice shut the door, and motioned for Mia to follow.

They went outside. At the back of the small compound, they entered a clay cottage through a wooden door made of rough and weathered boards painted over many times evidenced by the colors peeking through scrapes and chips. A teenage girl sitting at a table was idly thumbing through a colorful fashion magazine. Behind a partition was a small bed in the corner where Patrice withdrew a cloth covering a white head and whispered, "A surprise."

An old woman turned and sat up. Her clouded eyes squinted.

"Who is this?" Mia whispered.

"Inez. Isabel's mother, Rosalia's grandmother."

"*My* great-grandmother?"

The aged woman patted the pallet. Mia went to her and sat down. The old woman raised and settled wrinkled hands on each of Mia's shoulders. Inez mumbled rhythmic words, while her hands moved over Mia's face.

"Mia," Patrice said. "Maria Isabel Angelina."

A smile curved Inez's lips.

"Does she know who I am *really*?"

Patrice nodded.

"Does *Mama* know Great-grandmother lives?"

Patrice's eyes gleamed. "A surprise for Rosalia!"

When they returned to the bigger house, Patrice issued instructions. Multiple chairs and small tables were collected from the other houses and placed together to make a huge table. Chatter and animation filled the room. Table linens were placed, flowers were brought.

The bedroom door opened. "Why so busy?" Rosalia asked wandering out.

"Dinner for friends," someone answered. "Did you have a pleasant rest?"

Rosalia nodded, but said, "I miss much excitement!"

"You missed nothing," Mia answered with a shrug and a quick look to Patrice.

"Come sit." Patrice moved the upholstered chair closer to the kitchen where Rosalia could watch the food preparations.

But Rosalia shook her head. "I need walk for strength."

"Remember village?"

"Yes. I show daughter something."

Mia went with Rosalia through the neighborhood. Their eyes studied walls and fences and gates and houses along the street. Not far from the family compound, the road turned and thinned to a dusty trail winding up an incline covered in a few young trees. They followed around a corner and down a slope.

Rosalia ducked under branches of a large *ahuehuete,* and sat down on fine green grass next to the gnarly trunk. Resting her back against the tree, she smiled conspiratorially. "I hide here with Mano!"

"You were determined to be together! I wasn't able to be sneaky with Mother on watch! I think she knew everything I did."

"Good mother: keep safe."

Mia nodded, and said quietly. "My friend, Gerald, said the same thing."

"Good man? Have love with this man?"

Mia shrugged. "Something…"

Rosalia studied her with keen eyes. "Why leave good man behind?"

"He had work that couldn't be delayed."

"Man must work. Woman do what can." She shrugged, "Is life only."

"Tim and I worked together, but there was little else we enjoyed doing together." Mia glanced at her mother, "I realize now, we had no passion for each other. We were good partners, but the 'spark' was not there." She looked down at her hands, her bare ring finger. "I guess he found someone else to spark with!"

"Husband like what cook?"

She shrugged. "He never said much about it. I do cook well though. I do most things well," she sighed, "except make a baby."

"Some women old when make baby."

"Maybe I waited too long. Maybe it is too late for me, or was never meant to be."

Rosalia shrugged. "Words make wings."

"What do you mean?"

"Make wish. *La Virgen* listen."

Mia nodded. "I know *She* listens." A bird flying by landed up in the tree and began chirping loudly. Looking up at the bird, Mia replied, "Do you ever feel your mother near?"

"A mother always with daughter."

"I felt you," Mia whispered. "Even though I didn't know it was you, I ached deeply for someone who wasn't there. And I never understood why I felt so empty—as if I had lost something precious and dear. I tried to put the feeling away, but it persisted, returning again and again over the years."

They sat together a long time and were quiet with the sheltering tree and blue sky above.

On return to the family residence, they found the house crowded with people.

"Friends with whole village?" Rosalia asked.

She and Mia sat in two of three remaining empty chairs at the end of the table as Patrice began welcoming the group and all eyes were on her.

The girl from the clay cottage helped Inez slip into the empty chair beside Rosalia.

"Friends and family, please join hands."

Rosalia clasped Mia's hand and turned to clasp the hand of the person on her other side.

Patrice announced, "*Abuelita* Inez, here is Granddaughter Rosalia and Great-granddaughter, Mia—Maria Isabel Angelina..."

Rosalia wiped tears from her staring, astonished eyes.

Around the table, more wet eyes were wiped and Signs of the Cross were made with smiles.

Cheers followed a blessing. Food and drinks were served, eating commenced. Laughter and lively conversations filled the room. When finished with the meal, the group moved chairs outside and several men began playing guitars and other instruments. Woman and children clapped and danced and sang.

Later, sleeping on a pallet on the floor next to Inez and Rosalia, Mia dreamed.

He slapped her face…kicked her…she crawled from the blows…

River

The bus to Tlacolula de Matomoros the next day was crowded with vendors, and shoppers carrying bags to the weekly Sunday market. Sleepy heads bobbed against shoulders and seat backs.

Squealing brakes halted the bus. Riders filed out. Stalls were set up in attractive and painstaking arrangements of everything for home or farm or family—even freshly butchered meat hanging red and juicy. Also available was barbecue and practically any other food desired. Three-wheeled vehicles covered with canvas whizzed by live animals for sale. Shiny black pottery from San Bartolo Coyotepec was displayed, as well as other ceramic and wood pieces used in home cooking. Rugs, leather goods, decorative wooden figures were in abundance.

Local citizens were early shoppers. And then came tourists—buses and cars full of tourists. Some friendly and smiling, others irritable and penny thrifty.

Dressed in borrowed headscarves, aprons, skirts and blouses, Rosalia and Mia helped with sales in the family's booth.

Many tourists asked for photographs, but Patrice and the other "indigenous" women were quite skilled in deflecting thoughtless questions and comments from city dwellers.

A chatty couple purchasing several items said they were from Austin, Texas and just loved coming to Mexico.

"Like Austin," Rosalia announced.

"You might like it very much!" chimed the tourists. "If you come, look us up in our store, **Why Not Country**!"

"It *would* be wonderful if you come to America," Mia said as the couple walked away.

"Come last year," Rosalia added with shaking head.

"Last year?" Mia rubbed chill bumps from her arms. "I saw a woman at the mall in Austin. A familiar looking woman. I glanced away only a moment but she had disappeared. I thought my mind played tricks, or it was a ghost. I thought it might be Mother. Oh my GOSH! The shop was named ***Angelita***! Was it really you?"

"Name shop 'little angel,' name give daughter," Rosalia answered. "Hope name keep daughter safe. Hope also name make good business for shop!"

Mia's eyes sparkled with recognition. "Ohhh. When I began searching Mexico, angels seemed significant. And Joyce asked if *Angelita* and my grandmother's name, *Angelina,* were the Spanish and Italian versions of the same name. ***Angelita*** is on the scrap of cloth that led me to your shop! I think Mother changed our names to hide our identities and to keep us safe in the U.S. But I don't understand why, or how she escaped whatever she was running from."

Rosalia said softly, "Pray. Pray and more pray! *La Virgen* keep safe."

Mia nodded.

"Many thing different this country. Many work for little money. Life simple. Hard," Rosalia said with a shrug.

Other women eavesdropping nodded.

"My life in the U.S. is rich beyond belief. All the years I was working and working, making money, I didn't realize there was another way to live." Mia shook her head with wistful smile. "I knew something was missing, but I thought it was a baby. I see now, and hear when you speak of Mano and of Javier, there was so much more missing in my life than I knew, than I *allowed* myself to know."

Rosalia nodded, saying softly, "Family see marry?"

"Yes."

"With Mano, no family, no church give blessing," Rosalia sighed, "Is life."

"There are many things more important than the blessing of the church!" Mia stated loudly.

"Maria have blessing?"

"Yes, but it was based on a story she concocted. Maybe they said Angelo was my father and they had married in a civil ceremony. Maybe they said after I was born they wanted to marry in the church."

"Family see this?"

"Only Grandmother Angelina. From pictures, and what she said, I think Grandmother accepted the marriage with great difficulty. What *did* she know or suspect of Mother's true identity and heritage? Maybe her objection was only that Mother was more than twenty years younger than Papa. On the surface—with the concocted story—Grandmother Angelina had an Italian daughter-in-law to marry Papa and carry on the family name."

"Mothers have ideas for life of children."

"That's certainly true!"

"What is true?" Patrice asked with meddling smile after finishing up with several customers.

"Oh," Mia sighed. "We were talking of how mothers and children have different ideas how they want to live."

"True! My children dress modern. Hair, makeup! *Ay*! Too much! Why children fight tradition? Television fill minds with city ideas! Always talk: money, money, money. 'Why stay in village and work hard for little money? Come to city: more fun, make more money!' *Ay*! See city! Is much crowd and stranger. Frightening."

"It can be."

Rosalia interrupted, "Village small! Everywhere eyes, ears! So much talk!"

"Is true." Patrice's head bobbed up and down.

"And nothing for help."

Patrice replied evenly, "Some things difficult. Private."

"What does a village say if a man beats his wife?"

Eyes riveted to Mia's face.

"Just wondering what is considered acceptable behavior between husband and wife. In a disturbing dream…I..."

"No business of others," Patrice answered carefully. "Some talk, advise, but do nothing."

Rosalia glanced around, then said in half-volume, "Parents work hard. Father drink. Sometime too much drink."

"Many have that problem," Mia said softly. "Did he ever show anger to his family?"

Rosalia nodded with grave expression. "Mother. And when sister say too much. Father make big trouble."

"Ohhh," Mia sighed. "How upsetting to watch and hear!"

Her mother nodded, lips pressed tightly together.

And Patrice turned to attend to more customers.

The day became busy; little time was left for talk. Rosalia and Mia helped with sales. In a lull between surges of customers, finally Mia was able to break away for a walk through the market. Her eyes were drawn to colorful spices and fruits and flowers. Her ears listened through a cacophony of sounds: calls and pitches of vendors vying for attention, conversations of shoppers, squeals and cries of children and animals. She wandered, searching for something her eyes did not see and her ears did not hear. A familiar ache burned inside her. But she found nothing to buy to fill the void, nothing to eat to quell the longing. She forced it away and went back to work.

Riders on the evening bus returning to San Bartolome Quialana dozed with arms around sacks of leftover sale items, heads leaning against seats. Perhaps the road was familiar: traveled often for the weekly market. Perhaps they did not care to see known landscape. But Mia stared out at the grassy land stretching toward the mountains and something again gnawed at her.

Later, in the home of her ancestors, she slept restlessly on the pallet on the floor next to Inez and Rosalia, and dreamed.

He cried for a mother…arms for comfort…

Mia forced her eyes open. She was alone in the clay cottage, she drew a ragged breath. "Why didn't my parents come back here? Was the shame of going against family wishes so great? Did something else prevent their return? I might have grown up here with all this family, all these kind and loving women to teach me about love. Maybe I would have been happier." More questions flashed in her mind. "Who is the boy I dreamed? Why does he break my heart so? Is he one of my lost babies?"

She got up and splashed her face with cool water to wash away tears, then went to the larger house where several family members were busy in the kitchen.

"Late sleep," Rosalia stated with motherly concern.

"I'm still tired," Mia sighed.

"Coffee? Oaxaca best!"

"Maybe not. My stomach feels shaky. I don't know why it's bothering me—maybe from disturbing dreams."

Rosalia squeezed Mia in a hug. "Be okay."

"Ugh. I feel squishy. I've been eating too many sweets and not getting enough exercise."

"No worry," Rosalia chuckled with a gleam in her eyes. "Men like soft."

"Oh, my gosh!" Mia laughed, deciding after all to fix a coffee with cream and sugar. She sat down.

Across the table, Patrice smiled while wrapping a granddaughter's braids in fresh ribbons.

Rosalia came over to stand by Mia. "I brush hair?"

"I guess so."

"I put ribbon?" Rosalia teased, briskly running a bristle brush through Mia's hair.

"No ribbons for this old girl. We missed that phase, *and* I was a married woman!"

"American women color hair?" Patrice inquired.

"Many do. I did. But I'm letting it grow out natural so I can donate for wigs."

"Wear hat, scarf. Why wig?"

"It's more than an expression of personality or uniqueness. Hair is important to sense of self, a sign of good health. Some patients have hair loss or are undergoing medical treatment and lose all their natural hair.."

"Tradition important. San Bartolome Quialana women cover hair. Respect for church, husband."

"In America, that is not a tradition I've seen except within a few cultures and ethnicities. There's so much diversity there, it's hard to know what should be worn."

"Ahhh." Heads nodded. "See magazine."

"Don't believe everything you see. The media can be misleading. Much of what you see is advertising for products, not necessarily how most women really dress."

"Where Mia and family live?" Patrice asked, piquing the attention of several lingering family members who had not gone with them to Tlacolula the previous day.

"I live alone now in Texas," Mia answered, her eyes scanning the faces around the room. "I wrote a novel and hope to make money on it. I was working in a bookstore when I left. But I don't know what I will do when I return. I had just moved into a new condo and was nearly finished decorating when I went to San Antonio to follow clues I thought Mother left for me. A few days later, I came to Oaxaca. That all seems ages ago, and worlds away."

"What condo?"

"An apartment I bought."

"One person? Like cottage of Inez?" Ofelia, wife of Victor asked.

Mia shook her head. "There are more rooms. And space for others, but I'm the only one to live there."

"Sad," Patrice commented with sighs around the room agreeing. "Lonely one person."

"I guess it can be…" Mia sighed.

"Have big work?"

"No, not right now."

"Maybe stay in Oaxaca?" one of the girls interjected with hopeful smile. "San Bartolome Quialana?"

Mia smiled back. "Maybe. I don't really know what I will do…"

"Have big work here!" Patrice announced suddenly. "Tomorrow market. Today make tamales. Need help!"

"I'd love that! But I've never made them."

"Much work. Many hands. Many steps. And HOT!" Rosalia said.

"Easy but long," the other teenage girl offered. "Work of women of Oaxaca!"

Chickens were butchered and cooked in pots of water making broth. Mia was assigned to chopping. Several different moles were prepared in a lengthy process with various ingredients. Chilies, lard, onion, garlic, tomatoes, tomatillos, chocolate, and spices: cumin, cloves, and thyme. *Masa,* meal made of ground corn, was spread thinly on two softened banana leaves. A bit of shredded cooked chicken was laid on top of the masa. Mole was spooned over the other ingredients. Then the banana leaves were folded so the masa made a case around the chicken.

The women worked in an assembly line, dispatching dozens and dozens of tidy green packages into a large pot. Mia observed each of the steps and worked side by side with the women. She helped build a wood fire contained by a circle of bricks. The two strongest women, faces red and dripping sweat from the hot work, lifted the heavy steamer pot and placed it on the bricks.

The fire was continually fed with small sticks to keep water boiling for two hours in the bottom of the covered steamer. While the savory tamales cooked, additional tamales were assembled with raisins, vanilla, sugar, and mole.

"Smells delicious!" Mia said breathing deeply, "This seems such a large number of tamales. How long do they keep?"

"One week. Fourteen people this house."

"Do you eat them every day?"

"Also men take to work."

"Oh, of course. Tamales are portable. And with the lard and chicken plus the tomatoes and spices, they must be quite satisfying," Mia commented. "I'm amazed at how much work they are to make."

The women exchanged looks, and shrugged. "Work of women."

"Do any women have jobs in the village or other towns?"

"Enough work home and market. But some women work in field with men." Patrice looked at the gathered faces. "Isabel, Rosalia's mother work in field. Hands hard and black with soil. Father work at bottle."

Mia glanced over, but Rosalia's expression was unreadable. "When living in a family compound like this, do you all share expenses? Do you help when there are financial problems, or when some can't work?"

Patrice's voice sparked with passion and vehemence, "Yes! *Pero...eh, lo siento* (But...eh, I am sorry). Help some, not all. Some take too much, problems too many years!"

"Do you offer opinions and advice to each other?"

"Of course! Sometime too much!" several said with a mixture of humor and complaint.

Rosalia added, "Small town. Many mouths! Always someone say something!" She placed her hand on her ears and shook her head.

Laughter sounded all around and heads nodded. "*Que es tan cierto* (That is so true)!"

"I see how that could be helpful, and irritating," Mia chuckled. "If advice is refused, or not followed, what is the attitude? Is more help offered?"

"If change nothing, no."

"Like this with mother, Isabel," Rosalia said quietly.

Looks were exchanged. Finally, Patrice said diplomatically, "Help Isabel after husband gone."

"Didn't she need help all along and especially when her children were small?"

Faces were set, but eyes darted around.

Rosalia answered, "Respect. Woman have husband. Family no interfere. Woman do what must, no complain."

Mia silently considered this, and then said, "It seems the marriages here are set in traditional roles."

Heads nodded.

"Do most women stay home except for working at market, and shopping?"

Patrice answered, "Some men take wife and daughter everywhere, always watch. Even make fight with other men."

"Ahhh," Mia sighed. "Some relationships in the U.S. have issues of trust like that."

Voices erupted, "*Americanas* have freedom! All do what want!"

Shaking her head, Mia replied, "Most relationships are more traditional than you might think. And some men treat their women suspiciously or try to control them."

"Mia's husband do this?" Katia asked. Harsh looks from others caused her to apologize for the bold intrusion. "*Lo siento* (I am sorry), Mia."

"It is okay. A fair question," she answered, eyes reassuring the girl. "I want to learn about the culture and expectations of relationships here. And I understand maybe you want to know about the U.S." She glanced about for affirming nods. "My husband trusted me. I thought I could always trust him. We worked together every day at our store. Maybe something would have turned out differently if we had children." Her eyes jumped from face to face. "We…*I* lost babies. I was sad. I quit going to work, quit doing things I'd always done to make our life and work run smoothly. I struggled to get over the losses."

"A tragedy," the women offered with sympathetic nods. "Woman give life to baby. Baby make life of woman, too. What woman without family?"

Mia studied the faces looking on. "Those are old ideas entrenched in social roles and Catholicism. And I believed them, too. I thought a woman's most basic purpose is being wife and mother," she sighed quietly. "Now I'm neither."

"Men no understand. Woman ache for something. Most women want baby, need baby. Maybe some fill life with work, help others. Most women better with more family."

Tears glistened in Mia's eyes. "I might have been happier if I didn't push away even the family I did have. I don't know why I did that." She shook her head. "Something wasn't right between us. Now I know why. Our family was held together by a lie."

"Sad with little family!" the crowd offered.

"I wished I had more family while growing up, and again when my marriage fell apart…"

"What happen with this?" Patrice asked gently.

"I found my husband kissing another woman."

Gasps sounded through the group.

"Handsome husband?" one asked quietly.

"Handsome men sometime think too much of looks," Patrice said with heads nodding.

"Sometime men spread good looks around!" another said with a chorus of comments around the room.

"Not only handsome men!"

"Tim is handsome," Mia said. "But he did more than spread his looks around. He had a *baby* with *that* woman—a baby I couldn't make." Her eyes met sympathetic faces, and arms encircled her.

Pool

Market day in San Bartolome Quialana began: sale items were set out on tables or spread on fabric on the ground, produce was stacked in colorful and artful arrangements. The pace was calm industriousness. This was a village market. These were neighbors and friends and relatives.

A few tourists wandered the aisles and were greeted cheerfully. It was not crowded. And there was time to visit, joke, and pose for photographs which were accepted gracefully.

Rosalia sat at the back of the family booth and sewed. She helped Mia with stitches—much like she would have done when Mia was a girl if they had lived here.

Trying to duplicate Rosalia's stitches she was shown, Mia struggled at the effort.

The other women teased, "Need practice! Make little money this slow!"

"It's true," Mia giggled, opening and closing her hand that'd clutched the needle tightly.

Rosalia suggested, "Maybe rest."

Mia smiled, the crease in her forehead lessening. "Maybe if I take a break and walk around a bit I'll do better when I come back."

She strolled through the marketplace. Unlike the market in Tlacolula with many vendors and multiple choices for every item wanted, here each vendor seemed to have a niche. In years past, before the road to Tlacolula was paved and transportation was more reliable, all essential items would have been sold here in the village market.

As her eyes scanned available wares, Mia's attention was drawn to a long table at a booth displaying *alebrites*—carved and painted wooden figures. She examined the fine details of carving and decorative paint on the smooth figures. A cloth covered table off to the side was manned by a young girl sitting on a low stool.

"Do you make these?" Mia asked pointing to the roughly carved and crudely painted figures on the small table.

The girl looked down shyly, and nodded.

Mia picked up a smiling coyote with dancing eyes and pink flowers on its head. "I like these colors!"

The girl's face lit with a smile.

Another coyote wore a shirt painted deep blue. Mia bartered a little in fun for the two figures, but paid nearly full price to the girl, then wrapped the figures up in the bottom of her apron. "Thank you. I'm Mia. What is your name?"

"Marisol," the girl whispered.

The small table jolted, tipping the displayed figures.

"Oh, my goodness. What was that?" Mia asked.

A sound came from the table nearby, but when Mia glanced over, all eyes were averted. She bent down, glancing at below the cloth where it did not meet the ground.

Marisol's eyes grew large.

"I'm sorry," Mia said straightening up. "I didn't mean to be nosey."

A hand reached out from under the table. Marisol extracted a young child wearing shorts and a shirt with the bottom pulled up over his face.

"Benito," the girl said. "*Mi hermano* (my brother).

Benito lowered his shirt enough for one eye to look.

"Peek!" Mia said smiling.

The children giggled.

She said it again and they giggled louder.

Benito squirmed, Marisol struggled to hold him in her arms, and the bottom of his shirt fell, exposing the boy's face. Crooked teeth jutted through a large gap beneath his nose where a top lip should have been. Benito scurried back under the table.

"Thank you for the *alebrites*," Mia offered quickly, and returned to the family booth.

"What buy?" Rosalia inquired, studying Mia's disturbed expression.

Unwrapping the two figurines in her apron, Mia said, "From Marisol, and Benito."

"*Ay*, a tragedy," the women murmured.

"I've only seen such defects in pictures. Those horrible conditions are repaired early in the U.S."

Looks passed from face to face.

Finally, Patrice replied, "In Mexico, expensive. With no parents for Benito…" Patrice shrugged.

"No parents?"

"Sofia pass when Benito born."

"What about his father?"

"Say baby cursed. Drink much. Find in river."

Mia sighed loudly, "Ohhh! How sad! Orphans? How do they live?"

The women shrugged.

One of the girls said, "Village help. Each market give money, food."

"Where do they live?"

"With aunt, many cousins make hard."

"Benito is so thin," Mia murmured. "Maybe he doesn't get enough high quality food. I could give something to help." She rifled through her pocketbook.

"Better no give. When go away, too hard."

Later, Mia's mind troubled over the situation with the children. And when she slept, Mia dreamed.

A boy...clothes falling from him...a hand
reaching out...a face morphing into a skeleton...

Mia cried out in her sleep, "What happened to you?"

A hand patted her shoulder.

She startled awake, and told *Abuelita* Inez about the vision.

The old woman nodded. "Come for Benito."

"Who?"

"Mother."

Shrugging off a shiver, Mia said in wavering voice, "Comes to *take* him with her? Is he dying?"

Inez only gave Mia a look, turned over and went back to sleep.

Mia thrashed the covers the rest of the night as the dream played again and again in her mind.

She woke early, dressed, and rushed out, down the road, and followed the path she and Rosalia had walked.

Mia sat with eyes closed and drew breaths of calm beneath the old *ahuehuete..*

Leaves fluttered.

She glanced up to the spreading branches. Everything stilled.

"I'm so disturbed, unsettled."

Leaves fluttered again. A breeze lifted her hair.

"If only I knew what to do with my life," she sighed.

Images flowed into her mind—the photograph Gerald had shown her of the mural he painted—a stunning woman behind a veil of water or tears. "I don't want to be that woman."

The next day, Rosalia and Mia prepared to leave San Bartolome Quialana. Though they promised a return visit, the parting was drawn out with preparations for a large breakfast. Fruits were sliced: papaya, guava, banana, mango, *maracuya* (passion fruit), lychee, and pineapple. Powdered chili and lime juice was prepared to sprinkle on the fruit. Cooked pork was shredded and cooked again in juices under a broiler, then dressed with cilantro, avocado, and *crema* (slightly soured and thickened cream). Eggs were cooked, tortillas warmed. Hot chocolate and coffee was brewed in abundance. All the family gathered, along with many community friends. The meal had taken several hours to prepare, and the pace of eating was slow. It seemed they lingered, stretching out the animated conversations and laughter ringing through the crowd.

Rosalia described the house Javier was building in Puerto Escondido, and invited them all to visit. "See Pacific Ocean. Swim. Enjoy beach!"

The younger family members were especially excited about this and begged to hear more about coastal living and how Rosalia and Javier had come to settle there.

"Something say come." Rosalia shrugged. "Wind, water say, 'Here! Find what need, want.' And is true! Much work for Javier build, and money for sewing good."

Heads nodded.

"And daughter find!"

All eyes looked to Mia while their hands made Signs of the Cross.

The car had been arranged and would soon arrive.

Mia asked if someone might say a blessing for health and safe travel and continued happiness and good fortune for all assembled and absent.

The blessing ensued, followed by more Signs of the Cross, hugs, and pleas for quick return.

Tears and waves saw them off. As the car drove away from the family compound, Mia and Rosalia looked back and waved. Turning to look out the front window, Mia caught a fleeting glimpse of two small figures slipping out of sight.

The night was spent at Las Mariposas in Oaxaca City. After a light breakfast and coffee, they departed for a sightseeing trip.

"I'm so glad we're going to *Hierve el Agua* (the Water Boils)! My spirit longs for water. My mind needs the flow to clear and calm."

"Water good."

"You've never been there, Mama?"

Rosalia shook her head. "Tourist make much effort."

"Everything I've read says it is only a short distance from the parking lot to where the pools can be seen. I'd love to see the falls; the hike down might be too much for you though. *Any* view of the water will be welcome. I'm excited to see the carbonated spring water bubbling. White and greenish mineral deposits have built up over time making it look as if the water flows over the edge of the cliff like an infinity pool."

Rosalia nodded. She closed her eyes and napped with head resting against the seat.

Staring out the car window, Mia watched the landscape passing by. "Infinity," she whispered. "Does one *go* to infinity or become infinity? Would it feel like floating or flying?"

The highway became a road, and then a *very* bumpy road winding uphill. "Ohhh, I hope this is not a mistake," Mia whispered, stomach flip-flopping.

Rosalia pointed to the front of the vehicle, "Look there."

Mia stared ahead and ignored the mountainous scenes in her peripheral vision. She breathed deeply and slow, and her stomach began to settle.

At last, the car pulled to a stop at a parking lot.

They went to use restrooms charging a small fee.

"So much better than a port-a-potty by the side of the road!" Mia gushed.

Rosalia only shrugged.

"That road was not good! Now that we're here and stopped, I feel better!"

They walked over to a small spring surrounded with an ironwork fence. Water bubbled up as if boiling, though it was actually quite cold. Nearby, a man-made pool formed of stones enticed a few to swim in the turquoise water.

"I want to try it!" Mia took off her sandals and waded in while holding her skirt out of the water. "OOOO! Cold! But it feels sooo good!" she giggled and splashed a little Rosalia's way.

"Mama, come in! At least put a toe in the water! Maybe you will never be here again. It's so beautiful! Isn't the green color just amazing?"

Stooping down and putting her hands in, Rosalia pushed the water around. "Good cold."

Mia stepped out of the water, and wandered over to the other pool. "OH MY GOODNESS! We have to get closer! I want to see it better!"

She slipped on her sandals. Holding Rosalia's hand, they baby-stepped toward the bluff drop-off where the spring water had formed dips and pools of green and cream and beige minerals.

"Incredible! Now let's get away from the edge!"

They found a stand selling drinks of cold *tejate* made on the spot. Roasted corn, fermented cacao beans, mamey seed, and flowers of a funeral tree—*flor de cacao* called *Rosita de cacao*—were ground into a paste, and mixed carefully with cold water in a large ceramic pot until a perfect foam rose to the top. The woman kneading the paste had strong hands and wore a determined but peaceful look.

Rosalia took a sip from her cup, and wiped a bit of foam from her lip. "Good!"

"A drink of royalty in olden times!" Mia chimed.

They sipped and sat on rustic wooden benches on the grassy bluff with a view of the cliffs tumbling down to valleys. Tamales made with the family a few days before in San Bartolome Quialana were unwrapped.

"At the edge of the world," Mia mused. "My life is also on the edge of something." Her eyes settled on the pools of turquoise water catching light. Her hand stroked the moonstone beads on her chest. "My heart is beating as if it has wings."

Rosalia smiled and drew a breath. “Every wish a prayer.”

“My prayer now is gratitude, an acknowledgement of blessings pouring over me.”

“Much sweetness.”

Mia looked at Rosalia. “After so many hard times, you should have more!”

“This moment happy. This moment everything.”

Nodding, Mia whispered, “You’re right. Each moment we live anew.” She smiled, and drew a breath. “You’re so very wise.”

“Eat. Then try waterfall.”

“We could go down a little if it is not too difficult to climb back up the hill.”

“I try,” Rosalia shrugged. “Stop and rest if need. Maybe big man help up!”

Mia laughed.

Going down the trail, they did stop to rest and enjoy sights of a verdant valley. Petrified minerals of the cliffs appeared like green water cascading from the top. The actual waterfall was white like fluffy clouds or snow.

“Simply spectacular!” Mia gushed. “We have to bring more people to this place!”

“More people make less peace.”

“True,” she sighed.

On the return trip to Oaxaca City, they stopped at Mitla.

“I want you to see the market stalls where I searched for fabric and embroidery like the scrap of cloth. I was sure I would find something in the market to lead me forward, but there was nothing. I had such a sense of imminent discovery, and then it vanished.”

Rosalia said quietly, "Maybe hear what I think and pray. When I sleep, maybe feeling go away."

Mia's eyes sparked with recognition. "You were communicating directly with me? I believe it!"

They wandered through the ruins. Rosalia pointed to intricate designs and color variations in the immense stones. "See? Pretty."

"The stones radiate. Not just heat. They…" Mia paused. "I 'feel' them. They speak to me."

"Story stone," her mother replied. "Listen."

Back in Oaxaca City, they spent another night at Las Mariposas, and in the morning, walked the cobblestone streets of the historic district to Museo Textil de Oaxaca, the Textile Museum of Oaxaca. The façade of the colonial building was green quarry stone dazzling in morning light. Inside, the extensive collection of textiles from around the world showed commonality of creativity. Colors danced. Designs stunned with simplicity, dazzled with complexity in a variety of embroidered, woven, and beaded pieces.

Again and again Rosalia exclaimed, "Favorite! Another favorite."

"I LOVE LOVE LOVE these!"

"Learn this?"

"To embroider or weave? Maybe in a hundred years with a hundred gifted teachers!" Mia laughed. "I do love museums, love seeing collections. So stimulating! Now my mind is running amok with words I can't put down and can't exactly remember."

Rosalia studied Mia. "Mind create stitch."

"What do you mean?"

"Remember word when stitch."

The next day they flew to Puerto Escondido.

"Much money for fly. But good," Rosalia sighed. "Road over mountains too much curve."

"That's for sure!"

On arrival, as previously arranged, Rosalia went directly to the hospital for a check-up.

"Everything looks good," Dr. Grimaldi said. "There is improvement. I'm pleased with your progress. The vacation seems to have been quite healing."

Rosalia smiled with relief showing on her face.

Dr. Grimaldi studied Mia's look and said, "Something else on your mind?"

"Something I'd like to ask about. Can we talk later?"

His eyes lingered on her face. "Possibly."

Mia's cheeks colored. "I could offer something sweet…"

"Dr. Grimaldi, Dr. Grimaldi. Report to ICU!" sounded the loud speaker.

"If I can, I'll come by," he said hurrying away without looking back.

Mia went with Rosalia to the villas and got her settled for a rest. Unable to relax, Mia walked to the traffic-less street of shops on the Aldoquin. The vendors greeted her with courteous gestures and comments, but they studied her dress and their expressions seemed to say she was only another *gringa* raised with privilege and education and advantages they did not have.

She quickly completed her errand. "I'm a stranger here," she said under her breath as her feet tromped down the dusty road back to the villas. Powdery dirt puffed up onto her sandals. Her eyes looked to the clear blue sky. Tides rushed the shore. "Is this my place, where I should be? Or is it somewhere else? With someone else?"

Over a light supper, Javier told them he was making great progress on the house, but did not give details. He asked to hear about all they had seen and done in the days away.

They recalled for him the smells and sights of the Tlacolula market. "Animals, food, people, noise! Busy!"

"*AY*! Miss large markets!" Javier said with great enthusiasm. But his expression dimmed under Rosalia's close study, and he shrugged, "See many like this."

"What plays in my mind are special moments with family. When great-grandmother Inez placed her hands on my shoulders, I felt something shift. She has strength and power in those thin dry. I have no words for it." Mia looked at Rosalia. "The feeling was surprising, but also settling somehow."

Her mother nodded with wistful smile. "*Abuelita* Inez have mystery. Too old to sew secrets, but hands give something."

"What do you mean?"

Rosalia's eyes conveyed a look of mystery. "*Abuelita* pass gift. Blessing of secret."

"She gave me a secret or blessed a secret?"

But Rosalia only laughed, "Sweet gift come soon!"

Later, as Mia settled into her bed, her mind was filled with images.

Sweat glistened on his skin…his deep brown eyes met hers…with recognition…a hesitant smile…

A knock sounded on her door, faint at first, then loud enough to rouse Mia from the dream. She pushed back her hair and crossed the dark rooms. Gripping the knob, she pulled the front door open.

Lanzo came in. He walked with her over to the sofa. They sat down.

"I forgot you were coming," she spoke quietly.

He whispered. "I'm sorry. It's very late. I had a critical patient to stabilize."

"Thank you for coming. I really appreciate your follow through," she yawned.

"I can't stay long. What was it you want to ask?"

"Ohhh," she sighed and yawned again. "I'm sorry. I was sleeping, dreaming, and now I'm too muddled to discuss anything. I bought some cupcakes from Pasteleria Reyzi. Double chocolate with walnut filling." She stood and headed for the kitchen. "I'll make fresh coffee." She placed the cupcakes from the refrigerator onto plates while the water was working up a steam. The brew filtering into cups filled the room with strong aroma.

They sat side by side on stools at the counter and ate the very rich cakes.

"Oh, my goodness! This is sooo good! Sinful!" Mia smiled. "I should not be having even a sip of coffee so late!" She got up and poured a glass of milk.

Lanzo finished a bite. "Long hours ahead. I'll drink your coffee, too." A few minutes later, she sat down and he leaned over, kissing her on the cheek. "I appreciate this. Long shifts are the worst. Almost forgot how pleasant late night sharing can be."

She smiled at him. "Yes, I enjoy the comforts of home—even a temporary one."

He gave a look, followed her with his dishes to the sink. He reached out, pulling her close. "I like this. Kitchen warmth and creature comforts."

Arms limp at her sides, she managed a smile.

Lanzo relinquished his grip, kissed her head. "Have to go." He walked toward the door.

"Yes," she whispered.

He slipped out the door with barely a sound.

Mia set the lock on the door, and went to bed. Each time she drifted to sleep, her mind returned to disturbing images. When the sun was finally up, she dressed in a white blouse with rolled sleeves, a pair of tan capris, flat sandals, the moonstone beads, and went outside. Javier and Rosalia were already up.

A horn honked beyond the front gate and Javier hurried away.

"How are you feeling today, Mama?"

"I rest. No work."

"Will you be okay alone if I run some errands?"

Rosalia nodded. "Sit here. Or go inside."

"No pain? No tightness in your chest? No fast heartbeat or other symptoms?"

Rosalia chuckled, "Only tired after much excitement and travel."

"I won't be gone too long."

Her mother nodded and waved as Mia headed away.

Along the way to the business district, Mia paused at a fenced lot where a sign for Rotary Clubs International was posted.

"A park for children," she mused. "Rotary Clubs make many community contributions..."

Her steps quickened.

In town, Mia asked questions, and was directed to one business after another in search of Rotary members. She gathered names and information, but was unable to make any direct contacts.

After shopping for needed grocery items, she caught a taxi back to the villas and picked up Rosalia.

They went for comida at Mario's Pizza Land restaurant.

"I love this décor! The ochre colored plaster, dark beams on the ceiling, square tables with red and white checked cloths transport me to Italy."

"Go see?"

"It was always a dream to meet family living there," Mia sighed.

"Italy not in blood, but family in heart. Heart move blood."

Mia stared at her mother. "It all seems strange now. When I was younger we celebrated everything Italian. I thought I was Italian. And it was a lie."

"Lie of love," Rosalia scolded. "Italy mean something."

"You're right. So right and wise. Maybe I *will* go to Italy sometime. I'd like to take Papa and Maggie and Grandmother Angelina. Wouldn't that be a wonderful surprise? Would you and Javier like to go, too?"

Rosalia grinned and nodded. "I go anywhere with daughter. Success and beauty. And so generous!"

Mia laughed.

After the meal, they took a taxi over to the house Javier was building. Glancing through the iron gate in a high wall, Rosalia rang the bell.

Javier rushed forward, and stood blocking their view of a courtyard and workers scurrying about. "No see now!"

Mia handed a to-go box from the restaurant through the gate. "I didn't know others were working with you. I would have brought them something as well."

"Many wife make food for men."

"I'm making a special dinner for us tonight."

"Special?" Rosalia asked.

"Invite friend," Javier said with a grin.

Mia laughed, "Maybe I will."

Javier went back to work, and Rosalia returned to the villas for a nap while Mia went on another errand.

At the hospital, she asked about Rotary Club activities.

A clerk at the front desk confirmed local projects for hearing and vision, and upkeep of the park. And perhaps some would help with a future medical mission rumored to be planned for Oaxaca City. Mia thanked her for the information, and was walking down the hall when a familiar voice caught her attention. She wandered around a corner, and halted.

A woman seemed to be leaning back against a gurney parked along the wall, but a man in white coat obscured Mia's full view of the woman. She saw only the woman's feet moving up and down his leg.

Mia's heart pounded. Words stormed into her mind. She swallowed, drew a breath, and let it out.

Dr. Grimaldi turned. His hands went quickly to his pockets. His face registered surprise seeing Mia.

"I…I heard you," she stammered.

The woman clattered away down the shiny tiled floor.

"I wanted to invite you for dinner with us. I'm cooking something you might enjoy. Seven o'clock."

"If I can, I will," he smiled, and walked away.

Later as Mia stirred a boiling pot of potatoes, her mind flashed back to hot summer days at Gerald's cabin. So many miles traveled since then. Fall. Winter. Spring. Another summer of surprise, others to care for...

When summer came ‘round
When the sun stood high
I looked upon your red tanned skin
With glad and favoring eye
Now winter wind cools me
Time for other things
But I hold you in my mind
And thank you for my wings

Well

Peeled and sliced russets were cooked. After letting the potatoes cool, Mia began shredding them with a fork. Her mind drifted to a pasta mill and other gadgets left behind in the Portland house shared with Tim before the divorce. "I once had so many nice but unnecessary conveniences," she sighed, and continued shredding, then mixed the potatoes by hand with egg and several cups of flour.

A wooden board was dusted with flour, then she kneaded the ingredients until thoroughly blended into a white mound similar to dough.

Watching from a stool pulled up to the counter, Rosalia asked, "Sister make this?"

"Yes," Mia answered, pushing back a tendril of damp hair with the back of her flour-coated hand. "Just like this, just like Grandmother Angelina taught us. Italian recipes are passed from one generation to another."

"In Mexico, too."

Mia smiled. "It's hard wrapping my mind around having relatives in Mexico. I longed for and wished for more family but…"

Rosalia replied, "Believe. Wish make true."

"Where do you get so much conviction? Is it individual emotional strength? Is it religious faith, and being a better Catholic than I am?"

"Here," Rosalia patted her chest. "Woman know many things. Maybe know everything!"

"Maybe," Mia sighed loudly.

"When a girl, I have no strength. Sister Maria show so much."

Mia's eyes studied her mother. "Maybe *I* can learn strength. I want to get beyond my disappointments—especially not having a baby. Now that I'm single, and forty, any possibility of having a family is dimming. Somehow though, I haven't quite given up."

Rosalia only listened.

"If only I settled *some* of my questions. Are children really that difficult? Is having a baby really so hard? Is that what *I* feared? Is that why I put it off? Is that why *Mother* didn't have children? Did she ever try?"

Rosalia's face paled.

"Mama breathe! Think of water, waves rushing the shore and slinking back to the sea. Breathe in, out like the water."

After a few breaths, color returned to Rosalia's face.

"I'm sorry, Mama. I didn't mean to upset you with questions."

Rosalia nodded gravely, drew a deep breath. "Answers easy. Understand hard."

"What answers?"

"I tell before—our mother Isabel suffer with baby. No want more, keep husband from bed. Father angry. Drink. Sometime angry, yell, hit, kick."

"Were you safe?" Mia asked with shaky voice.

"Say nothing, father no bother. Different with Mother…" Rosalia continued with wringing hands, "And Maria no quiet. Father make trouble with sister."

"That must have been horrible."

Rosalia only nodded, her mouth quivering.

"After your sister left home, did you become a target for his anger?"

"Learn hide good. But much yell. When Mano say leave family, go to city, I think easy."

"Maybe that is why Mother wanted to leave so badly. Though it must have been hard leaving your mother, grandmother, home and village behind."

"Sick, maybe for home," Rosalia answered. "Even Mano make no better. Here thin," Rosalia pinched her arms. "Then grow here," she patted her middle. "What do with this? No go home. Family send away. Mano say find cousin, maybe Guillermo help. Then surprise! Mano say maybe Maria there! *Ay*, this make happy!" Rosalia smiled, but then she shook her head. "Many days travel: walk, ride wagon with smelly animals or in back of trucks. In north, ask where find cousin. People say want no danger, 'Be careful.' No say why."

"I dreamed that! I wrote it in my novel, *Mending Stone*!"

Rosalia's eyes sparked with emotion, "Many times I tell story in mind. I pray daughter hear story."

"I did hear! What happened when you found them?"

"Find shack. Mano knock at door. Woman say, 'Who there?' Door open. See sister! Maria grab and pull inside."

"How thrilling to finally be together!"

Rosalia nodded. "Rest in hut. Maria give food and drink." She paused, and then said with gleaming eyes and shaking voice, "Guillermo say, 'Go.' Maria say stay, rest. He say, 'Woman quiet!' Sister no listen. Guillermo hit Maria. Again. Again." Rosalia shook her head. "Sister no quiet. I beg Mano, 'Do something!' Mano take Guillermo to cantina for drink."

"My father was a strong man," Mia sighed. "And he listened to you."

Rosalia smiled. "Guillermo have work for Mano. Work no good. But Mano must do. No other place can go." Rosalia looked up at Mia with sorrow in her eyes. "What work, Mano never say. Sometime go many days, weeks. How I ache for Mano! And in small house with sister, girls fight."

Mia nodded. "I worked every day in our small gift store with my husband. At home, I kept busy with projects: redoing the house, decorating, gardening, shopping, cooking, cleaning, laundry. Tim and I got on each other's nerves, but we didn't fight." She looked at her mother. "Maybe we didn't fight because most of the time, we were in separate rooms or doing separate activities."

"Mano miss Feast of *La Virgen*, miss more than this…"

"I can't imagine how hard that must have been for you, Mama, in a strange place, without more family and friends for help and comfort." Mia's hands had been still while they talked, but now she finished kneading the dough, broke off pieces, and rolled them into thick strands. She cut these into inch-sized pieces. Pressing each one with the tines of the fork, she made indentations for catching sauce.

Mia dropped ten little "packets" of potato dough into heated cooking water.

"One day pain come! *Ay*, such pain. I think maybe I die with pain! I cry for Mano! Maria say man can do nothing for this. I cry to Mother, Grandmother, *La Virgen*! Maria say, 'Be strong. Do work of women. Work hard!'" Rosalia was standing over the pan of boiling water and watched the potato packets pop to the surface one by one and she laughed in surprise.

Mia used a spoon to fish the cooked pieces from the water and set them on a paper towel to dry.

This process was repeated again and again until all the dough was cooked.

"While they cool, we'll make sauce. What do you like? Basil, tomato?"

Her mother shrugged. "No cheese?"

"We can make more gnocchi with cheese inside. You start peeling a few more potatoes. So, where did you find Guillermo and Maria? Northern Mexico?"

Rosalia nodded, "San Bartolo."

"'A town with a name like your villages!' I wrote that! You told me. I heard you. And I dreamed it. Mother told me with clues she left."

"Think name sign maybe *La Virgen* keep safe."

There was a knock at the door.

Javier came in. "What smell good?"

"Italy!"

"Boot like this country."

Mia looked up and laughed, "Boot?"

He nodded with enthusiasm, "On map, see boot like Mexico."

"I think that, too! The two countries seem a little similar."

"I like maps. See roads, city, river, mountain."

"You like mountains don't you? The high country…"

"I like hunt game."

Rosalia interjected, "Javier so much hunt. Make money with game: horn, bone, meat, skin. Man of country do anything," she said smiling at him, her voice sounding appreciation. "Great luck I find this man."

"A man of talent is a man to keep," Mia suggested.

Rosalia's face colored.

Javier's eyes were on his feet, but he wore a smile.

"Mama, since you were not legally married to my father, and he is lost—or dead—couldn't you and Javier marry?"

Rosalia's eyes looked at her hands. She answered quietly, "Maybe."

Javier replied, "Mountain, river and wind make beautiful music like Rosalia make my heart!"

"So poetic! Javier, you are such a surprise!"

He quipped, "Surprise cooking! Maybe never finish. Too much talk!"

They all laughed.

Rosalia had finished peeling, cutting, and cooking the potatoes she set aside to cool.

Mia opened a bottle of wine. "I searched stores and finally a restaurant to find my favorite Prosecco. I wanted everything Italian today!" She poured them each a small glass.

After sips of the light sparkling wine, Javier smiled and said, "Mouth funny."

Mia and Rosalia shredded the cooked potatoes into two mounds. A cup of flour was sprinkled on each, then a well was pressed in the middle for an egg and a pinch of sea salt. Each mound was kneaded until the ingredients were bound together smoothly. Long fat strands were rolled, then short segments cut, and filled with chunks of Oaxacan cheese. The dough was pressed around to encase the cheese. A thumb well was made in the center and tines of the fork pressed around the edges of the dough to catch sauce.

"Fun make this!" Rosalia grinned. "What other kind can make?"

"One favorite I make with spinach or zucchini inside. More often, I grill the zucchini, and serve it on the side with sauce."

"Have this?"

"Oh, yes! I nearly forgot!" Mia retrieved several large zucchinis from a shopping bag on the counter.

"Ahhh," Rosalia nodded. "*Calabaza*! Some make soup: *sopa de flor de calabaza.*"

"*Flor*? Flower? Zucchini flower soup?"

Javier asked if Mia's friend would arrive soon.

"Hopefully. I invited Dr. Grimaldi. He's Italian. I thought he might enjoy the meal."

"Good doctor. Maybe good man for you?"

She shook her head. "He's only a friend. And he might not come. He's very busy."

"I no like man too busy!" Rosalia pronounced.

Mia's brow furrowed. "He's interesting though."

"Many men interesting."

Javier added, "Every man interesting!"

"To self!" Rosalia retorted, laughing good naturedly while pressing fork tines around the edges of the cheese filled potato packets.

Javier watched as these cooked. After about a minute, the packets popped to the surface and he laughed in surprise.

Mia stirred the pan of sauce, browned the zucchini.

Dr. Grimaldi arrived with flowers and dessert.

"Welcome!" Mia smiled, "Thank you! And pastries from the *pasteleria*! Wonderful!"

Dr. Grimaldi nodded. "Nice to see you again, Rosalia and Javier."

"Mama, Javier, Dr. Grimaldi requests we call him Lanzo outside of the hospital."

"Welcome, Lanzo," the couple said.

"Please, sit down and relax." Mia poured him a taste of Prosecco. The trio sat down at a cozy table while she finished dishing up. She brought over bread, two kinds of gnocchi, the cooked zucchini, and a bowl of sauce.

They were mostly quiet while they helped themselves to the food and ate the first bites.

"What work do you do Javier?" Lanzo inquired.

"Construction. Many business buildings. Also, house for Rosalia."

"That's ambitious."

"Like work hard! Good for man work much!"

"Agreed," Lanzo chuckled. "Work is good for most people!" He flashed a cautionary look to Rosalia. "Not for you quite yet, though," he said with kind concern.

"No," Rosalia grinned, "much resting, learn something."

"Today Mama learned how to make gnocchi!"

"Fun!" Rosalia beamed.

Lanzo glanced at Mia. "What are you learning?"

"I'm not very good at sewing. Even with Mama's great instruction and patience! Actually, I already knew that—when I was little, Mother also tried to teach me. I can do machine sewing; hand work is very difficult. I doubt I will ever be proficient at needlework."

Lanzo smiled. "Most of us are lucky to find one or two things for which we have a talent."

"I guess," Mia sighed. "But I've always wanted to be good at many things. Not just good, really good!"

"I have to say you have a talent for gnocchi! I especially enjoyed the one with cheese."

"That was Mama's idea!"

"Quick study!"

"She *is*. Mama is amazing! And seeing how quickly she learns, gives me hope for what I might be able to learn about *her* culture. Ehhh," Mia looked about uncomfortably, "*my culture* in Mexico. I learned to make gnocchi from my Italian grandmother, Angelina."

He nodded. "My grandmother was a superb cook! And her baking was unparalleled! Not sure the pastries I brought are on par with hers. Hopefully they will not disappoint."

"Surely not. I love most every bit of sweetness I ever eat," Mia gushed while clearing away their plates. "Javier makes good desserts."

"Hats off to you! That's something I have not tried," Lanzo complimented with appreciative nod.

Javier shrugged. "I like happy smile on pretty faces!"

They all laughed while Javier jumped up and helped Rosalia clear the table of serving dishes. "Need time to settle meal before sweets!"

Lanzo patted his belly. "I ate much too much."

"Go out—get fresh air," Rosalia commanded as she and Javier began washing dishes.

"Are you sure, Mama? I don't want you to get tired."

Rosalia waved them away.

Outside, Mia and Lanzo watched water pull from shore.

"Lovely evening."

"Yes," Mia sighed. "The thing I wanted to discuss…"

"I'm listening."

"I remember something you said about medical school: you made friends in other specialties?"

"Yes?"

"Do you keep in touch?"

"With a few. What specialty interests you?"

"Pediatric surgery. Do you know physicians who are interested in organizing a team of medical personnel for work in Oaxaca?"

"Aren't the services already offered adequate?"

She drew a breath. "Maybe. But not in the rural areas. Not for indigenous peoples in some villages. I've done research on the internet. The diets of many do not include enough green vegetables to prevent birth defects. And prenatal care is often lacking. Quite a few children suffer physical defects, but don't get medical and surgical care needed because of cost and the hardship of travel to service. I heard Rotary has a mission possibly in 2008 or 2009, but I don't want to wait."

Dr. Grimaldi's dark eyes regarded her.

Mia added, "Sometimes care is not sought because of superstition: believing children with defects are cursed."

"A few colleagues may be interested in some sort of mission. But it would require extensive planning and support. It could take years to set up."

"Years?" Her face fell. "I am so tired of waiting years."

"Why does this interest you? I didn't take you for such a do-gooder."

"My interest is more than do-gooding! There's a boy in the village of my relatives; he has cleft lip. And he's so thin!

They say he's three years old, but he seems much younger. He doesn't really speak. He's so shy and is barely able to eat. His sister—only six years old—takes care of him. Their parents are dead. I want to do something. If I can convince the family…"

"Why?"

Mia sputtered, "Last year, I dreamed of a boy and also a girl. They were in my arms—I felt the weight of their bodies, the satin of their skin against mine. It was real. Powerful." Her voice shook, "If I can't have my own babies, maybe I'm supposed to help other children."

Grimaldi's look softened. "I do know a pediatric surgeon. I could contact him, test the level of interest, but no guarantee. I might get no more than a perfunctory response."

"Thank you. Please try. I'd be so very grateful," Mia gushed.

Later, Mia's heartburn after eating too much or too many sweets kept her awake for hours.

Her stomach was still unsettled in the morning. And a cup of coffee she drank did not help.

She took a walk on the beach, feet pressing down into the dry sand. "So much I want…" Each step seemed to add to longing. She whispered, "I hate that I am beginning to hope. Hate the tiny seed of an idea growing inside me. I don't want to suffer more disappointment. I'm terrified. What if…"

Mia glanced up.

The sky was blue. Very blue. Cloudless.

Bird wings flapped.

She turned to look, but there was nothing. Mia left the beach, and went into town, made a call.

Gerald answered after a few rings.

Mia told him of the trip with Rosalia to San Bartolome Quialana, the many relatives met, new friends made, and finally, the children.

He listened, barely able to interject more than, "Uh huh."

She told him about wanting to secure some medical care for rural Oaxaca. "But—if nothing else—maybe I can encourage families to seek services offered by some organization."

Gerald said quietly, "Why do y' want to do this?"

"It would feel good. Like finding another piece of the puzzle that is me."

"Might be big commitment, lots of time to see it through. Y' planning to stay there?"

"Stay?" She paused, the question hanging between them. Finally, she said softly, "A while."

He was quiet, and then he said, "Easier doing something for others than deciding what to do for y'rself?"

She could not answer.

"Hope everything will work out how y' want," he finally said.

The line crackled.

"I wish *you* wanted..." Mia said softly, but then the line crackled again. "Gerald?"

There was no response.

"Hello?" Hearing nothing, she set the phone down. "You're *there*, and I'm here. I'm not sure I could ever live in Oregon again…"

She walked back to the villas. Javier was away working. Rosalia was napping. Mia looked around the unit, thumbed through a brochure, washed up a few dishes. Finally, she slipped off her clothes, and donned a dry bathing suit and shorts and t-shirt. She went down to the beach, slipped into the water.

It enveloped her skin like satin. Mia floated on her back, eyes closed, drifting, tide pushing her body like a rocking ship, a cradle.

When Mia tried to sleep later, words filled her mind.

> In darkness
> arms and legs
> like kindling
> ignite more than passion
> Ideas crackle

Mia sighed, "If only I can…"

Lake

They rode in the taxi over to the building site. Mia helped Rosalia from the car. At the gate, they rang the heavy bell.

Javier ran towards them. Smiling, he undid the latch, swung open the gate, and ushered them into the small brick courtyard. "No wind. Grow garden?" he said pointing to wide planters lining the high wall surrounding the courtyard.

Rosalia smiled.

A wooden gate in the curved opening of a low wall invited them to a wide patio stretching from one side of the property to the other. Half the patio was shaded by overhanging thatch of a portico attached to the house. The southern-most section of the patio closest to the beach was rimmed by a low wall of sun-warmed bricks and block.

Eyes scanning the horizon where surf met sky, Mia sighed, "The view is stunning! How I love seeing the water. This is magical!"

"See house—inside good, too!" Javier led them through French doors surrounded by windows. A kiva fireplace in one corner of the living room next to the window was flanked by a curved platform.

"Make cushions for here?" Javier asked. "Sit, see out windows."

Rosalia nodded, her eyes studying the view.

A large plank table with benches occupied the other side of the room. The kitchen stretching across the back was separated from the living area by a wide countertop bar and a center passageway with posts up to the high ceiling. Sink and stove were to one side of the passageway, bare counter on the other.

Rosalia chimed, "Many cooks make food, watch ocean!"

"Yes, how lovely."

Shelves, cupboards, and another wide counter lined the back wall containing a refrigerator.

"Set package here! Easy," Rosalia cooed opening and shutting a door leading directly out to the entrance courtyard, then patting the counter.

Beneath a stairway at the side of the living room and kitchen was a half-bathroom. A utility/laundry room equipped with a long narrow shelf and a drying rack was tucked between the kitchen and outside wall. A door led outside to a small area where laundry could be hung to dry without view from the windows.

"Javier!" Rosalia exclaimed. "What women want! Make work nice!"

Smiling, he led them upstairs to the second floor bathroom complete with double sinks in a long vanity, a walk in shower and built-in tile tub with view of the ocean through large windows, and toilet enclosed in a cubicle with a door.

Rosalia clasped her hands over her mouth. "Javier! Where come these ideas?"

He laughed. "Men talk of many jobs!"

"This so good! No right for this!"

"So not true, Mama!" Mia exclaimed. "You deserve this, and so much more."

"Yes!" Javier chimed.

Rosalia did not continue protesting for she was attracted by a large walk-in closet with built-in drawers and shelves. "Big! Save many things!" She wandered into the large bedroom.

"Paint pink like sunset?" Javier suggested.

Both women nodded.

A platform bed was built-in with side tables and wall sconces at each side. Small windows above the bed allowed light to shine through the room. Tall windows on the ocean side could be opened to bring in breezes, and a French door led out to a balcony lined with a wrought iron balustrade. A long wooden seat with curved back and generous arms was adorned with hand carved vines and leaves.

Rosalia sat, looked out over the water below.

Javier perched beside her. "Like this?"

She nodded. "Perfect."

His arm swept across the stunning view of the beach below, then reached for her hand. "Perfect for husband and wife?" Javier's brown eyes begged for response. "This man and woman?"

Rosalia clasped a hand over her mouth.

"Mama!" Mia exclaimed. "He's asking a question! Give the man an answer!"

Eyes gleaming, Rosalia nodded with a sweet smile curving her lips.

Grinning, Javier stood and said, "Show something more!" He led them back downstairs, out to the side patio, and into a narrow building along the property's perimeter wall. Windows in the end looked out to the beach. A bench with underneath storage lined one side of the room, a platform for sleeping with side tables were built into the opposite wall. Closets separated the space from a bathroom. "Comfortable?"

"Terrific for craft room or work space and guests."

"For family stay?" Javier suggested quietly. "Daughter?"

"Javier!" Rosalia exclaimed.

Mia gulped down emotion.

Finishing the house filled many hours over the next weeks. Walls were painted cream in living/dining/kitchen area, pale blue for downstairs bathroom and laundry, pink for upstairs bedroom.

Rosalia bought cushions, and made slip-covers for seating in the living area. She constructed floor-length draperies to soften light coming through the tall windows and curtains to cover open shelves and storage beneath countertops in the kitchen. Bedcovers were pieced in long strips of colorful fabric, some she embroidered with intricate designs. Table runners were made in bright nature-inspired colors of sky and grass and flora. She worked hard pumping the treadle machine to sew together all the fabrics.

When the next medical check-up came around, Rosalia might have suffered from exhaustion, instead she grew stronger.

Dr. Grimaldi advised, "Keep with *reasonable* sessions of work and rest. Come back in another month or if you have ANY new or significant symptoms: pain, weakness, dizziness."

"Fantastic progress, right?" Mia asked the doctor after Rosalia joined Javier in the hallway.

Grimaldi nodded. "I have other information for you. I contacted my colleague in pediatric surgery. After much urging, I convinced him…"

"Oh, my gosh!" she interrupted. "When will they be able to come?"

Dr. Grimaldi held up a hand, and replied with an air of importance, "They will *consider* one case. A full medical assessment including tests and imaging is needed."

"Where would the assessment take place?"

"This could happen in Oaxaca City, the largest and closest city to the boy."

"Could you help make arrangements at the hospital? I'll see to lodging for the team. Would they stay then to do surgery?"

"*They're* not coming. If surgery is to happen, it would be in Washington."

"D.C.?"

"Seattle, Washington."

Mia's brow furrowed.

"Completing the necessary steps will take a good deal of commitment. And there are no guarantees for services."

Mia nodded, answering with reserve, "I didn't envision medical care in the U.S. That makes it much more complicated."

"And there's the financial consideration."

She sighed ominously. "I was hoping it would be a medical mission to help other children as well. A good will mission funded by some community organization, donations…"

"Unless you have many connections, that's unlikely. It could take years to arrange. If you're not fully committed to securing care for the boy, I suggest dropping this idea before starting something you can't finish."

Her eyes flashed back at him.

Mia flew a few days later to Oaxaca City, and booked a car for the trip to San Bartolome Quialana. As it drove, she glanced out at the flat lands of the valley. "Green, this time of year at least. I like green. It's just different vegetation," she mused. "Different country, different people than I grew up with. I do like it, but is it *me*?"

Passing through Tlacolula de Matamoros, she asked the driver to stop at the Church of the Ascension. Sunday, market day in the village, but the church was not crowded. She prayed and marveled over incredible décor of the Baroque Chapel of the Lord of Tlacolula—famous for statues of saints depicted in the manner of their deaths, and a large gold crucifix of Jesus.

Silent prayers she'd whispered lingered on her mind for the remainder of the drive. Her heart was pounding and hands shaking as she rang the bell at the entrance gate to the family compound in San Bartolome Quialana. Greeted with surprise, she was welcomed, and joined the family in a meal of tamales, steamed vegetables, Oaxacan cheese. Mia told them about the beautiful home Javier and Rosalia were making.

"Daughter stay?"

"At least until Mama seems recovered," Mia answered sounding uncertain.

"Glad here for family visit!"

Mia smiled, "I love seeing you, getting to know you!" And then, she added, "I also came to see Marisol and Benito."

Looks were exchanged around the table.

"I'm worried about them. Benito is so frail; I'd like to do something to help."

Patrice interjected, "Pray."

"I…I want to do *more,*" she said quietly, but heads were already bowing and prayers began filling the room.

She did not speak more of the children as routines normally followed were abandoned and the evening hours were filled with laughter and stories.

Later, as Mia settled down on the pallet in Inez's room, the rhythm of the aged woman's snoring made steady noise like ticking of a clock.

My heart beats for you
Little ones
Light of love
Wrapping you in care
Like arms

Preparations for market occupied the next day; Mia helped with chores. On Tuesday, after the family booth was set up, she slipped away.

At the same small table as before, Marisol was sitting with her *alebrites*. Her face registered surprise seeing Mia.

"I missed several weeks. How have you been?"

"Benito sick."

"OH," Mia sighed with concern.

Distracted by his small hand patting her leg, Marisol reached under the table, and pulled the boy into her lap. He snuggled against her, his eyes open and the corners of his mouth curving.

"Peek," Mia said.

He giggled.

She hid one eye behind her hand. "Peep."

Benito put a hand to his eye, then pulled it away.

"Peep!" Mia said, and they all laughed.

"Live here now?"

"No, I live in the United States. In Texas," Mia answered warmly. "Many years ago my mother and aunt left here. I was raised by my aunt, Maria, but she called herself Victoria Maria. Now I have finally met their family—*my* family. There is much to learn about Mexico."

Marisol nodded.

"Your English is very good."

"Tourist teach much," the girl replied. "Woman from Australia, stay months." Marisol looked down. "Adelaide say sometime come back. Never see again."

"Would you like to come over to see my family?"

Marisol pulled Benito close, "Maybe they no like."

"Ohhh," Mia sighed. "I think they like you both."

"Maybe eyes look too long at Benito…"

Pulling a cloth from her bag, Mia said, "You can wrap him in this *rebozo* (a shawl used by country women for wrapping babies, carrying items from market, shielding from weather). "

Marisol smiled, pointing at the shawl and saying a few words to to her brother.

"Benito like." Marisol placed the blue scarf on his head, wrapped it across his face and to the side.

"I bought it in Oaxaca City. Have you been there?"

"Some people say big, many buildings."

"It is an old city with beautiful buildings. There are many stores, a large indoor market with flowers, food, and everything for a house, even toys!"

"Ohhh." Marisol smiled.

"Look what else I have?" Mia pulled another *rebozo* from her bag and held it out to her.

"Green is good!" Marisol said accepting the scarf.

"You have natural beauty—green is perfect for you!"

Marisol grinned and wrapped it around her shoulders. "Let's go show my family."

Through the market, Marisol walked proudly and carried Benito. But then, she slowed while struggling to hike him up on her hip.

"Are you getting tired and hungry? We can go to *Tia* Patrice's house for tamales. It is not far; I can carry Benito?"

Marisol nodded and relinquished her grip.

Benito held tightly to Mia and cast an occasional glance at her as they proceeded on.

The house was quiet with the family away at market.

Mia helped Marisol form a piece of plastic wrap into a container like a funnel with a closed top to hold milk for Benito.

Benito drank from the opening, wiped his face, and smiled, then ate a mush they made from crushed maize.

Marisol nibbled at one end of a tamale.

"Don't you like it?"

"Save for later."

Mia wrapped up another tamale. "Take this for later."

Placing it in her pocket, Marisol finished eating. "Go now? Maybe customers come!"

"Your work is good. There should be many customers!"

Marisol beamed, and was a bit chatty as they walked back to the market. She removed the *rebozos* and held them out to Mia.

"Oh, no! Gifts for you."

"Like very much! Thank you!" Marisol gave Benito his blue one, and he ducked under the table.

At the end of market day, Mia walked with the children to a ramshackle fence surrounding a dilapidated house where a small dog yapped at her ankles.

A teenage boy came out. His name was Eber. He led Mia inside a messy house where seven children lingered near an obese woman he introduced, "My mother, Elodia."

Mia was offered a rickety chair.

Elodia shoed away the children with a wave of flabby arms and staccato orders.

Glancing at the woman, Mia drew a breath, and said, "I'd like to help Benito. I want to take him to Oaxaca to see a doctor about his face. Will you give permission for him to go with me? I will take the utmost care of him."

Eber translated the request to Elodia who only shook her head while fanning with a piece of newspaper.

Mia swallowed hard, and added, "Did I say it won't cost you anything?"

With a piercing look, Elodia delivered a string of words.

Eber explained, "My mother says Benito is much trouble. Attention not good."

"That is why he needs help: if his defect can be repaired, he will look more like other children. He can eat more easily. His life will be easier. Caring for him will be easier. *Your* life might be easier."

After animated discussion with Elodia, Eber said, "My mother gives permission only if you also take Marisol."

"Oh, yes, of course!" Mia smiled. "We'd be gone a few days, perhaps longer, for the first assessment."

Eber relayed this, and the woman shrugged, then pushed away a child creeping onto her lap. "*Quando*?"

"Soon," Mia answered. "As soon as I can arrange it."

Marisol and Benito watched out the windows of the car as landscape flew by. Passing through Tlacolula, Marisol told of a trip once to the Sunday market. "Animals everywhere. Some run free!"

Benito suddenly whimpered and clutched his belly.

"Hungry? I have food!" Mia unpacked several items, including his mush which he only looked at until she started telling a story.

> "Once, there was a girl who lived in a big house, with a shady yard and gardens where she liked to make plays. Flowers were her ladies, thorny bushes were devils. Grass was her mother, and the sky, her father. A large oak tree was audience. He could not laugh, but he shook his branches and fluttered leaves. Sometimes he whined with the wind, and swayed his branches as if dancing. The tree could not move his roots. The girl thought *she* was like that tree: with roots sunk into that one place. But when the girl grew older, she did move away. Years later, during a powerful storm, the tree's long branches shuddered and snapped. He tipped and fell, uprooted from the earth!"

Tears swelled in Marisol's eyes. "What happen to tree? Die?"

> "Men came with machinery. Broken branches were shredded into small pieces that were sprinkled over the garden to keep it moist after rain and warm when it is cold."
>
> "The broken tree trunk was cut to make a chair with a high back topped with a bird house. When spring arrived, birds began nesting there,

hatched young and fed them there. A large log from the tree's trunk was taken to a mill and planed into long boards for a furniture maker. Beautiful shelves and tables to hold books and dishes and food for feasting were made. Smaller scraps of wood were burned in a blazing fire to keep people warm and their faces glowed with beauty in the dancing light made possible by all the tree shared."

"Tree is hero!" Marisol beamed and wiped away her earlier tears.

"The next summer, when the sun was warm and full, it shined down on bare ground covering the spot where the tree stood many years. Twigs grew from the ground, sprouted leaves and fattened. The single old tree grew again in a ring of sprouts!"

"Many babies! No he! A *SHE* tree!" Marisol smiled and leaned her head against Mia's shoulder.

Benito had snuggled into Mia's arms and was sleeping—warm and sweaty resting against her chest. She cupped her hand to his head, kissed his dark hair, and then Marisol's.

The car parked at Clinica Hospital Carmen, a private hospital in the center of the historic district of Oaxaca City. Mia wrapped the *rebozo* around Benito's face, and carried him inside with Marisol clinging to her skirt.

A pretty nurse in crisp whites greeted them. Paperwork was completed. The doctor had a gentle manner and spoke Zapoteca, English and Spanish during the examination. Curls of Dr. Alvarez Romero's long mustache quivered while he asked questions.

They went to the laboratory. Benito cried loudly when held down for a blood draw. When another nurse offered colorful suckers, he became so involved with his sugary treat, he barely gave notice to the vials of blood being drawn.

When it was time for x-rays, the doctor explained what Benito would need to do. Benito's eyes were big and his hands clung tightly to the arms of the wheelchair as Marisol pushed him down the hallway to the x-ray room door. He made no complaint when the nurse took hold of the chair and pushed it into a room, and closed the door.

Mia and Marisol watched through the window from an adjoining room.

Benito held himself still and allowed positioning and repositioning for multiple x-rays.

"*Bueno* (good), Benito, *bueno*!" said the technicians.

"So brave, Benito!" Mia and Marisol exclaimed when reunited with him.

He smiled while shielding his face with the *rebozo.*

They waited on stiffly upholstered chairs in a lounge area. The children played peek-a-boo: leaning down and looking at each other under the metal chair arms.

"Shhh," Mia warned but smiled with her eyes.

Dr. Alvarez Romero appeared after many minutes. They were invited to his office. "We have gathered much information to send to Seattle Children's Hospital. When we hear from them, we can discuss the case in detail."

On the edge of her chair, Mia asked, "When do you think they will respond?"

He shrugged. "A few weeks, months."

Mia whined, "I was hoping much sooner—possibly a few *days*."

Dr. Alvarez Romero only shook his head and fiddled with the ends of his mustache. "A difficult case. Much time has already passed. And there is the matter of the family's commitment…"

"What matter? I obtained permission from his aunt Elodia for Benito to come." Her eyes puzzled over his inference.

"Payment for services…"

"Oh. Of course, I *could* take care of the account today if that would speed things along."

Charges were tallied. Mia paid the bill using nearly all her travelers checks.

Riding back to San Bartolome Quialana in the car, the children ate the last of the food Mia had packed. Benito snuggled up on one side of Mia, Marisol on the other.

Later as Mia drifted to sleep with the see-saw rhythm of Inez's snoring, her mind danced with images of children rocking back and forth in branches of a leafy tree high above blue water of a lake.

Cradle me
safe in your arms
wrapped in love
your lips on my hair
gentling me through the night
chasing away dreams of worry and weeping

Spring

The route over the forested mountains was curvy, and at the back of the swaying van, Mia fought indigestion and second guessed the decision to travel by road instead of flying—sacrificing comfort for price, because she was low on traveler's checks and even her bank account was low.

Mia fixed her eyes on the road ahead, the lush vegetation beside it. So different from spare and windy stretches of road along the Columbia Gorge National Scenic Area. The river had stretched out, grey and choppy under cloudy skies when she'd driven the road the dark night after finding Tim with Valerie. The sun had been high when riding another day with Gerald in his old Ford. And the water appeared blue—oh so blue.

"Gerald," Mia sighed. "So far away. Our lives so different. *We're* so different. What is between us—besides miles and miles of air and water and sand?"

Her mind spun out other questions hinging on doors she would not open.

Every dream I dream is you
arms sheltering like cover
smile warming like sun
reaching my depths with honeyed voice
You—you who require so little
You who throw my mind into a spin of questions
How can it be enough?
Or is it too much?
How can feeling like this be lived
or forgotten?

Mia woke with a jolt. The vehicle was turning at Pochutla where the road split along the southern shore of Oaxaca: west toward Puerto Escondido, east toward Huatulco—the stretch of Pacific coast promoted for stunning views.

She sighed, "So many things to do in Mexico—more things to see than in a whole lifetime."

Back at the villas, Mia showered and turned in. Sleeping restlessly, her mind was filled with dreams of money woes. Light poured in the windows. Something else woke her: a repeated sound. She rubbed her eyes, listened, followed the sound to the door, opened it a crack. "Yes?"

"Much carry? Rosalia say come," a helper from Javier's job site said.

"Now?"

"Make ready. I carry," Hector replied with a smile.

"Thank you. Really, I don't have much. I can do it myself later."

He lingered, his face eager and uncompromising.

She sighed, "If you return in in two hours, I'll be ready."

Grinning, Hector nodded, and went away.

Mia prepared coffee and stood watching it drip. Her eyes turned to the window. Outside, blue sky met blue-green water. Waves moved to the shore in rhythmic movement. "Nature's lullaby," she whispered.

She gulped down coffee and a few bites of stale donut, threw on her clothes, and walked briskly to an ATM, then stopped at the market before rushing back to the villas.

Hector was already there waiting. They went over to the new house. Hanging beside the bell next to the gate was a hand carved wooden sign: *Casa de Graciosa*, (House of Gratitude).

Rosalia rushed out the kitchen door. She opened the gate and grabbed a sack slipping from Mia's arms. "What this?"

"I brought more food and drinks." Mia followed into the house and set the remaining packages on the cupboard. Noticing new décor in the living area, she praised Rosalia, "Oh, Mama! What gorgeous bench cushions! I love the green fabric with the pinkish-coral piping! Such lovely colors! They'll be especially beautiful in the firelight. And the clean lines look simple and classic!"

Pride showed in Rosalia's smile as she began stowing away the purchased items.

"I like the plaid you chose for this," Mia said pointing to the gathered curtain beneath the countertop.

Rosalia paused. "House with Mano—no money for curtain. Sell every cloth I sew. House of Maria only scraps at window…" Rosalia spewed, "keep out nothing."

Staring at the strange look on her mother's face, Mia whispered, "What terrible thing there caused you such terror?"

"Devil," Rosalia rasped.

"Who?"

Rosalia did not answer.

"Was it Guillermo? Were you frightened by the work he and Mano did?"

Rosalia nodded, but her face showed something more.

"Husbands must provide for family. If Mano did something *bad,* wasn't it out of love? And commitment to you?"

Tension stayed with Rosalia and her voice was strained, "One day, Guillermo send Mano work. Sister go market. Guillermo say woman in house do what man want…" She shook her head as if to shake the memory from her mind. "Something ugly then…"

Mia stared at the stricken look on her mother's face.

"Maria…" Rosalia said in barely a whisper.

Just then, Javier arrived at the house and Rosalia quickly put on a smile.

They made food and ate out on the patio with the sound of waves rushing the shore.

Weeks went by. No word from Gerald. When an answer came from Seattle Children's Hospital, Mia made quick arrangements, then traveled back to San Bartolome Quialana.

Before seeing the family, she walked the trail to the old *ahuehuete.* Beneath the spreading branches, she breathed in and out, hands on her belly and rocking back and forth. "Why did I think I could do this? I don't know what is the right thing. God, Mother Mary, do you listen? Can you help me? Tell me what to do. I thought I knew, but now I'm not sure…"

She glanced up at the leaves overhead. Green. Green and fluttering. One leaf dropped from the branch. She caught it in her open hand. The skin of the leaf was smooth, but it's veins and stem were bumpy, the edges definite. "Oh, little being, you separated from your mother tree. We share this existence. You let go of safety, cast yourself into the wind."

Another leaf fluttered down to her hand.

She held the leaves to the light. "Similar, but different. Similar, but separate." Lines of a poem she had written ran through her mind.

We are not separate
nor dream alone
beneath the blue blue sky

With ragged breath, Mia said, "I do want to do good. I want change for Benito, even if he does not want it for himself. I can dream it, even if he does not dream it. I can make it happen." Straightening her spine, she glanced up to the sky. "I do want it for *him*. But I also need it for myself." She pocketed the two leaves, and walked the short distance to Elodia's house.

"Please. I must have your signature to take Benito for medical care in the U.S.," Mia begged with Eber translating.

Elodia shoved the paper back at her.

"You've taken care of Benito. Good care. He flourishes, as much as he can with his condition." Mia smiled.

Hearing this translation, Elodia nodded ever so slightly.

"You have been generous. You share all you have with Benito and Marisol. And with so many other mouths to feed! So many of your own to care for, yet you find it in your heart to care for niece and nephew."

Pride coloring her cheeks, Elodia smiled showing missing and darkened teeth.

"Let me help you do your best for Benito! Think how proud you can be doing this—allowing me to pursue special procedures for him! Think what joy there will be for his changed appearance if it can happen! Your efforts will be praised and remembered."

Elodia glanced at the paper and pen.

"Perhaps nothing can be done. If that is the will of *Dios…*" Mia shrugged. And then she whispered, "We can try. Maybe *Dios* will grant a blessing on Benito, on this family."

Elodia reached for the paper, and scribbled her signature.

"Thank you. Thank you for allowing me to play a part in your family. I will keep you informed when it might happen."

Even Eber beamed. "Hope soon!"

"Any number of days we might wait for clearance from Immigration. But hope and prayers for quickness are welcome!"

Days turned into weeks as more papers were completed and filed. More waiting. More questions.

"Thank goodness it is not a medical emergency!" Mia exclaimed to Joyce in a phone call.

"I'll say! Once cleared to travel, will you go to Seattle?"

"The team scheduled a conference in two weeks! I hope the clearance comes in time. I'd hate to reschedule."

"Sending thoughts for speedy resolution."

"Thank you, Joyce. You are a Godsend. Thanks for listening. I'm getting so nervous about it all. I just had to talk to someone."

"No word from Gerald?"

"No. Maybe it wasn't what I thought. Maybe not a relationship to," Mia sighed, "go the distance."

"Likely something unforeseen intervened for him."

"Is that 'Sage of the Cafeteria' or 'Wise Woman on All Things Love and Beyond' speaking?"

Joyce chuckled, "Whichever! You're headed for Washington and I'm off on a trip with Tony. Let's pray for smart decisions and awesome adventures."

"Yes," Mia sighed.

"You've gained a lot of courage. Keep up the spirit."

"I'll try."

"Will you also be *trying* to reach Gerald?"

"I don't know what I want. Maybe best to leave it…"

"ARGH! When will you get out of your own way, girl? It's not complicated. Do you want Gerald or don't you?"

"In a way...But I don't think…"

Joyce interjected, "*You* said you're not thinking so far ahead. What is more NOW than letting yourself care about someone who cares about you?"

Mia had nothing more to say about it and friendly good-byes were soon voiced.

Benito's head and shoulders were covered with his blue *rebozo*. He wore a navy shirt, khaki pants, and brown leather sandals still squeaking with newness. Marisol wore a dress in red and pink flowers on white polished cotton. Heels of her new red patent leather T-strapped shoes clacked up the metal stairs of the plane.

They took their seats, looked out the window, exchanged animated smiles, kicked their legs back and forth, and giggled.

"Listen when the flight attendant begins speaking," Mia said. "If you don't understand, I'll explain after."

Marisol relayed information to Benito. They seemed concerned by the instructions, then watched out the window as a plane touched down on the runway.

Benito hid his face and leaned his head on Marisol's shoulder.

"Don't be afraid." Mia reached over and patted his arm.

He lifted his head, his eyes still showing concern.

"Doesn't scare me!" Marisol pronounced.

"If you sit by the window, Benito can sit between us. Maybe he would be more comfortable."

"Yes, I like by window!"

Benito crawled over the seat arm while Marisol squeezed into the seat beside the window.

"Time to buckle up." Mia helped fasten their seat belts.

The crew prepared for departure; Benito rested his head against Mia's arm. On take off, he clutched at the armrests and squeezed his eyes closed. When he finally looked out the window, Benito pointed at fluffy clouds so very near.

The flight from Oaxaca to Mexico City was uneventful. And as the city was neared, the children looked out and squealed, "*Mira* (Look)!"

"The city sparkles like jewels," Mia said.

"Tell story about this!"

Her brow furrowed. She thought a few moments before beginning.

> "Once there was a girl—hardworking and obedient. Also she was an admirer of things and exclaimed with great joy and wonder over colors and form and textures.
>
> 'Too much!' said her mother. 'Tone down your enthusiasm.'
>
> 'But such BEA-U-TY!' the girl exclaimed.
>
> 'Don't touch,' warned shopkeepers displaying delicate wares.
>
> Still the girl bubbled over with delight.

If she had a thought of worry, she replaced it with reassuring words. 'Mother, your sky surrounds me like arms. Wind like your breath fills me with sighs of happiness. Stars guide like your eyes lighting my way.'

The girl's mother did appreciate her daughter's cheerful attitude, but villagers did not act kindly to the girl. Sometimes they said mean things, and their words were like blows pushing down her enthusiasm and confidence. This happened many times. Again and again the girl rallied.

But even strong girls sometimes grow weary. This girl took ill. She could not help at market. She did not work at chores. She did not even eat. The girl took to her bed and it seemed the life in her was dimming.

She drifted in sleep and in waking. One night—or perhaps it was day—a woman in a shimmering gown appeared above her.

The girl drank in the beauty of the glimmering figure and said with tears in her eyes, 'Oh, Lady! You shine for us.'

'I shine because of you,' the glowing lady replied. 'Your light comes back to me. Your light is shared with the world. You are needed by the world. Love lives in you like a mirror. Beauty is reflected by you. Be healed and know you are living love.'

The girl's spirit was renewed. She put away her pain. And moved beyond it."

Marisol blinked her eyes several times. "Is that the end?"

Mia shook her head. "It is never 'The End' because love lives in all of us. We have only to let it shine out, letting our lives be reflections of beautiful thoughts and kind actions."

Benito clapped his hands.

The plane touched down smoothly on the runway.

They wandered through the airport to waiting chairs in a corner with a television droning voices of sport announcers. The children slept with their heads in Mia's lap. When Priority Boarding was announced, Mia coaxed them into line.

"*Estados Unidos* when morning?" Marisol asked, yawning.

"Yes, when it is morning, we will be there!"

The children fidgeted in line, then walked fast down the ramp to the airplane. Their restlessness settled after take-off. Snacks were offered, they waited to watch the movie *Happy Feet,* and giggled at the lively music of ads.

"You go that place?"

"No. It's far to Antarctica, and difficult to get to."

"What city we go for doctor?"

"Seattle," Mia answered. "But we have a couple days before we need to be there. I thought since we are stopping in San Francisco, and it's also my first time to lay eyes on California, we can stay in a pretty hotel near the water and explore the area together."

Marisol's eyes widened. "See ocean?"

"Yes, and a bay, not as big as the ocean, but pretty."

Benito patted Marisol's arm, and pointed at the movie coming on the screen.

The children watched the movie and Mia pulled out paper, and pencil—yellow #2. She wrote one word followed by another.

Rolling
Rolling hills of dough
Rolling pin
Pressing mounds
Golden dough
Buttery
Baking
In sunny heat of your touch
My fruit sweetens
Ohhh... How I melt
Running over the edges
Bubbling out
You like rain to rare-kissed land
One splendid sweet downpour

Mia shoved the paper into her bag, closed her eyes.

The movie ended. They all looked out the window as the plane approached the runway.

Marisol pointed at the blue water below and the golden land. "California?"

"The United States of America," Mia smiled.

They were shuttled a short distance to the Bay Landing Hotel. Mia led the children into the lobby. The décor was classic and warm with meticulous woodwork in dark tones, old-world marble floors. They marveled over views of the bay from the room as they ate purchased snacks. Benito ate his cereal bar squashed into mush with a banana and some milk, and drank a bottle of juice.

Hunger assuaged, they yawned and went to their room. After showering and donning pajamas, the children settled into a soft queen sized bed.

"Sleep tight!" Mia said tucking their covers snugly beneath the mattress; she leaned down and kissed each forehead. They smiled up at her, then closed their tired eyes, and were sleeping before she could draw heavy drapes.

Mia crawled into her bed, and closed her eyes. Words were in her mind.

How my heart strings
Across the distance
But I pull back
Puddling rope at my feet
Severing strands with jagged fear
Allowing only
Now to occupy my mind

Hours later, they awoke, dressed and went out. It was a short distance to the wharf. Mia held the hands of the children and they walked over to the piers.

Benito squealed loudly and ran ahead to look at sea lions longing on the wooden dock.

Several large sunning bulls awakened and lumbered over to the platform's edge. Pouring themselves into the water, they submerged, and came up floating on their backs with ease. Others barked, some flapped flippers or clapped or romped as if entertaining the onlookers for treats.

Laughing, the children breathed moist "fishy" air into their lungs and clapped like the giant mammals.

They walked and gawked at more animals and people.

"Ehhh," Mia sighed, suddenly forcing down a wave of nausea. "Marisol, Benito, are you hungry? Let's find somewhere to eat." She turned, her eyes scanning businesses along the wharf. Spotting a restaurant with view of the water, they hurried over and went inside. Mia ordered chicken and waffles.

Marisol ate eggs and hash browns drenched in catsup—so much she had to continually wipe red splotches from her mouth. She polished off several slices of bacon and worked on two link sausages. "Mmmm. I like," she claimed with a radiant smile and popped another bite into her mouth.

Benito demolished a bowl of oatmeal with diced fruit and cream.

When cups of hot cocoa with whipped cream arrived, the children tapped their spoons together and giggled.

"Would you like to see more of the city? We could ride the electric trolley cars, or see the downtown buildings?"

Marisol only shrugged.

As she cleaned Benito's hands and face with a wet napkin, Mia said with sudden exuberance, "Oh! I have a better idea! Let's have an adventure!"

Back at the hotel, she arranged for a shuttle to take them to rent a car.

"Where?" the children asked, squirming and staring out the window.

Mia only shook her head and made a locking motion with a hand to her lips.

"What this?"

"Oh," Mia smiled. "It means, 'My lips are sealed.'"

"Why?"

"A secret, *un secreto. Es un sorpreso* (It is a surprise)!"

"See soon?"

"Yes, but if you are a bit tired, close your eyes for now."

The children shook their heads, and though yawning, continued to watch out the windows at buildings, traffic, and oddly dressed pedestrians crossing the street.

Marisol said with sober expression, "Is much different in America."

Laughing, Mia answered, "Especially here in San Francisco!"

"Why?"

"Why…" Mia considered. "Hmmm. Maybe some different families settled here."

"Why?"

"Uh, I think maybe the air or the water here is just right for enhancing personal expression."

"And sun?" Marisol suggested brightly.

"Yes! Definitely the sun brings out something different in people! Perhaps the energy of the sun fuels their ideas. Maybe it enhances the colors and makes them feel very creative."

"People make something here?"

"Yes. Many are artists. Like you!"

"Paint?"

Mia nodded, "Oh, yes. I'm sure many do! And they do other creative things to make money to live."

Benito dozed while Mia drove, but woke at loud exclamations from Marisol on seeing the sign for the San Francisco Zoo.

"*Mira!*"

Benito pointed at the outline of a lion, giraffe, an antelope or deer, and a gorilla on top of the metal sign.

"Animals here?"

Mia laughed, "Oh, yes! And many more!"

Inside the zoo, they quietly viewed each exhibit and listened to audio descriptions. On the walk between exhibits, Marisol peppered Mia with questions and relayed answers to her brother.

At the amphibian enclosure, Marisol stared at a red faced creature. "What this?"

"Chinese fire-bellied newt. Isn't he cute?"

Marisol giggled. "Is like me?"

"Hmmm," Mia pondered. "He does have a nice smile like you!"

"No *he*! Is girl!"

After reading more information on the exhibit sign, Mia answered, "You're right! It is a girl!"

Marisol studied faces and colorful bodies of other species, then insisted, "Fire Newt is best. A princess!"

Refreshments of root beer floats had Benito laughing at the fizz tickling his tongue.

They watched some of the big rides. The roller coaster terrified Marisol, but Benito looked with exhilaration as the coaster rolled up and down the metal waves.

"Spinning teacups were my favorite as a girl," Mia said smiling as they boarded a small train for a short ride around and around with Benito as the engineer.

"What next?" Mia asked.

Eyes lit with excitement, Marisol pointed to a carousel. Benito rode a stunning tiger and held himself proudly; Marisol beamed from the back of a prancing white horse while the carousel spun, the animals rising and falling like their laughter. They rode again, and again—a giraffe and alligator, ostrich and reindeer. Mia snapped photos of them on each animal and when the ride was done, they laughed at their expressions.

As they were leaving the carousel, a white-haired gentleman walking toward them staggered. Mia caught his elbow enough to stabilize his balance.

"Thank you!" the man sighed.

"You're welcome."

"New hip. I still get a bit of a hitch in my git-along," he smiled, heavy white eyebrows raising comically.

The children giggled, then sobered.

Marisol whispered, "Sorry."

"The gentleman meant for you to laugh. Right, sir? You were making a silly face for them?"

The man nodded and smiled with apology. "Maybe I am a scary old stranger."

"No," Mia shook her head. "Their first time to the States. They're just learning our language and humor and customs."

"Have fun," he responded, stopping at a bench in the shade and taking a sit.

"Take care of yourself!"

They all waved, and Mia continued on with the children to see more animals.

"It's a Kunekune," she said at the pen of a wiry-haired pig with pug nose and split little feet.

Benito stared into the small dark eyes of the snorting pig and laughed, then whispered to his sister.

"Benito say he like him!" Marisol grinned. "Sometime sound like this!"

They posed and hammed with the pig, then went on to see giraffes, black rhinos, gorillas, big cats, penguins and other animals before leaving the zoo.

"This place a miracle!" Marisol pronounced.

"Yes, it was wonderful to see."

Loaded into the car, they were headed for the hotel, but Mia made a wrong turn with traffic squeezing around the car preventing lane changes. Soon they were passing over the Golden Gate Bridge. "I've always wanted to see this," she cooed glancing at the children: Marisol yawned and closed her eyes and Benito was sleeping. "Might as well keep going."

Following the highway north, Mia drank in the views—architecture of buildings, branches of trees, colorful flowers. Passing Petaluma, a quaint town with historic buildings, she craned her neck to see the clock tower—maybe similar to the old clock tower in The Dalles. It was a reminder of time passing, and Gerald. Her eyes caught a view of the domes of a white church similar in grandeur to the ancient churches of Mexico. Could faith be found and replenished, as needed? She'd asked those questions before. Still, the answers were not clear.

The road stretched out ahead: a grey ribbon with a backdrop of blue sky.

Seeds of ideas sprouted in her mind.

Ahead was wine country. Prosecco. Her favorite Italian sparkling wine. Ahead, Hispanic migrant workers tended fields and orchards. Maybe these workers were illegal—with false identities and desperate to succeed—maybe they escaped some tragedy in a country left behind.

Could their lies be excused? Could lies and make-believe lives invented by others be explained and forgiven? Even if by those very close—family, parents?

"If I let go of confusion and untruths tying me to the past, who will I be?" Mia sighed. "Who can I be? What am I most? What do I want most?"

Changes to old lines she'd written bounced through her mind.

My heart strings
Across the distance
I want to pull back
Puddling the rope
Severing the strands with jagged fears

Ahead is unfamiliar
Behind are parts unknown
I'm lost on the road
Longing for a sign

Pond

Nearing Glen Ellen, Mia read a sign for Bouverie Preserve. "535 acres, once home to writer MFK Fischer."

She drove to the Preserve only to find it was closed. "Inspiration needed," she whispered glancing at a map. Another garden was nearby: Quarryhill Botanical Gardens. Mia drove to it and paused at the entrance.

Marisol stretched. "What do here?"

"I want you to see American wild and beautiful as well as man-made. In Seattle, if Benito has treatments, we might not have the freedom to do much exploring. I thought we could walk and breathe in some nature before going back to the city."

The driveway was lined with vineyards carpeted in green grass. "Isn't this pretty? A brochure at the hotel said this garden is grown from seeds and specimens collected from Southeast Asia. We'll see many plants we might never see again," Mia said as they got out of the car. "I do so love flowers. They're miraculous mysteries."

Marisol ran a few yards ahead and back, ahead and back on the path while Mia walked with Benito, holding his hand and keeping pace with his small steps.

"Pretty!"

"Yes," Mia breathed. "Spectacular!"

They gawked at varieties of lilies blasting trumpets of gold. And there were many trees with interesting bark and beautifully shaped leaves.

Mia paused at a Japanese Maple—red and weeping—like the tree she had once loved in her yard in Portland. The yard and the tree now belonged to Tim and Valerie and *their* young child. "Will I have children to love and make a home with?"

They wandered to the Heritage Rose Garden. Complex scents filled the air with perfume. Mia bent over a China rose, "Bourbons Maggie" with a strong peppery scent. Her mind jumped to Gerald and the rose garden at Sorosis Park in The Dalles: the sweet scents they breathed with their faces smiling and close. Mia sighed.

Benito stopped at a wide stone set like a sign, its face soaking in sun. He fingered engraved symbols in the stone—Chinese words they couldn't read but imagined what they might be by the shapes of the words.

"Tree?" Marisol pointed to one looking like an evergreen with branching lines, "*Arbol*?" she said to her brother. "Mama with many babies!"

"Maybe symbol for a plant that reproduces freely," Mia answered eyeing the stick-like figure with little mounds attached.

"Benito a baby!" Marisol teased.

Mia picked him up, balancing the boy on one hip and grasping Marisol's hand. They strode along the path and studied more roses. "Mother loved roses. Grandmother does, too."

"Mother Rosalia, Grandmother Inez?" Marisol asked.

"Probably they do, too. Who doesn't love roses? Though I was thinking of other women: Mother who raised me and her mother-in-law, Angelina. It's confusing, huh? Even to me!"

"*I* love roses!" Marisol said loudly.

Benito nodded and kicked his feet like giddy-up on Mia's side.

"Whoa, boy!" Mia laughed setting him down. "I especially like rambling roses. I'd love to re-create a garden like this! In Portland, my gardens were precisely arranged with grouped flowers. This is so free and enchanting."

They wandered the grounds kept in wild state like in Asian woodlands. There were many rhododendrons. Like the "rhodies" in lush Portland, Mia noted with a sigh. Other beauties: peonies, camellias, magnolias, and shrubs of many varieties were sprinkled throughout.

They paused at a pond, saw a waterfall cascading over the rocky remains of an old quarry. Again Mia's mind went to Gerald—the day at Multnomah Falls on the Columbia Gorge where water poured over rocky cliffs towering above the gorge. How her emotions had poured like that water and the rain. Her marriage seemed then as treacherous as the rocky crags. But now her life was different. "*I'm different*. Maybe I'm like stones and plants placed in a new environment. Can I settle into foreign soil? Or am I the gardener? Can I nurture transplants in my home garden? Can I make a whole new plan that is my life's creation?"

"We're hungry and thirsty!" Marisol whined.

Startled from reverie, Mia led them back toward the car.

Blue dragonflies flitted over a shimmering pond. A breeze lifted Mia's hair. She turned to look, but there was no one. Her eyes lingered on delicate Himalayan Blue Poppies at the edge of the pond. "I love these wild transplanted blooming plants, the water like satin…"

"Seattle have water?"

"Water and more water! Photos of Seattle show many big trees, mountains in the backdrop, rivers, and lakes…"

Marisol pointed at the pond. "Like this?"

"MUCH bigger!"

"How long stay in Seattle?"

"I don't know. Days, weeks, maybe longer." Mia said grasping the children's hands and walking quickly to the car.

Fruit smoothies from a fast food restaurant soon allayed their hunger pangs for the drive back to San Francisco.

After they freshened up at the hotel, Mia asked, "What would you like for dinner? We could eat at El Torrito Mexican Grill."

Marisol shook her head. "*Estados Unidos*! We eat American!"

"Then we have *many* choices!" She glanced at the list of local restaurants and descriptions. Unable to decide, Mia said, "Who wants to pick?"

The children hopped up and down.

She closed her eyes, spun around and pointed. "Benito picks!" Mia held out the list.

He pointed to Elephant Bar and Grill.

It was only a short drive away. Shining gold elephant heads for door handles of the restaurant had Benito squealing with delight!

When spotting an elephant's head and trunk dangling down a wall inside, he squealed again.

"It's decoration only. Not live."

"Not live? Ever?" Marisol asked scrutinizing it.

"Not ever. It only looks real."

While they were being seated, Marisol eyed the elephant head again. "Miss something."

"Yes, something big—her body!" Mia laughed.

Shaking her head, Marisol said, "Have soft eyes of mother. She miss something, someone."

Mia looked again at the elephant, and then at Marisol. "Her eyes are pretty brown like yours."

"And you! Soft eyes like mother."

"Thank you, Marisol. I do hope to be a mother—someday." Mia turned to the menu. "I'll order Italian and some other items for you both to sample."

The appetizers came: sweet potato fries with Szechwan chili-spiked ketchup, baked French Onion Soup.

Fries were mashed with a little milk for Benito, and he ate with enthusiasm.

Marisol shuddered over a bite of fries with the flavored ketchup, "Ehhh! Wrong spicy." After drinking some milk, she tried a bite of the soup, and did not like it either.

Wistful gleam in her eye, Mia said, "I had a fantastic bowl of French Onion soup with Gruyere cheese at the Baldwin Saloon in The Dalles, Oregon, with Gerald…"

"Who this man? *Husband?*"

"Friend."

"Have husband?"

"Yes, I did. But we divorced."

"Why no children?"

"I wanted them. Very much. But I lost the babies. I…"

The waiter brought bowls of creamy macaroni and cheese, and they got busy with eating.

"Soft enough for Benito?"

Marisol nodded, helping him with a trial bite.

Tuscan style shrimp, linguine with marinara, and Parmesan chicken dishes arrived.

After a few bites of each dish, Marisol said, “Mmmm!”

Mia smiled, her hand smoothing over the tabletop with inlaid flecks of gold and red in the wood. Ambient lighting sparkled on the glass candleholders on the table.

“Not hungry?” Marisol asked eyeing Mia.

“Oh, sure, yes…” Mia smiled and took a few bites. “Just a little upset stomach.”

The night was fitful for Mia, and she managed only a few bites in the morning before they had to check out of the hotel and catch a shuttle to the airport for the flight to Seattle.

“Did you enjoy San Francisco?”

They nodded while coloring pictures. “California fun!”

“I liked it, too,” Mia smiled.

As the plane flew from California to Oregon, Mia searched the ground for landmarks. The peaks of the Cascade Range were topped in summer white. Unknown lakes and rivers dotted the landscape. Nearing Portland, finally she could identify the Willamette River, and then the Columbia. Her eyes followed the wide blue line to the dry lands of the east and the golden hills.

So much new
So many things different
But land
Red-brown like a hand
Gentles me
Breathe
Oh breathe

Breathe me
Sway my heart like wind
Whispering
Love
Come to me

Mia sighed loudly, "Oh, for goodness sake! I can't keep pining for what was probably only an interlude or two." She drew a deep breath, and looked over at Marisol who wore a pinched brow. "What's troubling you?"

"Worry for Benito. What happen at hospital?"

Mia wrapped an arm over Marisol's shoulder. "They will ask questions and look at him. Maybe they will make some tests. And they will answer our questions."

Marisol whispered this to Benito.

He hid his face.

"Don't worry," Mia soothed, patting his shoulder. "We are in this together."

Nearing Seattle, they watched out the plane's window, "Oooed" and "Awwwed" at the many sparkling bodies of water, mountain peaks, and hillsides covered in evergreens.

"Not California," Marisol stated.

"No," Mia laughed. "Beautiful, and different. You'll also notice differences in architecture: Sea-tac has Northwest style." While steering the children through the crowds in the terminal, Mia added, "The people here dress in different styles than in California, too. Maybe due to the climate."

After bathroom stops, and more walking, finally they reached the shuttle and went to the car rental facility. Benito was strapped into a car seat with great difficulty due to sobbing about not being allowed to sit on one of their laps. And Marisol was tearful over his upset.

Mia tried to restore calm with quiet words and smiles. When that did not work, she said, "Breathe deep, and blow, breathe deep, and blow." Exaggerating her example, Mia had them giggling and they smiled all the way to the hospital.

Gleaming windows and the stair-stepped design of the exterior of Seattle Children's Hospital was interesting, and the inside of the ambulatory care building was more so. A large sculpture of a mother and baby whale delighted the children, and a colorful mural of Puget Sound wildlife enchanted.

"Like zoo, not hospital!" Marisol stated.

"Yes, I LOVE all the colors!"

A nurse dressed in scrubs patterned in giant yellow flowers greeted them, "I'm Nancy. I'll help you get checked in. Whatever you need, just tell me, and we will do our utmost to make it happen. Okay? Promise not to suffer in silence?"

"Of course," Mia answered.

Nancy directed them to a small area where they waited on comfortable chairs.

A very short time later, a man in a deep blue lab coat came in. Smiling, he said, "Ms. Casinelli, I'm Dr. Vincent Andrew Rayburn. Some call me Dr. Andy." He shook Mia's hand, then turned and smiled at the children while bending on one knee and holding out his hand.

Marisol shook it and grinned, saying her name. She reached for her brother's hand, and helped him off his seat without tripping on the dangling end of the *rebozo*. "Benito."

"Pleasure to meet you," Dr. Andy said soothingly.

"Benito no talk much."

"Yes, but you understand?"

"Not English," Marisol offered.

Protesting, Benito nodded.

"For comfort of the children, Ms. Casinelli, we do have the interpreter you requested. It will help them understand more fully the various aspects of care."

"Thank you so much, Dr. Andy," Mia replied, her voice calm and warm.

"Come and I'll show you around." He led them down the hall, up the Frog elevator to Level 4 and the inpatient playroom. "Both children are welcome to enjoy the activities, toys and books. We're staffed to meet your needs. Just let us know."

"Thank you. I'm impressed with this beautiful facility. It really helps calm our worries, and everyone is so friendly."

Dr. Andy smiled, "This building just opened! We're quite proud of the way it will allow better delivery of care and more comfort for patients and families. The staff is excited and proud to be part of such a forward thinking expansion. Already exemplary, Seattle Children's Hospital is ranked number 9 in the nation this year, up from 12 for 2006."

"I had no idea this hospital was so outstanding when Lanzo—Dr. Grimaldi—said he had a classmate here."

"How is Lanzo?" Dr. Andy asked smoothly.

"He was a great deal of help with my mother."

Dr. Andy eyed Mia's wrinkling forehead and lip biting. "Is she doing well, now?"

"Oh, yes. Improving every day."

Dr. Andy rounded up the children and said to Marisol, "Up on Level 6, Ocean section, is a playroom for siblings. Marisol, you're welcome to use it in two hour segments while Mia and Benito are busy with appointments."

"Ohhh," Marisol sighed, grinning with bright eyes.

They followed Dr. Andy to a small exam room where information was gathered with the help of an assistant, Jojo, whose long hair with a streak of purple and rainbow covered smock seemed to captivate the children's interest.

Benito was examined thoroughly. Several scans were ordered for additional evaluation.

While he was in the friendly and capable care of professionals, Mia and Marisol went up to the playroom where several little girls about Marisol's age were sitting around a small table.

"Come on over," smiled a dark haired woman wearing a printed nametag: 'Liz—Art Therapist—I specialize in fun!' Liz wore a bright orange and red dress with bold pattern, and a necklace of large stones circled her neck.

Marisol edged toward the table.

"See if you can find a crayon matching each of my beads," Liz suggested, holding out a large box of crayons.

One of the girls turned to look.

Marisol dropped her eyes.

The girl pushed aside a straggler of hair from her messy blond braid and said, "I'm Bridget. Come draw. It'll cheer you."

Across the table, a smaller version of the blonde and another girl continued to watch Marisol.

"Pull up a chair over there beside Natalie or Grace," the therapist said, "while I put your mom's phone number in my phone. I'll let her know when to come back for you."

"Oh, I'm not…"

Marisol turned, eyes begging Mia not to say more.

"Enjoy a few minutes to yourself," Liz said to Mia. "Grab a coffee. Make some calls. We'll be fine. Right girls?"

"Right!" echoed the smaller girls.

"Definitely!" stated Bridget.

Marisol nodded, smiling.

After exchanging numbers with Liz, Mia wandered around the corner and over to a bench along a wall of windows. She glanced at the contact list in her phone. Her eyes stuck on a name: Gerald.

An image flashed through her mind: a small woman wrapped in wool blanket, back to the sun, eyes on a river.

"Charlotte," Mia whispered.

Heaviness bore down on her chest and she fought back tears while dialing Gerald's number, waiting for the answering click of a connection. "Ger? I'm really worried about your grandmother. Everything okay? Just thought I'd call…"

Before she could finish, there was another click, and a recorded electronic message played.

Her voice wavered, "Gerald, it's Mia. Call me right away if you get this. Morning or night, I want to talk to you about your Gram. Tell her I'm thinking of her. Give her my best."

At the cafeteria, Mia purchased coffee, cherry pie, and a glass of juice. Seated at a small table, she consumed her snack while watching other patrons across the room, mostly women, mostly with children, mostly quite busy tending to a myriad of needs.

Her phone was on mute, but she checked it several times. No calls. No emails. No messages.

Later, full of pizza and root-beer floats, Benito and Marisol yawned and prepared for bed in a motel near the hospital. Outside the window, leafy trees waved in summer breezes. The room had the essentials and comfortable beds with many squishy pillows the children enjoyed plopping against and smiling.

Mia kicked off her shoes and turned down the lights, stretched out fully dressed on top of her bed.

Marisol whispered, "Benito sleep?"

"Yes."

"Nice place."

"Yes, comfortable. I like it."

"You like Benito?"

Mia answered, "Very much."

"You like Marisol?"

"Yes," Mia said softly. "If ever I had a daughter, I'd want her to be just like you."

Marisol drifted to sleep with a smile on her lips.

A long time Mia listened to the quiet breathing of the children before getting up and showering. She slipped on a nightgown, and brushed her hair with the boar bristle brush used as a child—the brush found in the bureau at her parent's house after Victoria's passing—the brush that had stroked her head so many times, so many years before she had any inkling of the truth of her life.

No worry for past
Now time for loving
sharing
precious
hopes and dreams
of home

A sigh rose from deep inside her. Mia checked the phone again. Still no calls, no messages.

The next morning, Benito was checked into the hospital for tests and consultations with a team of doctors. "Take the day for girl-time!" Nurse Nancy said to Mia and Marisol. "Little man will be busy and sedated. Come back tomorrow morning."

Marisol wore a concerned look.

Mia took her arm. "A day to explore Seattle!"

"Okay."

"Don't worry," Mia flashed a reassuring smile. "Benito is in good care. And they can call me any time to come back if needed."

Mia rented a car. They drove through several neighborhoods, gawked at people in yards and walking down the streets, admired colors and shapes of houses. Suddenly, Mia pulled the car to the curb, and took a deep breath with hand to her stomach.

"Why stop here?"

She forced a smile, looked around. Mia pointed at a sign posted on a lawn next to the street. "An Open House. Let's see what kind of houses are available in Seattle."

Beyond a gated privacy fence and across a brick courtyard, they found a heavy wooden door ajar.

"Be right with you! Look around!" called a woman in business attire who was inside speaking on a cell phone.

They placed blue booties over their shoes at the door, and went in. Views of the bay attracted Mia to a corner window. She gazed at blue water and sunny skies. "Isn't this pretty?"

Marisol nodded.

Mia's eyes took in the home's features: hardwood floors, brick fireplace, coved ceilings, built-in shelves adding charm. They wandered through living, dining, kitchen, four bedrooms, three bathrooms, and a daylight basement walkout to a fenced backyard.

The realtor manning the open house caught up to them outside. "Hi! Sorry about that! I'm Deena."

"Mia. And this is Marisol."

"Can you see yourself living in this house?"

"Yes," Mia answered smoothly, her eyes catching Marisol's and winking.

"Are there enough bedrooms for your family?"

"We're just beginning to explore the area. I'm not sure exactly what we're looking for."

"Come inside. We'll make a list of possible requirements. I might have listings of greater interest. If you leave your number and email, I can keep you updated."

"Oh, great. I'll take your card and call if I want to see something."

"Of course," the realtor replied while jotting down information. "When will you be ready to move in?"

"I'm not sure yet."

Deena smiled, "Let me know if I can answer questions or be of further assistance. Take a brochure. Feel free to snap a few photos so you remember all the unique and beautiful features of this house! It really is special."

They shook hands, then Deena went on to greet a couple of lookers coming through the door.

Outside, Marisol silently got in the car.

"Pretty house, right?"

"*Si, pero grande.*"

"Yes, big with spectacular views! And the courtyard was beautiful."

Marisol said with shy smile, "I like house."

Mia smiled, and nodded. "I like it, too."

"Is much to buy?"

"Yes." Mia watched the road ahead. "What shall we do now?" Glancing over at Marisol, she noticed a sign for MOHAI:

Museum of History And Industry. "Reach in my purse and find some brochures—folded papers—I picked up at the hotel."

"This?" Marisol pulled out a stack of pamphlets.

"Find one with MOHAI."

Marisol held up the brochure.

"That's it! Is there a map of Seattle?" She pulled the car over to glance at the paper. "Let's go to the arboretum first."

They found the Graham Visitor's Center at Washington Park Arboretum, and followed the guide, Lorraine, around and listened to her relate interesting local history.

Evergreens mixed with deciduous trees formed a canopy of green overhead. Trails through the wetlands had warm woodsy smell of moist bark and needles. Marisol bounced from foot to foot and pointed with excitement at twittering birds hopping from branch to branch.

"I see!" Mia cooed, smiling.

Blooming flowers, vines and shrubs dotted the grassy landscape in a lush arrangement of color and texture like a living quilt. Her mind jumped to the winding stitches and colors on Gerald's old quilt—the quilt made by his grandmother, Charlotte.

Inside MOHAI, Museum of History and Industry, on Lake Union, Marisol admired an immense red "R" on display.

"It's an icon. A symbol for a beer: Rainier. Named after a mountain here in Washington. I guess it's a good beer," Mia said. "I don't think I've ever actually tasted it."

They went on through many interesting displays. A World War II era periscope grabbed their attention with views of Lake Union and the ships and boats out on the water.

After leaving the museum and driving north, Mia pointed to the Space Needle, "There's a tower like this in San Antonio where my parents met and fell in love."

"Rosalia mother? Who is father?"

"His name was Mano. He's probably dead. I was raised by my aunt and her husband I call—Mother and Papa. I didn't know anything about Rosalia until a short while ago, didn't know Mother even had a sister, or that she, *they*, were from Mexico."

"What think now? Is okay?"

Mia nodded, forcing a smile. "I thought I was Italian. That's the culture I was raised with and believed was my heritage." Mia looked over at Marisol. "I do like the people of Mexico very much!"

Grinning, Marisol watched buildings of the bustling downtown go by.

Though the traffic ahead moved slowly, Mia followed behind as if attached to a string of cars. She stopped when they stopped. Marisol was busy looking at brochures. A line formed. Mia realized it was waiting for the ferry at Mukilteo. She phoned to see how it was going with Benito and was informed he was sleeping between tests, doing fine. No need to return to the hospital.

She was snapping photos of the lighthouse and water when two incoming calls came at once and both were lost. One number showed up in recent calls, the other did not appear at all. Her voicemail had activated but malfunctioned and the message was completely garbled.

Mia stared at the phone and was startled when it rang again, vibrating in her hand. "Hello?"

"Hi, this is the realtor you met earlier—Deena?"

"Oh, sure."

"Say, I really enjoyed meeting you and Marisol, and I hope you don't think this is too forward. I have a little girl about your daughter's age, or maybe a year older—Kelsey is seven, nearly eight. Anyway, I wondered if you'd like us to show you around town a bit tomorrow? I have the day off."

"Oh. Uh, maybe."

"I was thinking we could go down to Pike Place Market. Also, we could check out the Moore Theater. It's only two blocks from Pike Place. You'd LOVE the interior décor: Byzantine and Italianate. Just fabulous!"

"It's sweet of you to offer. We would like that very much. But, I…"

"Just thought I'd offer. Always nice to welcome newbies to the city. No pressure. Not trying to coerce you into buying real estate from me!"

"No pressure felt," Mia laughed. "Thank you, Deena. That's very kind. And I'm sure Marisol would love meeting your daughter. I'm not sure yet if tomorrow will work. And I can't let you know until morning. Perhaps another day if tomorrow doesn't work?"

"You have my number. And I'll keep looking for suitable places for you, regardless."

"Thank you. I'll let you know tomorrow."

"Great. Look forward to it," Deena laughed. "Fun, fun!"

Mia drove the car onto the lower level of the ferry which was about to depart.

They went up narrow metal stairs to a glassed in seating area with many bench seats facing several directions.

Marisol pointed to the sun deck. They went out.

Warm wind caught their hair. Small waves bounced against the boat as the ferry got under way. They looked back at shore—the lighthouse standing on a curve of land next to the ferry launch.

"Pretty!"

"Very!" Mia snapped photos of Marisol with arms raised to the sky, sun shining on her face and wind in her hair.

"Where we go?"

"Whidbey Island."

"Island? Like boat of land with water around?"

Mia laughed, "Just like that! Only Whidbey Island has an interesting shape. We won't be able to see much of it today though with so little time for this adventure."

"Ferry is fun," Marisol replied, her hands clutching the cold metal rail and head bowed as she watched the vessel's wake.

Suddenly, Mia turned away with a hand to her stomach. "Let's go inside."

Puddle

Off the ferry at Clinton, Mia followed a road on the eastern shore of Whidbey Island. Blue water, blue sky, and the sound of wheels on the road beneath them made for pleasant driving.

"Go where?"

"Hmmm, not sure," Mia answered, flashing a smile to Marisol. "What do you think about just driving a bit, see if we find something interesting?"

"More adventure!"

"YES!"

They rolled down the windows. The road stretched out beneath a high canopy of old deciduous trees—large leaves dangling from branches gently swaying in a breeze. The air smelled of damp forest and grass. Here and there, small creatures—red-brown, black, and white—were seen moving in yards and along the road.

"Cats?" Mia looked again. "OH! Rabbits!"

Marisol giggled.

They went through a village and on to Langley. More rabbits, leafy trees, evergreens, and flowers, little old cottages and new construction huddled on narrow streets near the tiny downtown.

"Let's park and walk." Mia found a space along the sidewalk toward the end of the business area. "Oh, my gosh! This is so cute! Look at these storefronts. Darling! I love the intricate details and varied materials."

Marisol could only nod and gape.

They walked a block, passing small businesses and shops. Marisol hopped off the curb and over a small puddle, then back again onto the curb. Mia snapped photos of her posing with outdoor décor: stained glass windows, yarn art wrapping an ugly pipe, a metal gate fashioned like a leafless tree, a stump carved into a seat with a back of handsome fish leaping.

They went into the Star Store Grocery. Organic produce, household items, deli foods, and anything else one could want reminded Marisol of the markets in Oaxaca. "This where eat?"

"Let's go upstairs to Prima Bistro," Mia answered. "Maybe there's a view from there."

They were seated at an antique table next to a narrow window looking out on the street below.

"How lovely," Mia smiled, and glanced at the menu. "Oh, this is French cuisine! Mmmm. Shall we have the Penn Cove mussels?"

Marisol shook her head.

"How about soup with bread?"

"Cheese sandwich?"

Mia laughed, "A girl after my own heart!" When the mussels came, she showed how to eat them and Marisol tried a few, then filled up on her sandwich of thick whole wheat bread.

"Thank you for being so polite and sampling the foreign food," Mia cooed. "Let's share dessert." They had Crème Brulee with a perfectly golden crust of sugar on top.

Marisol was all smiles as they went outside. Mia wrapped her arm around the girl's shoulders and crossed the street to a viewing area with rail topping a vine covered ledge above a narrow beach. On the mainland across the water, the Cascade Mountain Range stood in the distance. "I like being near all this water. It's so soothing."

A small sailboat with diagonals of rainbow colors zipped by. Mia sighed, "On the Columbia River, there are many sailboards with colored masts. I like *watching* them move like toys on the water, but I think I'd be very sick riding on them. The ferry was bad enough."

Marisol raised her arms to the wind, swaying as if onboard the zipping boat. "I love wind!"

They wandered up the street one way, and crossed over to admire shops and artwork on the other side. Articles in a store, Sassy Siren, caught Mia's attention with spirited fashions. "Look at all the mermaid items," she pointed at a vibrant handbag. "That could certainly brighten a dreary day!"

Down an inviting alley, they wandered to a shop with brightly blooming flowerbeds and hanging baskets. A woman watering with a hose smiled and said, "Hello! Welcome to Langley Clock and Gallery."

"I love this twig furniture and the painted signs," Mia said glancing at the wares displayed outside.

"Hand crafted! We also have quite an assortment of rescued items, art, and collectibles. And many clocks of course! My husband specializes in repairing antique clocks. Lots to see!"

They looked about.

"Ohhh," Mia sighed, attracted to a gleaming side table stained reddish-gold.

"That's new to us," the woman replied following them inside. "Probably mid-century. Refinishing was done well."

Mia opened a drawer, her eyes scanning the inside. "Where did you get this?"

"I'll take a look and see." The woman thumbed through a notebook at a desk, then checked a computer screen. "Here it is. Sometimes we buy outright. This piece is on consignment. Came in about two weeks ago."

Mia's eyes widened. "From someone local?"

"Seattle, actually."

"A man?"

"No, a nurse. She comes over now and then."

Mia's hand traced the satiny surface of the side table. "I thought…" But she did not finish what she might have said.

"*Mira*!" Marisol said pointing at a tiny clock in an owl-shaped casing. "For Benito?"

"It is cute."

"Teach Benito time?"

"Yes, that's a good idea. Better though to have a clock with a timer," Mia looked through others, "so he can time our returns, or when procedures will be finished."

But Marisol was shaking her head. "This happy face for Benito."

"Yes, it is cheerful. I like the dial in the belly and cute little wings. How much is it?"

The saleswoman checked the price information. "My goodness, we've had this quite a long time. See the blue sticker? It's marked for seventy-five percent discount. Only $9.00."

"Sold!"

The saleswoman smiled, adjusting a wave of her blond head of curls. “A gift?”

Marisol nodded.

“I’ll wrap it up special.”

“For my brother. At hospital.”

“How old?”

“Three.”

“Let’s make this fun!” The saleslady opened a large cupboard filled with tissue. The owl was wrapped in bright yellow, then light green, dark green, and finally brown. The puffy package was placed in a bag printed with a forest of trees. Yards and yards of bright ribbon in rainbow colors was curled, and tied to the bag.

Marisol grinned with approval.

The woman made a long curl of fuchsia ribbon and tied it around Marisol’s head.

Marisol giggled at her reflection in a mirror.

“Enjoy Langley! Come back to us! Hope your other little one likes his clock!”

On the way out, Mia paused beside the side table, her hand sliding across the smooth surface, and words slid into her mind.

Oh my redskin
how you soothe
satin cool
captivating
more than this moment

They walked around several more blocks before stopping for ice cream—double fudge with mini-marshmallows on waffle cones.

Mia and Marisol sat on a bench and licked while the warm sun shined on their backs.

Continuing the exploration, they noted a library and also an arts center. "This is such a cute town. I love these little businesses. I worked in a store many years. I did like working in the bookstore in Austin, but I think I'd rather be writing."

"What write?"

"I wrote a long story about a girl growing up—her hard life, her hope, faith, and dreams. I'm hoping it will be published this year." Mia paused to lick a drip. "I should call to find out what is happening. I thought I'd hear from Dr. Farnsworth by now."

"Story doctor?"

Mia laughed. "Dr. Farnsworth works for a university. She's a doctor of literature."

"Why *Mending Stone*? Sounds sad."

"Broken hearts of stone cannot be mended. Not until softened with love and beauty and tears of gratefulness. Rough edges are smoothed. Pieces come together. Hope grows with healing. Or healing grows with hope—I don't know which."

"Both! Good story!" Marisol pronounced, and stuffed the last of her cone into her mouth.

Mia's ice cream dripped down her hand. She tossed it into a waste can on the way to the car. She made a call on speaker. "Dr. Farnsworth? It's Mia Casinelli."

"MIA! We've tried numerous times to contact you by phone. Even sent letters to your Austin address. Have you lost interest in the project?"

"Oh, NO! I've been out of the country. Apparently my cell phone is not messaging properly. I'm in Seattle, now."

"I could send the information via Facsimile."

"Can you give a hint what it is?"

"One word: publication," Diana chuckled.

"Oh my gosh! What about the changes you wanted? I haven't finished them yet, don't even know when I can."

"We went through the manuscript again, decided to publish as it stands, *if* you will write an epilogue."

"I can do that! Oh, thank you, Diana! So much!"

"My pleasure. Send me the FAX number. Get back to me as soon as reasonably possible with your response to the offer."

"I will! Thank you again!"

Mia set down the phone. "OOOO! Marisol! You bring me luck! I'm so glad you asked about the story and I thought to call!" Mia leaned over and kissed Marisol on the cheek, and they smiled at each other.

"Sell at store?"

"OH MY GOSH! How I hope so!" Mia giggled, starting the car.

While Marisol dozed with the hum of ferry engines beneath them, Mia attempted another phone call. There was a loud click followed by an automated response with abrupt termination. "Strange," she sighed. "What would I say anyway?"

Other thoughts were not so easily dismissed.

How I long for the honey of your voice
your eyes warming me
your lips taking me
somewhere
like home

Back in Seattle, before going to the hotel, they stopped at the hospital to look in on Benito who was sleeping.

A team was assembled the next afternoon to discuss his condition. After a promise of financial support from Mia, a plan was developed. Due to unusual availability of the surgeons and an operating room, in addition to the distance traveled to secure care, the first surgery was scheduled for two days later.

Heart pounding, Mia signed Marisol into the sibling play area, then went to a bank to request withdrawal of funds from the account set up after her divorce. She waited, foot tapping the leg of her chair in the busy lobby.

"Ms. Casinelli? I'm Thomas McAdams, bank manager. Please follow me."

She walked on stilted legs to his desk in a quiet back corner of the large branch.

"Please, have a seat. I'm sorry for the long wait. There are irregularities in your account."

Mia blanched at his words. "What do you mean?"

"No funds are available."

Her voice shook, "I don't understand. It was set up months ago and I haven't made any withdrawals."

"There have been no receipts."

"Payment was court ordered. Money from Tim was to come from the investment firm on a quarterly basis after the initial payment of $100,000. And there should be an additional $50,000 by now."

"No funds were received. Perhaps your attorney may offer additional clarification."

She stared at 'THOMAS McADAMS' on his nametag as if the tidy gold lettering could say something more. Maybe she muttered something in response before rushing to a bathroom filled with cool marble walls and floors, gleaming chrome fixtures, cold porcelain sinks. Mia leaned against a basin, hands shaking as she made a call to her attorney. "This is Mia Casinelli. I've been out of the country for several months."

"I've tried to reach you, Ms. Casinelli. A letter was also sent to your home address..."

"I'm in Seattle. I've just been to the bank," Mia interrupted. "The manager said there are irregularities associated with the account: no money has come from the investment firm. Do you know anything about this?"

"Unfortunately. After a lengthy investigation, action will soon be taken against the account executives of the firm."

Her heart was beating loudly and her voice was shrill, "The court ordered funds to be transferred from the investment accounts to my bank!"

"There's the rub. The money taken from Tim's account was never received into your account."

"What can I do?"

"You can sue. That will be costly. It is quite a mess. Could take years to track and unravel, with no guarantee of any recovery. It's just a piece of a bigger puzzle."

"What *bigger puzzle*?" she sputtered. "I know there is some sort of financial crisis going on overseas, but that shouldn't affect the payments made to me. How does this happen in 2008? Isn't someone overseeing these firms?"

"I can understand your dismay."

"I'm more than dismayed! I NEED that money! I made commitments! I'm not working right now and I..." her voice trailed.

"I'm sure if anything can be done, we will be hearing from the bank."

"Right." Mia ended the call. Everything in her was shaking as she made the way out to the car and sat with her head on the wheel. "Why? Why is this happening to me?" She whined. "I tried to do what I was supposed to do! I was FAIR! I was kind! I was a lady! And this is SHIT!"

She hit the wheel with the palm of her hand. "Is it *my* fault for not paying attention?" She sighed loudly, "I *was* foolish. I trusted too much. I'm too nice. I should have insisted Tim be personally responsible for depositing the funds instead of allowing the firm we've always used to handle it."

Anguish clenched her throat.

"Unless he's in on it somehow," she breathed.

Mia started the car, and drove into traffic, was swallowed up by the other cars. Words popped into her mind—words changing a poem written the year before.

Momma told me be a good girl
And I tried
Momma told me, "Be nice, be quiet, be a lady."
But such sad things came my way
And I cried
Momma said, "Be thoughtful, kind, and sweet."
And I tried
Oh how I tried
But deep down inside me a temptress whispers,
"Wake up!"

People rushed by on busy sidewalks. Mia parked the car, put money in a meter, and started walking toward Pike Place Market. Passing by fish vendors and numerous shops, something drew her over to the Steelhead Diner. She was quickly seated at a table near the window with a view of the street and words poked her mind.

Pushed across boundaries of herself
what she would do
who she would be
she found someone
someone worthy

"*I'm* worthy. But I'm still a woman alone," Mia whispered. Watching a ferry depart for Bainbridge Island, she studied the blue water. "Limitless blue—baby boy blue," she breathed.

"Need more time to decide?" the waiter barked, startling her from thought.

She glanced quickly at the menu on the table. "Water, and baby red and golden beet salad."

"Side of fries? Bread, or soup?"

"No, no. Just a pick-me-up snack," she sighed, glancing again at the menu. "After that, I *would* like the Olympic Mountain cranberry cider sorbet, please."

"Sure thing. Great choice!"

Soon eating, she mumbled, "Mmmm. So good! *Life* is good." But her stomach did a lurch, and she gulped down water.

Walking back to the car with renewed energy, Mia phoned Angelo. "Papa, I need to access the money you set aside for me after Mother died."

"It's yours to use as you wish, Darling. Are you feeling alright? You sound a bit upset. How are plans proceeding with the little boy?"

"He's scheduled for surgery day-after-tomorrow to repair his cleft lip. I have to pay up front for some estimated costs. Others will be waived possibly. But it's expensive. There will be another surgery soon to repair his cleft palate. And I've just learned there's a…" Mia swallowed hard. "There's a problem with the account for the money from Tim and it appears the investment firm is responsible."

Angelo said soothingly, "Perhaps, with a bit more time, things will straighten around."

"It does not look likely at this point."

"I'm sorry to hear that."

Mia blinked back tears. "I miss you."

"As I do you, Darling Mia. When are you coming home to Austin? You've been away much too long!"

"Yes, I know," she sighed. "With Benito's surgeries, we might need to stay in Seattle a while."

"I see."

"Would you do something else for me? Could you go over to my condo—check to see if all is well?"

"Of course."

"Ohhh," Mia sighed. "Never mind. Just feeling nervous about *everything*. As soon as Benito can safely travel, we'll come down for a visit. It'll help to see you."

"Wonderful! What will you do after that?"

"I have no idea."

The following day, Benito was sitting in the hospital bed surrounded with coloring books and had snacks on the over-bed-table.

"My goodness, so glad you are not bored!" Mia laughed.

He showed Marisol how to make the bed go up and down at the bottom and top, and they giggled. Sitting beside him, she operated the television remote and turned to cartoons.

Nurse Nancy came in to check his vitals and asked to speak to Mia in the hallway. "We still have a few tests we were unable to complete yesterday. We'll need Benito here again all day to fit his tests into the gaps between other appointments. You won't need to stay. In fact, we need to take him right now."

"Okay," Mia answered glancing into the room. "I'm sure we can find something to do."

Outside the Moore Theater, Deena introduced her daughter, Kelsey. "Let's go inside for a look. It's the oldest still active theater in Seattle. Too bad there's nothing showing today."

Mia gawked at the stunning architecture reminiscent of ancient cathedrals of Mexico, though less ornate. Black, reddish, and cream marble graced the entry and floors.

Deena and Kelsey told about performances they'd seen over the years.

"My favorite was Regina Spektor! I *LOVE* her!" Kelsey gushed. "Do you like music?"

Marisol shrugged.

"Here, watch this." Kelsey pulled out her iPhone and played a music video of Spektor's song "Fidelity" from 2006. "She's a singer-songwriter. I'm taking lessons to learn to play piano like her! Regina was born in Russia! Her family came to the U.S.A. when she was a little girl. I just love her!" Kelsey grinned and twirled one of her long red braids fastened with rainbow colored bands. "Don't you just love her? She's Jewish, you know." Kelsey began jumping around with dance moves while playing an imaginary keyboard.

A motherly hand rested on Kelsey's shoulder. "Easy." Deena opened a heavy door to an auditorium.

"Oh, wow!" Mia exclaimed. "How gorgeous and grand!"

"This is the 100 year celebration with fundraisers for restoration."

"A beauty worth reviving," Mia responded.

"You should hear how music sounds in there! Other-worldly!" Kelsey said with a dramatic swoop of her arm.

Mia laughed, "The décor would make anything seem elegant, almost ceremonious—like the pageantry of a Mass."

"Are you Catholic?"

"No, not really. Not for a long time."

"I thought once a Catholic, always a Catholic." Kelsey said. "Weren't you Baptized *practically* at birth?"

"KELSEY!" Deena chided.

Mia only laughed. "Practically! I think the Church would like to claim me. But I have claimed myself. I have my own beliefs." She pointed up to the balconies, "What a view that would be. It'd be fun to see every nook and cranny of the place."

"They have tours on Saturdays. Ninety minutes. A bit much if you ask me, but informative."

Intently watching and listening, Marisol was quiet and followed along as they wandered outside and toward Pike Place Market.

"Bite to eat?"

"Definitely," Mia smiled. "Hungry, Marisol?"

Both girls nodded.

"Piroshky! Piroshky!" Kelsey chimed.

"Kels is in the phase of 'Love all things Russian!' Thank, God for little girls and their exuberance for life and learning!"

"I don't love *all* things Russian! I'm not at all interested in the language," Kelsey huffed, grabbing Marisol's hand and racing ahead on the sidewalk.

"Not too far, Kels."

"She's so much fun," Mia giggled. "They look cute together."

"They do. Whoa, girls! Wait for us!"

"Wish I could keep up with them," Mia huffed. "I'm a little tired today for some reason."

"Not being settled can do that."

"Settled. That's a concept! Seems forever since I've been settled. Sounds appealing," Mia breathed.

"Oh, hey, I meant to tell you…Okay, this is a moment of business. I found an interesting new listing this morning. It has a peek-a-boo view of water. North Central Seattle, between Ballard and Green Lake, just north of Fremont. The Phinney neighborhood has Woodland Park Zoo and lots of character with old Craftsman style homes I think you would like."

"I haven't seen that neighborhood; it does sound lovely." Mia followed Deena and the girls into Piroshky Piroshky. Aromas filled their noses with pastry and savory herbs and meat and cinnamon. She glanced at a menu. "I couldn't begin to decide what to order."

"Let me! Let me!" Kelsey offered and stepped up to the high counter. "Today we would like a chicken with mushroom and rice, smoked salmon pate, potato and cheese, and Bavarian sausage!"

"Sounds like sampling the world with Piroshkys!"

When the food came, Marisol tapped Mia on the arm and whispered while pointing discretely, "What this?"

"It's a little pie you can eat with your hands."

"Ohhhh. Like tamale?"

"Love tamales!" Kelsey chimed with an approving nod.

"I make!" Marisol beamed. "Many kinds!"

"You can cook? We don't do that. We prefer our meals out. We're so busy," Kelsey sighed, and they all laughed at her dramatic tone.

"Lucky for us it's slow here today," Deena said as they pulled up barstools at the small counter along the window. "We didn't have to wait. I *do* know *how* to cook, but with just the two of us, and Kels in dance and piano lessons, soccer, combined with my work, we barely have time to catch up with ourselves, let alone wait through all the time it'd take to prepare our meals."

"Only two of you?"

"Yes, just us. Not married." Deena leaned in close and whispered. "Kelsey was conceived In-vitro."

Mia had just taken a bite, chewed and swallowed before saying quietly, "That's brave to take on by yourself."

"It was time. My latest relationship had ended. I just couldn't keep waiting for my one true love to want what I wanted."

Sighing, Mia said, "I was married. Fifteen years. I postponed having children. By the time I realized I wanted them more than anything, my husband and I…"

Deena interrupted, "Marisol's father?"

"OH! No. She's not my daughter. It's a long story. I met Marisol and her little brother recently—in Mexico—when I traveled to the village where my mother was raised. I also only just met my mother."

Deena took a bite, her eyes contemplating Mia.

"Can we get dessert?" Kelsey asked. "It's sooo good."

"Let's get coffee first. Then we can go to a park or check out that home just listed in Phinney neighborhood. We could stop at my favorite bakery later. Sound like a good plan, girls?"

Marisol's brow furrowed.

"We can call to see how Benito is doing," Mia offered reassuringly.

Marisol's look of concern faded.

"How old is your brother? Where is he? Pre-school visitation?"

"No, Benito *esta en hospital.* Tomorrow..." Marisol's eyes implored Mia to fill in the blanks.

"He's preparing for surgery: a cleft lip repair tomorrow."

Deena nodded. "Seattle Children's? Excellent hospital."

"Thank you for the reassurance," Mia smiled.

"Is that the only thing bringing you to the Northwest?"

"Not exactly. When I was married, Tim and I lived in Portland. We owned several gift stores..." Mia's voice trailed. As they tossed their wrappers and went out the door, she added, "I do have a friend a few hours away I want to look up at some point soon."

"That sounds interesting!"

Mia laughed. They went to Starbucks, ordered coffees, and apple ciders to go.

Deena drove and chatted en route to the house just listed for sale in Phinney. "I hope you like this neighborhood. We're right on schedule for when the listing agent said she'd be there. Not an open house, but we're welcome to drop in to see it. Don't worry, no pressure. I have to check it out anyway. Just thought you might enjoy coming along. But of course, if you like it..." Deena smiled.

A small yard with flowerbeds and maples on each side of a slate walkway led up to a porch. "Pretty. Not too much yard, just big enough to enjoy," Mia said, stopping next to a tall plant covered in white blooms. "This smells heavenly!"

"I think it's a Mock Orange shrub."

Mia breathed in the fragrance and was still smiling as she stepped inside the front door. Her eyes were drawn to a wood burning stove backed by a wall of river stones.

"A bit of a departure from traditional Craftsman which would have brick or tile."

"I like it. My friend has a beautiful stone wall like this."

"Same friend you mentioned before—the one you want to look up?"

Head nodding, Mia sighed, "A man I…" She did not finish what might have been said for Deena led them into the small but updated kitchen.

Quartz countertops, stainless steel appliances, gas range, a work/eating peninsula, and a cute little window with view of the yard and in what would be direct morning sun. "There are only three bedrooms, rather small actually, but the closets are surprisingly large. Sorry, no master suite and only one and a half bathrooms," Deena said. "But with small children, perhaps not such a sacrifice."

The hardwood floors were original but refinished, and the house was immaculate with fresh cream paint in all the rooms. "I love the built-ins and the dormers," Mia said. "I wouldn't mind not having a dining room. The views out the living room windows almost make up for the small room."

"Would be a cozy house for you. Not a lot of space to grow, but plenty of re-sale value."

"Yes," Mia sighed, "that's a plus. I like it. I just don't know if I could swing it financially. But good to see."

"Can we get dessert now?" Kelsey implored with a twirl, then a dash out the door while pulling Marisol along.

The mothers laughed and followed behind.

Deena drove to TM Dessert Works, and ordered an assortment of Petit Fours and Mini Pastries, plus drinks.

"Oh, my!" Mia gushed, sampling a square drizzled with raspberry. "So delicious! This reminds me of being in Oaxaca.

My friend Joyce brought back a dozen kinds of treats from the *pastelaria.* We ate every bite and were so full we could hardly move!"

"Sounds like a girl I would like!" Deena grinned licking sugar from her lips.

Mia flashed an appraising look, and replied, "You would. She's also a good baker herself, and lots of fun! She's on the road now in a motorhome traveling around to craft fairs with her boyfriend."

"Wouldn't you know it?" Deena quipped, smiling.

Channel

Mia paced the family waiting room. Marisol sat quietly in an armchair and was thumbing through glossy nature magazines. An hour stretched to two, three.

Punching numbers into her phone, Mia tried another call to Gerald. It would not go through. She sighed, and dropped to a chair; words she could not say lingered in her mind.

Cannot reach you
Cannot touch you
Cannot change you
My body is heavy with you
You who glides on gentle wind
Breath scented sweetness
Moves me
Ohhh
How you moved me

"Gerald," Mia whispered. "I need you. Do you hear me? Where are you?"

A hand patted Mia's arm. "What make sad?"

Looking up with glassy eyes, Mia pulled Marisol into her lap, hugging her close.

"Benito be good."

"Yes," Mia breathed. "I'm sure of it! Let's go get a snack from the machine? That'll make the waiting better." They split a candy bar and bag of potato chips.

"In Mexico, like chips with hot sauce," Marisol said while licking salt from her fingers.

Mia handed her a napkin. "I've seen that—dribbled right into the bag!"

"Yes! Good!" Marisol smiled.

Mia's phone vibrated. She stared at the screen, then answered. "Hi, Papa. No, still in surgery. Probably soon. Our nerves are a little frayed. I know. Thank you. We're sure he will be good." Mia smiled at Marisol. "Thank you for calling, Papa. It means the world to me. I can't wait for you to meet them. I love you, Papa. Talk to you again very soon." She drew several deep breaths, and got to her feet as a nurse walked toward them.

"Benito is out of recovery and will be up in his room shortly. The doctor will come talk to you soon. I can say it went well." The nurse winked at Marisol who clapped her hands together and drew them to her chest in a silent prayer.

Mia tiptoed into Benito's room with Marisol trailing behind. His hands were in restraints, face red and swollen, but with no gap below his nose. He had two full lips! She wrapped an arm around Marisol's shoulders. "He's just sleeping. They want him sleepy so he will not be restless. He has medicine for pain. When he wakes, you'll see he's the same Benito but better!

He's a little puffy. Soon that swelling will go down. And in about ten days or two weeks, he will be so much better we can take off the restraints."

Marisol's eyes were wide and watching.

"The head of the bed is up to help with his breathing."

"Look comfortable."

"Yes." Mia's brow furrowed. "We need to go right now to check out of our hotel. I found another that has a recliner chair that will be better for Benito." Seeing confusion on Marisol's face, she said, "I'll show you what it is when we get there, okay? Very comfortable for him to sleep on his back so his face won't rub on the sheets."

Nodding, but not appearing to understand, Marisol followed along to the car. They were soon lugging their suitcases from the hotel to the car and back out again at the new hotel, Marriott Residence Inn, Seattle Downtown Lake Union.

"Thank you for the early check-in. We have to get back over to Seattle Children's…"

The clerk interjected, "We have a discount for Children's Hospital."

"That's wonderful," Mia breathed. "Every little bit helps." She glanced again at the estimated charges for a week's rental. Her hands shook as she signed papers securing the room. "I'd like to be able to extend the stay indefinitely, if needed."

"Yes, very good. I will make a note of that. You can stop at the desk each morning and let us know your plans. A week at a time would be much better, if possible."

"Certainly. Thank you." Mia pushed the cart with their bags up to their room that was clean, bright, and modern with a kitchenette, leather recliner, sofa-sleeper, glass-topped desk, and a separate bedroom. The living room area had a small outside deck with several chairs, a round table, and stunning view of the lake and downtown.

Marisol bounced onto the sofa. "This good home!"

"Not home," Mia smiled. "We'll stay a while. See how fast Benito gets better. We might leave and take a trip."

"Mexico?" Marisol sighed. "Miss so much! Miss make *alebrites*."

"You are quite an artist! Creativity is so restorative and fun. Would you like to do some art? We can make something for Benito. First though, I need to take care of some business. Let's see what's on television." She flicked it on and checked the guide. "Oh! *Happy Feet*!"

Marisol grinned and stretched out on the sofa to watch the movie she'd enjoyed on the plane.

"It is worrisome how Antarctica is melting: channels of water running under the ice…" Mia muttered, glancing up from expenditure estimates covering the breakfast bar. "Everything is shifting." Her eyes wandered to the window. The Space Needle stood as symbol of Seattle, tribute to technology, innovation, transformation. The Tower of the Americas in San Antonio stood as a personal symbol—the beginning of Angelo and Victoria's life together in Texas. "I met and married Tim in Texas and ached for something somewhere else. Then I was in Oregon and ached for Texas. Now I don't know where my heart is, but I think again and again of the Columbia River Gorge—blue sky, wind, and water…" Words flitted across her mind.

Water
like cocoon
envelops
living tissue

"Cocoon? Cocoon like a giant tumor like Mother had?" Mia gasped.

"Okay?" Marisol wore a worried look.

She nodded, tried a reassuring smile. Mia reached for her phone. "Papa, I…I've just realized something...And I've been going over finances and I need to ask another favor."

"Anything, Darling Mia."

"Could you and Maggie go over and pack up all my personal items? Contact the realtor, tell her I want to sell the condo furnished for as much as possible, as soon as possible. Have a cleaning service come in to make it show ready. Put my things in storage, or if you don't mind, keep them for me?"

"Why now? Have you made other plans?"

"Not exactly. I…" Mia paused, "I may need the money soon."

He was silent a moment, and then added, "Of course, we will do whatever you want. And know that Maggie and I will always have room for you in our home for as long as you need."

Mia's voice quivered, "Room for me, and others?"

"Yes, Darling," he chuckled. "As many as you can squeeze in."

"Thank you, Papa. Give my love to Maggie." Mia set down the phone and grabbed her purse. "Marisol, we need to go get something to eat."

They bought food from the deli and ate at a tiny table in the noisy grocery store.

A while later, they visited Benito again at the hospital. He was awake and eating from specialized feeding tubes to protect his tender mouth from being damaged by metal utensils.

They chattered about what they had been doing in recent days: told him of Pike Place Market and Moore Theater.

Benito listened, yawning.

He was doing well, so well he was discharged the following afternoon. When they reached the hotel and Benito was settled into the recliner and the children were watching a program, Mia made a call.

Deena asked, "How's it going with the little guy?"

"He's doing very well. We've changed to a hotel more home-like. But I need a favor. Can you recommend a reputable and safe sitter? I need a couple hours at the most."

"Daytime?"

"Yes. Also, can you recommend a medical facility?"

"Not happy with Seattle Children's Hospital?"

"*I* need a check-up. I'm overly tired, nauseous."

"You can't go wrong with University of Washington; they offer anything you need for any condition."

"Thank you," Mia replied quietly.

"Would you allow Kelsey and I to be your sitter? We can bring movies, games, crafts, whatever you want."

"THANK you. YES! Do you like to paint? Marisol and Benito make *alebrites*, hand carved and painted wooden animals. She's been missing the creativity."

"I'm game for anything. I'll see what I can find."

"Deena, you are a Godsend!"

"It will be fun for us. It helps me to keep busy. I've been a bit down lately."

Mia sighed, "I know what you mean."

"Let me know when you have the appointment. I can arrange my schedule to accommodate."

A few days later, Mia was on the exam table—her hands smoothing the crinkly paper exam gown, her face a mask of tension.

The doctor came back in with several papers. "Ms. Casinelli, we'll put a rush on the blood work. The technician should be here in just a few minutes." Dr. Emerson smiled with calm assurance. "We have one result already back from the urinalysis." He handed her a print out.

Mia's eyes stared at the blurring lines on the paper he handed her. "I...I don't know what to say. I had a vision of something growing in a pool of water...My dreams often point to truth or something materializing..."

A bag was lugged from the car and through the lobby. As the shiny elevator door snapped shut, Mia glanced at her reflection.

Marisol jumped up from the floor as Mia entered the room. "MomMia!"

"I brought you all something," she smiled.

"Yay!" Kelsey squealed.

Mia set the bag on the counter, and went over to the recliner. "Doing okay, Benito?"

Corners of his mouth curved in a smile.

"Good." She went to the kitchen and reached into the bag. "I brought different foods for you to try. Apple and broccoli, pears and squash." Mia showed him packages of puree.

Joining Mia in the kitchen, Deena unloaded apples, pears, raisins, nuts, string cheese, and caramel corn from the large bag. "Nice assortment."

"We can make snack plates. Eating healthy is such a celebration of life," Mia answered.

Deena grinned without comment, only chopped fruit and cheese while Mia fed Benito. The girls opened juice boxes and milks and served up their own little plates, then settled on the floor to watch a movie, *Lady and the Tramp.*

Mia made herself a snack plate, and motioned for Deena to follow into the bedroom. They sat on the edge of the bed with their plates and talked in quiet voices.

"Was the doctor able to allay your worries?"

"Yes. He was reassuring. I'm only slightly anemic: that could have added to my fatigue. I bought vitamins, and more healthy snacks will help."

"Good."

"I was really worried about having cancer."

"Oh, NO!" Deena exclaimed, then lowered her voice. "Did he check out *everything*?"

"I had an ultrasound. No tumor. Thankfully!" Mia laughed, relief showing on her face. "Guess I'll have a new chapter to write soon…" Mia whispered more to Deena, and they smiled.

"You have an interesting story. You said you're a writer, of fiction? Truth is so much better! You should write a memoir. Start with this! Back track, then go forward."

Mia grinned. "I could do it. I could! It would be so easy! Do you think it'd sell?"

"*I* think so! You have a unique way of spinning out details—slowly, slowly and I am caught, waiting to be pulled in!" Deena shrugged. "Might be a best seller. You could call it *Hooking*."

They both laughed.

"There's so much to think about! Benito's surgeries need to be completed. And he'll require therapy and follow-up. I didn't know how complicated the condition can be and that it involves so much more than skin repair: hearing and speech can be affected, orthodontia might be required. And I don't know how I'll manage it: my financial situation is now complicated."

"Tell me about complicated," Deena commented wryly, then smiled. "Only days ago I was whining about an ended relationship. Now, the impossible has happened. My someone special came back! Now I'm filled with terror and joy."

"Can you tell me who it is?"

"Soul mate," she glanced at Mia, "my heart husband."

"OH! Hope you don't take this wrong, I sensed a vibe of interest in you for someone your own gender?"

Deena nodded, but said, "Not in the way you might think. Love doesn't always conquer all. We lived together ten years. I wanted to marry and have a family together, but Lon struggled with issues of masculinity. As time went on, I became more and more puzzled, and we fought about the strained physical connection. Finally, breaking down, Lon revealed a disturbing and deeply personal secret."

Mia waited silently for Deena to continue.

"He said he should have been born a woman. He wanted to *be* a woman."

"Oh, my gosh! How terribly hard!"

"My heart broke with his anguish. Still, I struggled with my own grief and disappointment over the illusion of a future together. I felt I had nothing more to give him, no way to help him. We went separate ways and have been apart since before Kelsey."

Gently, Mia said, "You had In Vitro Fertilization. You said you couldn't keep waiting for your one true love to want what you want. Was Lon the sperm donor?"

"How did you guess that?"

Mia shrugged. "Does Kelsey know?"

"Only that I had IVF and was previously unable to conceive. I couldn't conceive because Lon couldn't…"

"I'm sorry. How difficult that must have been to love the man and not be able to have the physical love you wanted with him. Now he's back in your life?"

"Not exactly." Deena sighed, then continued, "Lon is now Lonni."

Mia's brow furrowed. "As in cross-dressing?"

"As in sex change. I knew he was scheduled to have the surgery. I was so paralyzed with fear and grief, I didn't even send a card or find out how it went! I've heard nothing from him in all these years. But the other day I was shopping—reaching for a turquoise blouse—and I saw her. I knew it was Lon. My heart nearly jumped from my chest. She's stunning!" Deena's eyes filled with tears. "She saw me, and our eyes could not look away. Old feelings came leaping back as if the gap of more than seven years never happened! We went for coffee and talked for hours. Lonni answered my questions about the surgery, how her life has been since. As she talked, I could see the man I loved in the face of that woman. I felt such overwhelming love for him."

"Will you keep in touch?"

Deena nodded. "Lonni has purchased an historic home with three floors and fantastic views of water. She's deep into planning a renovation and wants me to help design the spaces—something we always talked of doing together."

"Sounds fun and exciting. Would the experience help with your real estate business?"

"It would enhance my portfolio of projects."

"Maybe you should do it. Can you afford the time? Would you enjoy working with her?"

"It's more complicated. She also asked me to live there in any capacity I feel comfortable, and I had to tell her I have a daughter. I didn't say Kelsey is *her* daughter, too. I'm in the grips of doubt and guilt. How could I have abandoned Lon when he needed me to be supportive and jump now into some association with Lonni?"

"Does she hold resentment for what you could not find a way to do back then?"

"No. She understood! She said she loves me still and wants me in her life in any way I can handle. But I don't know what that is! How can I move forward with her? Maybe it is only him I love? How do I know if I also love *her*?"

"My friend, Joyce, says you never know where you might find love. She says we should embrace all love and see where it leads."

Deena smiled, "I like that Joyce!"

Laughing, Mia said, "Me, too. She's wise. I nicknamed her, 'Sage of the cafeteria.' She helps me so much."

"Friends help make life wonder-full. I know that is true, but I don't know if I could be *just* friends with Lonni. We are such homebodies. How could we be roommates and have other relationships? How could we make room for intimate others? And if it doesn't work out, how can we part from each other again? I think it'd kill me to lose the relationship again. I nearly lost all will to live last time."

"I can understand that. I was devastated when my marriage broke up, when I lost the babies and Mother."

"It might be torturous to be in close daily proximity! Lonni says her interest hasn't changed—she still wants a relationship with a woman!"

"Ohhh, that is complicated," Mia said gently.

Deena was quiet a few moments, then admitted, "I can't envision a physical relationship with Lonni, no matter how much I might love her. I'm not wired to go that way. But if I had a relationship with someone else, I might feel I am cheating on her emotionally!"

"That's a tough one."

"Or if somehow we did negotiate the sexual issue, and made a commitment to each other, I'd have to give up the silly dream of *ever* marrying."

"It's not a silly dream," Mia whispered. "To declare love and commitment to each other, to celebrate with food and drink and music and all the beauty of gathering together with friends and family as witness..." Mia blinked away tears, "is just joyous!"

"It would be. If it were possible," Deena sighed, and finished the snack on her plate. "And what about Kelsey? How would it be for her? Can Lonni and I form some sort of cooperative parenting arrangement? And how would that feel? I have no idea how either of them will feel about all of this! I really did not think it all through before!"

"I can see the dilemma. But really, most complications we envision are not nearly as bad as we imagine. We just have to change our thinking."

Deena smiled. "You are a wise one, too. Guess we both have thinking to do about our futures: family, where to live... Really I would *love* living in that house and helping with the renovation! Though I do love living across the bay in Poulsbo, I wouldn't mind moving. And Lon—Lonni—is so much fun. Oh, hey! Lonni's house will have a separate apartment in the basement: three bedrooms, 2 bathrooms, laundry, kitchen, and living room! Maybe you could rent it! Wouldn't that be fun?" Deena's eyes were bright, then her smile faded and worry creased her brow. "I'm so torn! Seeing Lonni is such exquisite joy and pain!"

Later, as Mia listened to the sound of the children sleeping, her mind drifted to dilemmas her words clarified.

Marriage
not possible
But real love lives
through many years and many questions
with no model how to proceed
how to form a family
with untraditional bodies
but with the same need and want and desire
to be linked
hearts singing like no others
Marriage not an option
not legal
But if it was
would it be wanted?
Marriage
with ceremony and celebration
gathering friends and family under a canopy of trees
flowers and food
music and vows
and golden rings exchanged
showing the world how a pledge is more than words
how love restores
to the deepest level
how commitment is a treasure of immutable hope
and marriage bonds a family in more than love

Tributary

Benito hid his face and Marisol clung to Mia's side.

"Papa! Papa! Over here!" Mia called with raised hand.

Angelo grinned and hurried forward. "Darling Mia! And here are the little ones."

"Benito, Marisol, this is my Papa Angelo. And this is his wife, Maggie."

The children stretched out their hands and shook with the elders, then stood smiling and watching as Angelo and Maggie hugged Mia.

They walked with luggage toward the airport exit, and the car.

"You're looking well," Maggie said quietly to Mia with a tone of insinuation.

"Shhh. I don't know how Papa will…"

"How Papa will what?" Angelo asked. "Speak up! My hearing isn't what it once was."

But they only laughed. And Mia shook her head with a finger to her lips. The children made zipping motions across their lips, and grinned.

They chatted on the drive to the house; Angelo opened the front door with great ceremony and escorted them into the foyer. "Welcome to our home. And welcome to Texas!"

"*Ayyy*!" Marisol and Benito squealed over rainbow colored streamers stretching across the hallway. "*Bonita* (Pretty)!"

"Leave your bags right here for now and come into the kitchen," Maggie said. "Another surprise!"

"Stunning!" Mia giggled over a three layer cake in the shape of a star with yellow frosting on a plate at the center of the island. "Look, your names: Marisol and Benito." She held them each up to look and their eyes gleamed. "Thank you, Maggie."

"Maybe Papa made this!"

Mia turned to look at Angelo, "Did you?"

He only smiled and said, "We have ice cream, too. Benito can have cake?"

Grins and nods were the answer. The children perched on their knees on the barstools and waited quietly while dessert was dished up. They ate with sighs and smiles.

After refreshments, they were shown to a guest room.

"This is so cozy, thank you," Mia said setting their bags on a long wooden bench.

"It's a bit crowded. Perhaps tomorrow we can figure out something else."

"It's fine, Maggie. Really. Sorry for the last minute notice. Thank you for the reclining chair for Benito! He is in the habit of that positioning and when he has the cleft palate surgery, it will be needed again." Mia yawned suddenly, and sat down on a twin bed. "I'm sorry. Would you mind if we all take a bit of a nap?" Mia helped Benito into the recliner and tucked a blanket around him.

Tucking Marisol into a little bed, Maggie purred, "Little pea in a pod! It's fun playing Grandmother."

"GrandmomMaggie," Marisol offered rubbing her eyes.

Maggie smiled and quietly went out, shutting the door.

Yawning, Marisol said, "When we wake, will it be special day still?"

"Yes, sweetie. Even more special than you know."

Making up for the early flight from Seattle, they slept several hours. Later, they gathered for supper around the table—the children sitting on stacks of books from the library to boost them up. Mia waited until they'd finished eating, then tapped her crystal glass with a silver knife; it rang clearly, capturing their attention. "Papa, Maggie, children, I have announcements, and a question."

"Go ahead, Darling Mia. We're listening."

"First the announcements: my novel *Mending Stone* is being published!"

"My goodness, that is wonderful! We are so proud."

"Thank you," Mia beamed. "Also, I've sold the condo."

"That was quick! Congratulations!" Angelo and Maggie looked at each other.

Marisol looked confused. "Where live, MomMia? Not home with parents?"

"No, Marisol. I will make my own home somewhere. We'll be in Seattle for Benito's next surgery, and then…"

"Yes, Darling, what are your plans?"

"I need time to sort that out," she said, her lip quivering.

"Of course. I didn't mean to pry," Angelo replied.

Maggie jumped up and fetched dessert. "You mentioned you also have a question."

Mia nodded. "What do you think about adoption?"

"What this adoption," Marisol asked, looking from face to face to decipher the meaning.

"Adoption is when someone asks to become parent to a child, or children, who are not already hers. Like if I wanted to be your mom, not just for a little while, but for always. Would you like that?"

Concern showed on Marisol's face. "Where live?"

"Together, I'm not sure where yet."

"What about *Tia* Elodia?"

"If you want to live with me permanently, we would ask your aunt Elodia for permission."

"Much to discuss," Angelo suggested.

"Yes," Mia answered, and patted Marisol's arm. "We're only thinking about it now."

"Okay!" Marisol replied and dug into her bowl of applesauce.

When all had finished, the adults settled the children in the living room with a movie, *Finding Nemo*. Then they went to the study, and Angelo began pouring drinks.

"No brandy for me, Papa. Just water." When he was seated in a chair and Maggie on the ottoman, Mia drew a long breath, and said, "Papa, recently I had quite a jolting bit of news."

"Mia Darling, what else?" Angelo gasped.

"I…I have a condition. I was not feeling well. I'm anemic, and I…"

"Oh, my goodness. Are you feeling okay now?"

"Yes, Papa. I'm taking vitamins and getting more rest."

"That's good. Anemia is not so dangerous, is it?"

"In my case, no, that is not the biggest concern. You see, I'm also pregnant."

His response was guarded, "Is this something you have done with medical intervention—this *In*-something we hear about?"

Mia shook her head, "No, Papa, not InVitro. The natural way."

"I see." Angelo looked to Maggie, then turned again to Mia and asked, "Do you know who or are you in contact with the father?"

"Well, I…" Mia whispered. "I really don't want to say anything yet, just in case I might miscarry again."

Angelo's face tensed. "Oh, my dear, is that a great possibility?"

"I'm high risk because of my age and with my history."

"Almost forty is not so old."

"I'm already forty, Papa. The fabricated story of my birth was kept so long you've forgotten how old I was when we met!"

"My goodness. I am sorry. And of course, Maggie and I are very concerned with your welfare. Do keep yourself healthy."

"I hope you and Maggie are not shocked by this."

They looked at each other, and smiled. "A baby is an answer to prayer. How could we be shocked? We were sad and concerned for you selling your place here, and we worried you would be leaving Austin. Perhaps you need only a larger home for your growing family? How wonderful that would be!"

"Thank you, Papa," Mia laughed. "It is wonderful. Or it will be, if I can figure it out. I am actually terrified about the financial end of things, but feel I can work out something."

"How does your financial situation stand?"

"Bleak! The money that was lost—taken—may never be returned."

"Very disturbing."

"Yes. Benito's surgeries are expensive. And, of course, I'll need to pay for trips to Mexico."

"Tell us more about your mother, Rosalia."

Mia smiled. "She's hardworking, determined. She had a very hard life."

"And is she recovered from the heart problem?"

"She's somewhat weakened, but improving. Javier built them a big house, even with a small separate suite for me." Mia laughed, "That room will be crowded now!"

"What are your impressions of Mexico? Do you like the village of your relations?"

"Mexico is very colorful, with many contrasts. I like the slower pace, but for me, it feels foreign. I wondered, at first, if I would want to settle there, even for a few years to spend time with Rosalia, but now, I am sure I don't. I'm just not sure where I *do* want to be."

Angelo smiled. "Of course, selfishly, we are delighted if you would stay in Austin! And we meant what I said, our home is your home for as long as you like, with children, with children and baby. We can make room." His eyes glistened. He stood and went to her side, pressed his hands to her hair and kissed her cheeks. "Always our Darling Mia."

"Thank you, Papa, I adore you and Maggie."

A week later, Mia and the children were in flight back to Seattle. The pilot's voice sounded over the P.A. system announcing the flight was being diverted to Portland. Ticket agents would re-book flights to Seattle or arrange connecting flights.

"What man say?" Marisol asked.

"We get to see another city!" Mia replied with exceptional cheer. "Watch out the windows, you'll see the city where I lived many years."

As Portland, Oregon, came into view, Marisol said, "Green! Many trees!"

Mia nodded, her eyes following streaks of blue rivers stretching north and south, east and west. The wide Columbia stretched beyond the jagged peaks of the Cascade Mountain Range, beyond the green to the dry eastern lands turned golden.

Landing at Portland International Airport was smooth, and baggage claim quick. But long lines of angry passengers inched toward the ticket counter for re-booking.

"Why couldn't we just fly a few more minutes to get to Seattle?" a girl whined to a man who only shrugged.

"Why indeed," Mia breathed. Finally their tickets were arranged for a very late evening flight to Seattle. "What shall we do all day? I don't want to sit around here!"

Marisol said brightly, "Maybe do something else."

"Maybe that's the reason we were stranded!" Mia grinned, and headed for car rental.

After snacks of crackers and juice and yogurt, they loaded into a rented sedan and were on Interstate 84 heading east.

"This car is awesome!" Marisol grinned stretching her legs in the spacious back seat while Benito reclined and unreclined the wide electric passenger seat.

Mia shook her head in admonition.

He stopped for a moment. Started. Stopped. Giggled.

At Multnomah Falls, Mia parked and they walked the winding trail up toward the bridge. The water fell in a foaming tail of cold mist.

"Can we go?" Marisol pointed at the trail up the steep hillside.

"It's much too far. Let's go inside the lodge." Mia led them to the historic stone building. In the gift shop she bought coloring books of Oregon landmarks. Surveying the art work for sale, her eyes lingered on a display of small feathered and painted ceramic masks by Lillian Pitt, tribeswoman, artist. Especially captivating was a face like red stone: *Tsagagalil,* "She Who Watches." For the first time, Mia noticed the mouth she'd previously imagined to be smiling, was instead open and showed jagged little teeth. Mia shook off a chill.

Up the road a few more miles, they stopped at Cascade Locks to see the Columbia Gorge Sternwheeler. They admired the large black wheel that could move the riverboat through the water, then ran in the park covered with lush green grass.

They ate hamburgers and fries at Eastwind Drive-In. Mia might have crossed the street and walked over to see Lorang Fine Art and Gorgeous Gifts and look at the colorful and varied artwork, but the children were restless and wanted to color in their books. They loaded back in the car and headed again east.

Wind on the gorge was minimal, the pavement dry. Mia drove and watched the river for bright sails of boards she did not see. Mt. Adams stood white and proud beyond the hillsides on the Washington side of the river, and Mt. Hood in Oregon pointed to the blue sky. Signs announced: Hood River, Mosier, Rowena.

Vegetation on the hills became sparse. Across the river, the Klickitats were rounded and rumpled, shimmering gold in bright afternoon sun. Her eyes feasted on the sight and her mind said, "Creases in those hills are like creases of a warm body inviting discovery." And she sighed. Her heart beat loudly as the car rounded Crates Point where the horseshoe bend of the Columbia and The Dalles could be seen.

She turned on a street by an elementary school, then down a short gravel road, and stopped in front of the small house with peeling turquoise and fuchsia paint. Weeds sprouted from cracks in the concrete walkway and the small yard was dry.

Mia drew a breath, glanced at the sleeping children. She got out of the car, left the door ajar, traversed the walk, and mounted the stairs to the porch. The doorstep was littered with bits of paint. She knocked on the peeling door.

"No one there," a voice hollered.

Mia turned.

"Lookin' for the old lady?" asked a woman next door.

Mia nodded.

"Died. Couple, three, four months ago."

"Ohhh. What about the man that came by to help: her grandson?"

"Haven't seen him in a good while." The woman tugged at a bandana on her head. "Wish he'd come and clean up the yard like he used to."

Mia nodded, edging down the sidewalk. "Thank you," she mumbled getting into the car. "I've come so far, and found nothing, heard nothing. Maybe it was only something to help me through. Is that it? Mother? Mary, do you listen? Can you answer? Was it only meant to help me pass from one stage of my life to another?"

There was no answer, only the sound of children breathing in sleep.

"Was it not meant to last?" she whispered.

Mia started the engine, drove to downtown The Dalles, circled the end of third to second street and headed west.

Her eyes watched for the painted mural capturing local history on the side of a building. She glanced at Klindt's Booksellers where the book *Inanna, Queen of Heaven of Earth*, had been found, where she had chewed sweet gum and showed a colored tongue to Gerald, where the saleswoman—Ms. Wande—had seemed to step out of pages from the past. All that only a year and some months ago, now seemed a great distance of time.

"Maybe that was some other life…" she murmured.

Taking the curve of road looping back around to the east, she headed toward Interstate 84, and passed by the orange metal bridge beside the concrete dam spanning the river. Half the gates were open, water rushing down as if unending, as if electricity rushing through lines could not disrupt and burn, as if white wind turbines stacked along the ridges did not look like skeletons or headstones, as if propellers spinning around and around could not kill birds sucked into their whirl.

Mia shuddered.

She watched for the sandy hills where green vegetation clung for life, where rocks jutted in jagged teeth and dangerous crags. "Hideous," she cried. "It seems so strange and frightening now. How could I think this was somewhere I might consider living?" She breathed, in, out, in, out. Her hands steeled to the steering wheel. Gusts of wind pummeled the vehicle.

"What?" Marisol rubbed her eyes awake.

"Nothing."

At Celilo, sailboards were hopping and twisting in gusts of wind on the river.

"Pretty!"

Mia breathed, "Yes! See the rainbows on their sails? Rainbows are signs of new beginning."

"What begin?"

Mia only shook her head and kept driving. She did not turn to cross over to Washington on the arching bridge named for Samuel Hill. And at the Rufus exit, her hands could do nothing but turn from the freeway and head south.

The wind quieted between mounds of earth where her car had broken down the night Gerald found her on the ridge above the river. She had wavered at the edge—blood and tears on her face, bruises and abrasions marking the pain of finding Tim in the arms of another woman. Gerald had carried her to safety, comforted with slow words and gentle looks. How he melted away the hurt, mending the ache in her heart.

That was over a year ago—a year of loss and change.

The car wheels turned into the driveway. Crunching gravel might have brought him out on the wooden porch. She watched for his long dark hair to appear behind the wooden screen door. She waited and watched. But the door did not open.

Mia looked to the garden. Dried stalks of last year's sunflowers stood against the wire and wood fence like garden sentries with giant drooping heads. Rows of vegetation were clogged with weeds, and the watering hose was tightly coiled as if poised to strike. "Gerald, where are you?" Mia asked aloud.

"Benito hungry," Marisol whined, "Me, too."

"Yes," Mia sighed, "we're all hungry for something." She backed the car from the drive, went to the mini-mart in Rufus, purchased food and drinks they consumed while she drove. "Look, we're crossing the Columbia River! Did you ever see such a big river?" Mia said on the Samuel Hill Memorial Bridge. She glanced down; there was only the sparkle of sun on the water, not the long-lost wedding ring she'd cast out.

Stonehenge stood on the hillside to the east of the winding road up the hill. A memorial to war veterans of Klickitat

County, this Stonehenge was not as majestic as the original Stonehenge in England—this was man-made of concrete not stone. Perhaps it would not be as enduring against the elements of sun and wind of the area. The dry climate could strip the land bare, strip a heart bare of nourishment, too.

Even Maryhill Museum of Art, Sam Hill's dream home where he never lived, standing stately and bare on the cliff above the river, did not capture her imagination now. No voice called to her, no whispers tickled her ears, no wind echoed like a distant ocean tide.

Travelling toward Portland on the Washington side of the river—the reverse of the route that led Mia to Gerald—she reviewed all that had happened before and since. New words found a way into her mind.

Letting go
requirements
Letting go
resentments
Letting go
judgments and wishful thinking
Allowing
more
Oh so much more

Mia drove on, passing through the five tunnels carved through rocky fingers of land stretching out into the river. "Five tunnels, like stages of darkness in my recent past: losing the babies, finding Tim with Valerie, Mother's death, the end of my marriage, losing the money promised me—money I worked hard to earn all the fifteen years with Tim."

She settled those events in her mind with a breath, and a long release.

Mia crossed a bridge over the wild and scenic Klickitat River. A few more miles west, she crossed the White Salmon River. "Reminder of life flowing—constantly changing. Every drop of rain like tears adding to the all. Flows swelling over bounds, molding and softening edges, sweeping away what was, transporting all to another shore."

Further west, she drove through tidy upbeat Stevenson. She did not cross the river at the Bridge of the Gods where an ancient land bridge may have linked Washington and Oregon. That was a story passed down in telling, like many stories, perhaps with details altered over time. Perhaps no truth is absolute. What was fades in a haze of looking back. What lies ahead also is unclear. "There is only now. Only now..." she whispered.

The cycle of a year and some months was completed in reverse as she crossed over the Columbia to Oregon on I-205, and went back to the Portland Airport.

"A loop of my life journey gone full circle," she sighed as the plane lifted off the runway in flight to Seattle.

Reservoir

The holidays were rapidly approaching. Deena helped Mia and the children find a rental house. Marisol was enrolled in school. Benito's first surgery had healed, and they were at the hospital waiting to hear results of the second surgery.

Joyce said, "So glad to be here with you."

"Yes, so glad you are and I don't have to wait alone!"

"You know *I* don't mind hospitals. And it's such a perfect coincidence: Susan's internship in Seattle so I could come for a visit and help you, too! Couldn't be better."

"Ehhh, better if preeclampsia hadn't developed."

"True. I'm glad to be here, and you look good, look like you're behaving."

Mia sighed, "They say I'm doing okay, and the baby is doing well, but I've been terrified I'd miscarry or have a seizure or something else horrible."

"That's exhaustion talking: wearing down your filters so anxiety overflows. I'm here to help you get rested and stop trying to do everything yourself. No shame in needing help."

"Asking for help—or asking *at all* for what I want—has always been hard for me."

"Live and learn," Joyce chuckled.

"How long are you staying?"

Joyce shrugged. "Waiting to hear how benefits will work out my pay and vacation accrual."

"What about Tony? How's that going?"

"Not."

"Ohhh, what happened?"

"Nothing. I simply did not enjoy the lifestyle: living in a motorhome, staying in RV parks or by the side of the road! I like solid foundations of stone under me, not rolling wheels."

Mia chuckled. "Did you break up, or how did you leave it with him?"

"To be determined later. But he'll stay on the list." Joyce smiled mischievously. "Good in the RUMBA department. And a girl can always use a little rumba!"

"Joyce!"

"Except you! You don't need anything to make your blood pressure go higher!"

"That's for sure."

A nurse came over to speak to Mia. "Benito did well. It will be a little while yet before you can see him."

"Thank goodness! After these months of preparing and healing and waiting for the surgeries, finally they're done. I hope this will be the last one for Benito."

"Hope so," Joyce chimed.

"Even with all he's been through, he's so cheerful. And Marisol is so creative and helpful. I don't know how I will manage with three children, and I never imagined trying to do it single, but there must be a way," Mia said without pausing.

"Breathe, breathe!" Joyce made gestures with her hands rising and falling like a conductor.

Mia did draw a number of breaths, letting each one out slow. "I imagine we're swimming in the little bay at Carrizalillo. We're floating on our backs, faces to the sun, lulled by the waves and sound of water lapping the shore."

"Ahhh, Mexico. That was a sweet time."

"Even though I didn't know what I was about to find just one beach over at Puerto Angelito, I felt something, some anticipation, some 'knowing' that my dreams were close."

"Intuitive. Psychic even."

"Why then didn't I know this little one was on the way?" Mia's hand gently made circular motions on her extended belly.

Joyce shrugged. "The air did seem filled with mystery there, as if anything could happen."

"You felt it, too?"

"Yes! It was so powerful! And the moonstones I bought for you seemed to magnify everything. The energy coming off them radiated straight through me."

Mia laughed.

"Didn't you feel it when you put on the necklace?"

"I felt some kind of stirring, but I thought I was just lightheaded from being in the sun too long."

"For being in tune with the mystical universe and having as much faith as you do, sometimes you sure do doubt what you feel!"

Mia sighed. "There was so much going on. Ever since I went to San Antonio looking for answers, it has been one thing after another—the sudden trip to Mexico, the shock and surprise meeting my mother, her heart problems…I guess I was much too preoccupied to notice what was lingering inside me." Mia shook her head, a look of amazement on her face. “But four months of it not even crossing my mind?”

“Perhaps it was better that way, so you didn’t worry. Body and spirit knew what to do without your active participation. You set the desire in your mind for wanting a child, and the universe, God, Mother Nature, *whoever*, figured out the details!”

Mia pushed herself up from the armed chair with effort. “That’s one way to look at it.”

“Feeling okay?”

“I need to walk around.”

A short while later, the doctor came out to speak to them. “Benito’s surgery went well. We don’t anticipate any problems. There will be some pain for the first few days, possibly some sloughing of old tissue as the palate heals, possibly a bit of bleeding after a week or two. This is normal and part of the healing process. He will be on IV for today and tomorrow. Following a liquid to soft diet for the first several weeks is best. He should continue to wear the soft restraints on his hands to keep from touching his mouth as it heals. Head should be elevated, especially when eating. We’ll keep him here until late tomorrow, see him back in 5-7 days and again in two weeks.”

“What about speech therapy?”

“He’ll be evaluated in a few weeks to determine if additional surgery to correct any structural problems could be of benefit. Working with a therapist will help him learn sounds and how to make them. Benito is very lucky! He does not appear to have accompanying defects often associated with cleft lip and cleft palate: sight and hearing test fine.”

“That’s good,” Mia sighed with a look of relief.

“Throughout the follow-up, you’ll be given instructions on how to help him with language development.”

"How often will he need to be back here?"

"Yearly, or if other problems arise, though follow-up could proceed adequately wherever there are appropriate services and care."

Mia nodded. "We aren't sure yet where home will be."

"When are you expecting the new little one?"

"Trying to hold off at least another month," Mia answered with apprehension.

Joyce interjected, "We're keeping a close eye on her so she doesn't do too much."

"Good. I'll check in on Benito again later." The doctor started to walk away, then turned. "Do we know—boy or girl?"

Mia grinned, "I know, but I'm not saying."

"I've been trying to entice a hint from her, but she's strong minded," Joyce said smiling.

The doctor nodded and waved.

They went down the hallway to the elevator.

"Isn't this the most beautiful hospital? I love the murals. They add so much life and color."

"Speaking of life and color, what are you thinking about the father situation?"

Mia gave Joyce a look.

"You've been silent on the subject. Thought I'd acknowledge the elephant in the room. Not that you are required by friendship to give explanations, but wouldn't it help to talk about whatever dilemma you are having? What does Lanzo say about it?"

The doors closed, and Mia answered, "I have an uneasy feeling about him. Though chemistry is certainly there, I fear it would end up as heart break."

"Why?"

"I happened down a hall one day; Lanzo was around a corner with one of the off-duty nurses, and his hands weren't exactly in his pockets."

"That's quite an insinuation!"

Mia burst out laughing. "You should have seen the look on his face! We were barely dating, but it was startling, and reminded me of finding Tim with Valerie."

"But you *were* 'seeing' each other?"

"Yes, in a manner of speaking."

"GOSH! WAS there RUMBA or wasn't there?"

The elevator doors opened before she could answer. They stepped out.

Marisol was in the lounge at a table with the art therapist. Mia introduced Joyce and sat down in a child's sized chair. "What is this picture?"

"San Bartolome Quialana. See Benito? Every face smile to him."

"Both your smiles are big and beautiful," Mia said.

"You drew a large sun shining down. Is it very warm where you live?" the therapist asked.

Marisol nodded with downcast eyes. "Bare feet walk and run everywhere. Seattle not so warm."

"What else do you like about your village?"

The girl whispered, "Everything."

"I can frame this picture to hang in your room," Mia offered.

Marisol shook her head. "Make for MomMia to smile more! Have too much trouble now with Marisol and Benito."

"No, no," Mia soothed. "Only my own body is trouble. It is only a little difficult for me right now. After the baby comes, I will be better."

Marisol wiped away a tear. "Benito get better soon. Then can go home? Or have to wait for Mia get better, too."

The therapist eyed Mia, and asked Marisol, "Do you have family in your village?"

"Maybe family and village like Benito better when fix."

Mia studied Marisol's downturned mouth, and then she said quietly, "When I was a little girl, I dreamed of a big family. I had only Mother and Papa and Grandmother. I was lonely. I had no village to care for me. But now I know I have family in Mexico. *Abuelita* Inez and *Tia* Patrice and my cousins can help your aunt Elodia and cousins watch over you. They wait for you to come home and to hear of your big adventure."

The girl brightened. "MomMia and baby visit?"

"Yes," Mia smiled, eyes glistening.

Marisol nodded and smiled.

"Benito might be back in his room now. We could go see him," Joyce suggested while Mia dabbed at tears.

Blue sky hung above the blue-green ocean. Javier held Rosalia's hand. His face was stiff and his back was very straight sitting on the seat's edge. He scuffed his foot back and forth, back and forth on the white marble floor.

Their flight was announced. They carried two small bags out to the airplane, and were seated: Javier by the window, Rosalia on the aisle. They stared out as the plane rose from the runway.

"Rosalia! *Mira*!" Javier exclaimed.

The plane circled Puerto Escondido, and headed inland over emerald land. Rosalia glanced down, her eyes scanning tree to tree with no glimpse of *ahuehuetes* like the old one in San Bartolome Quialana with spreading branches—a living shelter from the world. Closing her eyes, hands clutching the glass pendant with tiny pink rose inside Mia had given and her rosary with sky blue beads, she whispered prayers.

"Rosalia," Javier whispered. "Wake up. See the city."

Brilliant sunlight glistened in a million windows reflecting like diamonds from Mexico City below. The land was a hilly patchwork of structures on small plots, roads and fences making lines like stitches connecting patches of color.

The layover in the city was long enough for a brief excursion to La Villa de Guadalupe, once a separate town now a neighborhood of Mexico City. In ancient times, a shrine there was dedicated to Tonantzin, mother goddess, until Spanish conquerors destroyed it. Ever since the Virgin of Guadalupe appeared to Juan Diego on the hill of Tepeyac in 1531, it has been an important pilgrimage site also for Catholicism.

Rosalia and Javier pushed through the quiet crowds on the Plaza of the Americas. The old basilica—built on a former lake—was sinking and access was now limited. Beside it, a new shrine housing the cloak of Juan Diego with the image of *La Virgen de Guadalupe* was constructed.

Inside, the air was sweet with a hint of rose scent and Our Lady seemed to linger like a mother watching over her children. Rosalia prayed with great emotion and expressions of thankfulness. And they went away with a sense of accomplishment.

They landed in Phoenix, ate cheeseburgers and fries in the airport, before continuing on to SeaTac. Late in the night, they arrived in Seattle.

Glimpses of Mia were not seen in the greeting crowd.

At last, a woman with reddish hair held up a sign printed with their names, and they walked toward her.

"Welcome to Seattle!"

They smiled.

"Remember I'm Joyce? I met you months ago when I came to Puerto Escondido with Mia?"

Javier and Rosalia nodded.

"I volunteered to pick you up so she could stay with the children."

Rosalia stifled a yawn. "Good."

"Only a little longer now then you'll be to the house and beds for sleeping!" Joyce said leading them to the car.

They watched out the windows at the sparkling lights of the city and sometimes yawned on the drive to the well-lit house.

Mia had been dozing on the sofa. She sat up as Joyce unlocked the door. "Mama! Javier!" She threw off a fluffy comforter, and stood up.

Rosalia gasped, "*Ay, Dios*! Baby!"

"Good surprise, huh?" Joyce giggled.

"When?"

"At least one month, hopefully two."

Rosalia and Javier grinned with excitement.

"Fun being in on the big reveal!" Joyce chuckled. "I'd better be going now. Get some sleep all. I'll check on you tomorrow," she said giving hugs.

"Thank you, Joyce," Mia said with great warmth.

Rosalia and Javier clapped.

Joyce bowed, smiled and waved as she went out the door.

Mia helped her mother and Javier get settled into the spare room. She fetched a drink of water, turned out the house lights, and went to bed, but did not sleep right away. Her mind was filled with words like a nagging pain in her body or stitch in her side.

How I have
waited and longed for you
Others pulled into my life
like tiny stitches holding me together
maybe my heart is mended
But oh how I long for you in my arms

The children were up early and running, feet padding down the hardwood floor of the hallway. Mia opened her eyes as her door was pushed open. "Come in," she yawned.

Marisol and Benito rushed to the bed.

She patted the side and they hopped up.

"Mama Rosalia come with Javier? They like surprise?"

"Yes," Mia whispered, putting a finger to her mouth. "They got in late. And it is such a long trip. Let's be very quiet so they can sleep." She got up and went out to the kitchen with them. The children sat on stools at the bar while Mia made oatmeal pancakes.

"When decorate for holiday?"

"We need to buy a few things. Maybe we can all go shopping this afternoon. Would you like that?"

They nodded with bright eyes and big smiles.

Several hours later, Rosalia and Javier woke and ate.

Joyce arrived, and they all loaded into the van borrowed from her daughter, Susan. They went to a large store. Mia filled a shopping cart with tinsel, lights, ornaments, and holiday crafts. Then they went to the grocery and stocked up on sugar and flour, food coloring and toppings.

"We can bake extra cookies to freeze and frost later," Joyce suggested.

"Make sweet tamales?"

"Yes, let's do!" Mia answered.

They wandered down an aisle of Hispanic foods.

"Different in Mexico, not so much American food."

"Probably not as many Americans moving to Mexico as we have Mexicans moving to the United States," Mia offered.

"Maybe MomMia move to Mexico?" Marisol asked. "Make house with baby in San Bartolome Quialana?"

"Or Puerto Escondido?" Rosalia asked with a look of hopefulness.

"Maybe," Mia answered hesitantly, then gasped and leaned forward.

Rosalia's brow furrowed with concern.

Mia steadied her hands on the shopping cart and drew a deep breath. "A bit uncomfortable for a moment. I'm okay." She smiled at Marisol. "I don't know yet where we'll make our home. Have to see how it all goes with having the baby. But for sure we will be there to visit," Mia soothed.

"Good!" Marisol beamed. "Soon! Before baby big like Benito!"

"Yes," Mia nodded. "Benito will be growing fast once he is all healed. He'll be big brother for the baby."

Benito grinned and nodded.

After the cartload was rung up and bagged, the group hurried outside into steady rain.

"I was hoping to drive by a holiday light display. Maybe another day might be better," Joyce said turning the ignition.

Mia leaned over and whispered to Joyce, "Could we stop?" She pointed to a tree sale.

After much debate and opinions by each member of the group, a nine foot Douglas Fir with one flat side was chosen.

"Perfect for my spot between the living room and dining room," Mia announced.

The tree lot attendant used a chain saw to slice off the bottom of the trunk. He loaded the tree into the back of the van where Joyce had laid out a blue tarp.

"You think of everything!" Mia exclaimed.

Chuckling, Joyce said, "Years of experience."

"We reap the benefit of your preparedness and willingness. Thank you, Joyce." Mia gave an appreciative look as they ducked into the van during an intense downpour.

"Smells good!" Marisol said loudly.

Javier joked, "Big tree. House big enough?"

"We'll make it fit!" Joyce answered confidently with a look and smile in the rear view mirror.

"Uh oh." Mia sighed. "I don't have any tools, and I forgot to buy a stand."

"We can swing back by the store. I noticed a display not too far from the front door. Probably a pair of limb cutters back in garden section. I'll just dash in so you all don't have to get wetter. And it'll be faster!"

Mia pulled out her wallet and extracted the last bills. "See what you can get."

While waiting, Mia and Rosalia entertained the children with holiday songs.

"Steamy group we have here," Joyce quipped on return to the vehicle. "Do we have any immediately perishable items—ice cream, something like that? The rain is letting up. Let's go by the light display. Shouldn't take more than an hour. She handed out snacks: a big bag of kettle corn, juice boxes, nuts, and several packages of pureed fruit and vegetables for Benito.

"Car party!" Marisol giggled.

Joyce looked over at Mia. "You're not eating? Need to keep up your strength."

"Waiting for my stomach to settle down," she answered, taking a number of sips and draining one small juice box, then opening another.

"Good, keep up the fluids at least."

The light display was several blocks long. The van moved slowly behind other vehicles stopping frequently for costumed carolers and other residents of the neighborhood handing out mini-candy canes to onlookers.

Marisol and Benito grinned at a puffy snowman waving and throwing handfuls of fake snow.

"Wish we could go to the Woodland Park Wild Lights display, but the charge for this group would be over $50. Hopefully this one will suffice."

"It's wonderful," Mia smiled, her eyes misty.

"Thank you for including me. With Susan so busy and my son on the East Coast with his fiancé's family, I didn't want to be alone for the holidays in Austin."

"Fiancé? I didn't hear this. Isn't he young to be getting married?"

"Probably." Joyce shrugged, "I raised children with strong minds they apparently want to use."

"He didn't finish college yet did he? It's so scary out there right now with the economy. How will they get by?"

"No doubt will figure out something. They're young and hard working. You remember those days."

Mia nodded, eyes on a towering figure in a yard. The face was golden lights, the dress tiny blue lights. Red lights at the center of her chest radiated.

"*La Virgen*!" Rosalia gasped.

"We missed the feast of *La Virgen de Guadalupe.* It was a few days ago on December 12, wasn't it?"

Rosalia nodded. "Mexico make big *fiesta*!" Laughing, she put her hands over her ears, "Much noisy!"

Javier made hand gestures and sounds like explosions.

"Fireworks? Sounds fun!"

"Best day!" Rosalia smiled. "Make special *vestido* (dress) for *La Madre.* I give in *Distrito Federal.*"

"Mexico City?"

"Wait for plane. Make trip. Have little time and much crowd."

"Joyce and I talked of going there sometime."

Rosalia looked to Javier. "All life, I dream of this place. So much thankful now."

"Me, too," Mia whispered.

Back at the house, after cutting branches at the bottom of the tree, Javier wrangled it into the stand and they hauled it inside. Mia put away the groceries and made supper while the lights were strung onto the tree.

They ate, their eyes twinkling with the colorful lights.

"If I'd been feeling better, I would have started decorating after Thanksgiving and put up the tree weeks ago."

"More tomorrow?"

"Much more!" Mia laughed to the cheers of the children.

After the children and Rosalia and Javier turned in, Mia sat at the table with paints. She freehanded names and designs onto glass ornaments while singing softly with the radio playing carols. "Where will you be Christmas?" and Connie Francis singing, "Baby's First Christmas" brought tears, and more words.

Have I lost you
You who warmed me
You who listened and did not comment
gentling and feeding and caring for me
You who saw no differentness
who looked on me with
sweetness in your eyes
Where are you?

My heart calls for you
but mind says
give it up
too late
too late
But how I long for your sweet quiet
wrapping me like welcoming arms
where I can rest

Pain radiated through Mia. She straightened in the chair, gulped down a glass of water. The pain persisted, but Mia worked to finish the ornaments. She cleaned up her paints, and went to bed.

But the night brought no rest or sleep, for the pain persisted, dull, sharper, dulling again as she watched the clock.

Swamp

Checked in, Mia climbed into the hospital bed. "This is not how I wanted the holidays to go," she whined.

"Not a decision how go," Rosalia clucked.

"But there are so many things I wanted to do! And now it's all on you! I think I could flip out!"

"Why here! Too much you do. No learn? Baby most important. God see through." Rosalia turned her palms to the sky, and shrugged.

"But I…"

"Family do together. Many hands make easy work."

Mia wiped away tears. "This is so frustrating! I had so many plans!"

"Plans make no happy life. My sister no teach this? Maria plan everything, but sister happy with only one man, mother-in-law, child?" Rosalia shook her head. "Small life. I want more for daughter! Life with people, laugh and love many."

"That's why I'm so frustrated. I wanted this to be the most special holiday ever for you. For everyone."

"Beautiful time here already," Rosalia replied quietly.

"I wish I had more money to pay for work you are missing so you could all stay longer. And there are so many things I haven't finished."

"Make list, can do anything," Javier offered, eyes bright with determination.

"Thank you," Mia smiled. "I know I'm a control freak. It's so hard to let go."

Rosalia's look was stern and her voice brusque. "Want healthy baby? Let go everything." She threw her hands in the air. "Here for help. No here for Disneyland. Come for daughter."

"I'm sorry, Mama, I just…"

"Listen Mama! I say something never before…"

Mia nodded silently.

"Only a girl with Mano. Think only of him. How smile warm. No think of mother, grandmother, father. Only Mano, how much I want him. Mano say leave family, and good every day I see Mano's smile, but heart break for home. Life hard. But I pray for happiness. And God give something from suffering—baby Angelita! Such sweetness," Rosalia's eyes were soft with love.

"I dreamed that. I wrote it."

Then Rosalia's face changed. "One day Guillermo send Mano work. Have wild look. Maria say husband must be hungry, but Guillermo no want what Maria make."

Rosalia steeled her shoulders, and continued.

"Guillermo yell. Maria say, 'Maybe husband want drink, more rest.' Sister go market. Something in Guillermo's eyes make me afraid. Guillermo say baby take too much time, too much money. Guillermo say woman in house do what man want.

Something ugly come then…" Rosalia paused and wiped away tears.

Mia watched her gather a breath.

"Hands of Guillermo hold down. I fight hard, but when man use fist to face of woman…*Ay*...man use force…" A sound of agony escaped Rosalia's throat. "Then Guillermo say, 'Make no baby!' and Devil push knife inside…" Her voice became a whimper, "*Ay*, so much blood."

Javier and Mia could not move or make a sound.

"I pray, '*Virgen, save me.*' And baby cry. I beg, 'Let me quiet baby!' Finally Guillermo let go." Rosalia stifled a wail. "I try clean blood away. But when Maria come, sister *know* what Guillermo do. Maria have look of anger, no surprise." Rosalia glance at them and asked, "Why sister make no baby? Maybe Guillermo do this to Maria. Maybe why Maria stay. What man want woman can make no baby?"

Javier protested, weeping, "This man! Baby, no baby, no matter."

Rosalia soothed him, patting his hair. "Javier, a saint."

Mia nodded, her eyes gleaming.

But Rosalia was not finished telling. "Maria give much drink for Guillermo sleep. Maria say must do something before Mano come. When blood stop, Maria say, 'Go to village, come back with more drink and sweet candy. Go fast, leave baby.' Afraid for leaving, I say, 'What if baby cry?' And sister say, 'If cry, like mother—cry too much.'" Tears sparkled in Rosalia's eyes. "Maria strong. Eyes and heart like stone."

Mia nodded.

"At market, children play. Not long ago, I play like girl. I watch, eat candy."

"I like sweets, too," Mia whispered.

"Eat all candy! Buy more for Maria. Carry package much work and hot with pain. Inside cathedral cool, quiet. Since go with Mano, I pray no rosary, but carry beads always. I try then, but even beads blue like sky and prayers make no calm. My heart beat fast. Something say, 'Go!' Outside…" Rosalia drew a ragged breath.

"Just like I dreamed!" Mia exclaimed.

"I see fire. Flames in sky—Maria's hut burn! I run, scream, 'Do something!' But people do nothing, only hold back. 'Too late,' they say. 'Is what happen when do evil.' But I cry, 'I do nothing.' But this a lie." Rosalia's face lined with anguish. "I know Guillermo's work no good and I tell Mano he must do for family."

"You were young; you needed money. You did what you could to survive."

Rosalia's eyes softened on Mia's face.

"How did the fire start? Do you think Maria—Mother—was cooking?"

Her head moved side to side. "Sister have plan. But I think Maria never do."

Mia rubbed her arms to dispel a sudden chill. "Mother said, 'I have lived on what I plan.'"

Rosalia nodded. "Maria say, 'No sin stop Devil.'"

"What do you *think* she planned?"

Her eyes leveled with Mia and Rosalia whispered, "Maria strong girl, fight father. Then she stop Guillermo."

"You think she KILLED him?"

Rosalia shook her head slowly, and said with great conviction, "I k*now*." She steeled her voice, pointed to her chest. "Is sin here, too. Maybe God punish for this. Maybe years I suffer for this. Maybe heart break because of sin." She braved a look at Javier who was weeping, his face wearing a look of caring.

"I knew Mother was strong, but I didn't think she could...I didn't know she'd fight so hard to protect us. I didn't know she cared so much."

Rosalia's voice was barely a whisper. "Fire out, I search. Find body of Guillermo. Look for Maria and baby, but no find. I cry so much. I think my heart break open, no can breathe. Arms pull away! Mano! Maria say go to town of name like our villages—San Bartolo Coyotepec and San Bartolome Quialana. Wait and wait with Mano at San Bartolo. Maria never come."

"I found that clue in the words Mother hid in her name on the marriage license with Angelo! She claimed her name was Victoria Maria Bartolomeo from Salina, Italy. In the old atlas, I found a spot on the map of Mexico where the paper was torn. It was near San Bartolo in Durango!"

Rosalia nodded. "I pray *La Virgen* keep Maria safe. But men Guillermo know also know Maria. Maybe follow, maybe think Maria have money from Guillermo. Maybe why sister never come."

"What did Guillermo do—drugs, smuggling?"

Rosalia shook her head. "Mano never say, but dream something terrible and cry out..."

"Mother must have known Guillermo's men would be after her. That's why she kept going to San Antonio, why she hid there and created a new identity and hid the clues."

"Always pray sister safe. Pray daughter safe. Pray happy." Rosalia's eyes glistened.

"Mother had help in San Antonio. A woman gave her work as a hairdresser. And after she met Angelo, they moved with Grandmother Angelina to Austin." Mia stared at Rosalia.

"Grandmother *must* have known! At least some of it. Grandmother helped keep the secret! When Mother died, Grandmother said, 'Secrets like illness kill.' Maybe Grandmother thought the secret had worn Mother down. Maybe the thing that seemed to torture Mother was for all she had done and what she left behind. Maybe she really *did* miss her family and her country, but was too frightened to go back." Mia searched Rosalia's face as if the past could be read there. "And maybe," Mia whispered, "maybe she did it all for love—for loving her sister, and me."

"Wait years for Maria." Rosalia shook her head. "I have Mano. I pray Maria come. Pray come with daughter. Sister no come. And Mano go so much. Then Mano no come." Rosalia bit her hand in anguish. "Maybe Mano take some woman. Angry, I wish Mano burn in desire! A terrible wish."

"*I* wished Tim would burn when *he* cheated!"

Nodding Rosalia added, "So much suffer! Then, I think maybe Mano suffer, maybe sick. Maybe need woman care for him! How much heart break! I pray, '*Virgen*, *Dios*, forgive me!' Only Devil listen. Tears fall from my eyes. Hands grab cloth and candle tip. I pray, 'Take me. Take me.' Already heart broken and black with sin. But someone push from fire. Running, I look back, and see…" Rosalia's voice choked with horror, "Mano burn!"

"On a hill, etched in red?" Mia gasped. "I dreamed that."

"Little life here." Rosalia tapped her chest. "But *La Virgen* send Javier. A good man. 'Work make life better,' Javier say. 'Make beauty, life good.'" Rosalia laughed, "A smart man."

"Work *is* good for heart and soul. What a blessing you found each other," Mia said quietly. "But oh, how terrible what happened to you! I don't know how you survived such horror."

"Mother do *anything* for love of baby. Rest now."

"But I wanted to make…"

Rosalia was shaking her head. "Important what baby need. Family everything! You have already! Have much love."

Mia brushed away tears.

"Joyce have children outside. Take all home. No worry."

Laughing, Mia said, "Okay, I'll try not to. But call when you get there!"

A week passed. On December 20, Mia dreamed deeply and long.

How you warm me
Your eyes a caress
Voice plumbing my depths
How you reach me
My heart leaping to meet you

She awakened with a stirring: a foot or hand stretching inside.

Pushing back on the spot, she sighed, "How I long to count your toes and fingers, little one. Please be healthy."

And she said a prayer, "Mother Mary, please help me be a good mother. I didn't know what that was. I didn't know how much Mother loved me. I didn't know how much she had done for me. And I said terrible things to her. I hurt her. I held my love from her. I was a terrible daughter. I don't know how I can ever make up for it. I've tried to do good for Benito and Marisol. I cared for them in the best way I can. I wanted to keep them, watch over them. But it's not what they want. They want to go home to *their* country. I have to let them go. Please watch over them. See them happy. I'm afraid. I thought I had everything figured out. I thought I was living my life and being strong on my own. I thought I could do *this* alone. But we never really do anything alone do we?" She wiped away a tear. "I've been wrong about so many things…"

"Have I failed at love? Will any man love me and want to stay with me?" She rubbed her belly and whispered, "Little one, will *you* love me?"

Mia drifted to sleep and was deemed stable enough the following afternoon to be discharged from the hospital.

Marisol and Benito were outside, hands open, faces turned to the sky when Joyce dropped Mia at the house.

"What are you doing?"

"MomMia! Catching rain. Maybe grow big like trees."

She chuckled, "Maybe."

They went inside. The children led her immediately to the bedroom, pushed pillows behind her, and said, "Rest!"

Mia smiled. "You take such good care of me."

"You take good care of Benito," Marisol said, looking at her brother who nodded and smiled. "Thank so much for this."

"My pleasure," Mia whispered, patting their small hands before they went out. The house quieted. She could hear a fire crackling in the fireplace. Mia closed her eyes, let out a sigh.

She awakened to the smell of warm sugar, and the sound of voices in the kitchen. Mia wandered out. Rainbow colored crepe paper streamers strung like rays of the sun hung from the pendant lamp. All eyes turned to her.

Rosalia smiled, "Party!"

"We make surprise!" Marisol said with glee.

They gathered around the table. Rosalia and Javier brought over a covered pot and a basket of warm tortillas.

"I make meatballs!" Marisol said, wiggling on her chair. She poked her brother, "So did Benito!"

He nodded and grinned with a hand shielding his mouth.

Rosalia removed the lid. Rich aromas rushed out. "Make with tur-key."

"Oh, thank you, Mama! So much easier on my stomach."

Rosalia nodded. "No onion. No spicy. Better for baby." She filled their bowls with the meatballs, broth, and strips of vegetables. "Celebrate birthday! And holidays."

They passed around a bowl of finely diced onion, garlic, cilantro, and another bowl of white topping, *crema.*

"This soup is so delicious! Did you look up the recipe in my cookbook?"

"No. Computer."

"You, did?" Mia laughed. "You're learning so much!"

"Fun," Rosalia smiled. "Find anything."

"I'll try a tiny bit of *crema,*" Mia said. "Mmmm. Sour cream with cilantro and chipotle?"

Javier answered, "Good for cold night."

"It is chilly outside. Did you get dry?" Mia asked the children.

"Hair wet a little," Marisol replied. "Was cold rain. Not like home."

"Yes," Mia sighed. "The temperatures in the valleys of Oaxaca are so mild."

They had finished supper and were clearing the table when there was a knock at the door. Mia answered it.

"You're looking good! A little color in your cheeks again," Joyce said giving a hug to her and stepping inside with Susan, her daughter.

They said, "Hi everyone!"

Dripping coats were hung on a rack.

Joyce carried a dome-covered footed dish to the table and said, "Hi, MiMa," to Rosalia who laughed and smiled.

The children wore excited faces while Joyce removed the dome with great flourish. “Something light and just perfect for Mia—*angel* food cake for ‘Little Angel’—*Angelita*!”

“I love coconut frosting! How lovely,” Mia purred.

“And,” Joyce said pulling cartons of ice cream from a brown paper bag Susan carried, “low fat chocolate marshmallow or old-fashioned butter pecan not low fat!”

Susan helped Rosalia pass out silverware, and napkins.

“Sorry I don’t have enough chairs,” Mia said bringing over the two wooden barstools.

Marisol and Benito hopped up. “Sitting high more fun!”

“Light candle and sing, ‘Happy Birthday,’” Javier said.

They sang as Mia blushed and blew out the flame.

“Thank you all for being here to share my birthday. I’ll treasure this moment always.” Her eyes were misty. “You give me more than you’ll ever know. And I have a little something for each of *you*! Excuse me a moment, please.” She went into the other room and returned with a box. “Let’s start with the youngest first.” Mia handed a yellow package to Benito.

He tore away the tissue cushioning a bright blue glass ornament.

“I painted your name. Therapists will work with you on sounding out each of the syllables and learning the letters. Soon you’ll be able to say ‘Benito’ well. Do you like it?”

Benito nodded, beaming.

Marisol helped him down from the stool. He carefully hung the ornament on a branch near the bottom of the Christmas tree.

Marisol opened her package: pale pink tissue wrapping a green ball with many small glowing stars and one larger with ***Marisol*** painted inside.

"You are a bright light, Marisol. Keep shining for all the world to see."

Standing on tip-toes, Marisol hung her ball on the tree as high as she could reach.

Joyce opened a bright purple ball with her name in gold.

"Cool! I love it!" Susan said examining hers with painted books and a rolled paper like a degree. "This year I have my own tree and apartment, and now my first ornament!"

Javier beamed and thanked Mia profusely for his white ornament painted with sprigs of herbs beneath his name.

Mia handed a package to her mother.

Turquoise paper wrapped a deep pink ornament with painted blooming pink roses and ***Mama***. "Beautiful!" Rosalia pronounced, clutching it momentarily to her chest. "Wait all life for this!" She hung it on the tree next to Javier's, then hugged her daughter.

"Where's for Mia?" Marisol wondered.

Mia extracted another wrapped ornament from the box and unwrapped it slowly, then passed the white ball around for inspection.

Turning the fragile ball in her hands, Rosalia grinned, pointing to her design of a pink rose. The ornament went from hand to hand with oooos and ahhhs sounding around the table as each person found the individual designs painted on it.

Joyce smiled with a knowing look.

"Shhh," Mia said with a finger to her lip.

"Design for each. Where Mia's?"

"I'm the ball—surrounded by everyone I love."

Marisol counted the people around the table and the designs painted on the ornament. "More designs than people."

"Others are for those not here. And did you notice this?" Mia asked shaking the ball and making a jingling sound. "That's the baby inside me." Mia laughed. "Now let's eat this beautiful cake and the ice cream before it melts."

The following day, in the early afternoon of December 24, they gathered with friends: Joyce and Susan returned. Also Deena, Kelsey, and Deena's friend, Lonni came. *Ponche,* a Mexican fruit punch was made without alcohol so Mia and the children could enjoy it also. Chips, veggies and dips were snacked on while they played Candy Land.

Mia and Joyce took a break outside and sat on a bench.

"This porch is such a good feature to the place," Joyce remarked. "Nice to get some fresh air without getting wet!"

"Yes," Mia sighed. "I do like this house so much, but the rent is too high to keep it for myself," Mia sighed. "I've lost pretty much everything promised me from the divorce. And the money Papa set aside is dwindling fast with the medical expenses for Benito, and this baby." She rubbed her belly absently.

"Yeah," Joyce sighed. "Money woes…"

"Just when I think I've alleviated my worry, a new round of emotion comes up."

"The moonstones might help with that."

"I'll wear them more. Thank you," Mia smiled.

Carolers coming up the street reached the house and sang Silent Night, then Ave Maria. Everyone came out to listen. Marisol stood beside Mia; Benito squeezed onto the bench. Rosalia offered all cookies. Well wishes for a happy Christmas were shared and the singers went on.

"Mexico make big celebration this night," Marisol said.

Rosalia looked to Javier. "After eat, have surprise."

Marisol and Benito hurried into the house and washed up before the potluck supper: sweet potatoes with pecans and brown sugar, turkey and gravy, smashed potatoes, spinach salad, Brussels sprouts with bacon and mint, fruit salad, Parker House rolls with creamy butter, corn bread dressing.

When finished eating, Rosalia and Javier and the guests cleaned up the dishes while the children sprawled out on the floor to watch a movie on television: *Charlie Brown Christmas*.

Mia sat on the sofa. She yawned, closed her eyes, and rested until it was time for dessert.

Served family style at the table, everyone tried slivers of pumpkin pie with vanilla bean ice cream, peanut butter fudge, apple crisp with fresh whipped cream, and tamales with fruit and nuts.

"Oh, my!" Joyce commented, "I've done it again! Ringing in the holiday with pounds extra of deliciousness!"

Mia moaned, "That's for sure. I think my stomach has grown a full six inches since yesterday."

"That is as it should be," Lonni said smiling, brushing wispy black bangs from her dark eyes. "The holidays are all about sharing the sweetness of the season." She patted her diminutive waist. "We had special meals when I was growing up in Thailand, but this is my best Christmas ever! Thank you for inviting me for the celebration."

"Maybe all come next year," Rosalia sighed. "Make bigger party."

Javier tapped her arm. They both looked to the windows.

"What are you two plotting?" Joyce laughed.

Rosalia and Javier led them outside to the front yard. "In Mexico, celebrate like this."

Javier lit fireworks and carefully handed out sparklers. Some were white, others had brilliant color. The children twirled and twisted their hands and bodies to make dazzling light designs in the darkness.

"Mama, this is so beautiful! I wish Grandmother and Maggie and Papa Angelo could see it."

"Make a video on your phone! You can text it to them!" Joyce suggested.

"Oh, I do have Maggie's cell number!" Mia hurried into the house to retrieve her phone.

More sparklers were lit, and they sang, "We Wish You a Merry Christmas," while she filmed. They made another short video introducing everyone and offering more holiday wishes. "Oh, my gosh! This is the best!" Mia said with elation as she sent the message. "How fun!"

The next morning, Mia, the children, Rosalia and Javier went to Christmas Mass.

A choir sang. The vestments of the priest were white, altar cloths white, candles white and burning with flickering light. Mia sat with a child on each side, her mother next to Marisol, and Javier next to Benito. Recited prayers in hundreds of voices and the drone of the priest were somehow settling. Mia pressed her back against the pew: oak with seat covers of woven wool. Organic. Real. "Feelings are also real," she whispered with a pang of pain.

Two halves with my whole
Two hearts matching my beat
Three like a family
How can I let you go
Couldn't I make you happy

Couldn't I keep you safe
wrapped in my arms
and fed with love
your MomMia?

Mia forced down a lump in her throat and raised her eyes. She studied the stained glass scenes in the windows—dim and dark on a day of rain and heavy hanging sky.

After Mass, Rosalia asked, "What to eat?"

Thinking a minute, Mia finally said, "We could add cheese to the left over stuffing, potatoes, gravy, and turkey, then bake it until crispy on top."

Rosalia shrugged. "Make tamale, too?"

"Sure," Mia sighed.

"Tired? Maybe daughter rest."

"Yes, I think I'll take a quick nap after we get dinner in the oven."

When Mia awoke an hour later, the children were with Rosalia at the bar. Marisol held up her hand. "Don't look! A surprise!"

Laughing, Mia returned to her room. She patted on blusher and applied lip gloss. "See, better." She practiced smiles in the mirror while staring at her eyes. "Light brown like my mother. Will my little one have my color?"

"MomMia!"

"MomMia!"

She followed the voices. "I don't see you…" Mia looked behind a chair, around a lamp, over a table. "I can't find you."

Pictures in hand, the children popped up from behind the sofa that was angled out from the wall. "Surprise!"

"Ohhh!" Mia exclaimed.

Benito's picture was a tall peak colored dark, a boy with big white teeth and arms thrust into the air stood at the top.

"An adventurer, a conqueror. How brave, and how happy you look. What a beautiful smile," she cooed.

Marisol and Benito nodded with big grins.

"Now let me see what you have drawn," Mia said taking Marisol's picture. It was a rounded woman with glowing red heart and open hands. Her smile was wide and warming.

"MomMia give heart to Benito and Marisol."

Mia whispered, "Thank you, Marisol. This is beautiful."

"Look on back."

She flipped the page over. A smiling girl and giggling boy looked up at her with deep brown eyes and glowing hearts.

"For MomMia, Marisol and Benito give hearts."

Mia wiped away tears. "I will treasure these always."

After eating supper, they watched a holiday movie, and retired early in the evening.

Joyce rapped on the front door at 4 A.M.

Mia opened it. "Come in. I have to round everyone up."

Joyce helped lug three suitcases to the car. "Is that it?"

Rosalia nodded, following outside with Javier and the children while Mia locked up.

"Okay, we're off!" Joyce said cheerfully, smiling into the rear-view mirror, but the back seat occupants only yawned.

"How was your Christmas Day?" Mia asked quietly.

"First one in years not spent in Texas. Seattle is a bit damp for my taste, but I sure love all the water around. I'm planning a trip back in summer, if not sooner."

Mia glanced over at her. "That'd be great if you can."

"See how this vacation time pencils out," Joyce smiled. "Thankfully there was flexibility for the holidays."

"That's a benefit to working for a small company."

"I didn't plan to work in the field of health care, but it suits me. I feel a real connection with the elderly. I should! I'm not that far behind them!" Joyce laughed. "I think a nudge from my neighbor, Louise, prompted me to interview for the position. And I like helping people stay in their own homes as long as possible. I'd really love to have more training, possibly go back to school to get an R.N."

"Nurse Joyce. I like it."

"Just a small hitch in the plan. I'd be at least sixty years old before finishing the program, and thousands more dollars in debt. Now that I've had a chance to observe up close what they do in elder care, I think that's what I want to do."

"It's a worthy goal. Besides, you're hardy. Didn't you say your folks lived into their 90s and were healthy right up until their last year?"

"Yes, no guarantees for me, though. Especially with the extra weight I'm carrying. But I had a thorough physical and was deemed healthy as a thirty year old. My resolution for this New Year is to take off troublesome pounds. I've lost a few in the months since I started work. Four pounds a month is a good solid rate."

"Staying healthy is the main thing. Maybe eventually we can get into walking and do some charity events like the cancer walk I did in Austin."

"I did say I'd do it with you this year, but we've had a few changes of plans. Life intervenes!"

"Yes, many surprises," Mia sighed, lips quivering.

They pulled into SeaTac airport parking; everyone got out and luggage was dragged toward the terminal. Passengers were checked in. They stood together at the entrance to security.

Mia hugged Javier. "Thank you for coming, and for all your help."

Rosalia hugged Mia a long time. "Sorry can no stay more month to see baby. Be strong. Do work of women!"

"I *will* be strong. And I'll think of you, Mama. If you could do it, I can! Thank you for sharing your life with me."

"Greatest joy is mother!"

The children hugged Joyce.

"Work hard on your therapy. And have fun at the beach with *Abuela* Rosalia!"

Benito's eyes danced with excitement.

Marisol said, "See ocean! And Benito learn speak good, then we go home!"

"Maybe by summer, I can come down to see you!" Mia said with extra enthusiasm.

Marisol patted Mia's belly. "Baby be good."

Mia hugged each person again.

Rosalia and Javier led the children through security.

Joyce and Mia watched until they were out of sight, then went to the car.

"I thought Marisol and Benito would be *mine*. The baby girl and boy in my dreams were so real. I thought it must be a sign of something to come…I thought they were meant for me."

Joyce sighed, "You can love them from afar. And see to their care."

"I had to let them go back to the life they knew and loved. But I wanted so much to make a home with them here in Seattle."

"Maybe sometime in the future they will want to come stay in the U.S. with you. But Mexico is in their blood. It is their homeland, their culture, their roots."

"I know," Mia wiped away tears.

Joyce started the car. "For now, it will be this way. And soon, you will have a new little one to fill your life."

Long after the sun went down, Mia sat on the sofa and looked out on the small yard illuminated by the porch light. A blue spruce stood straight and tall, top pointing to the misty sky. In Portland, the rain and heavy skies had weighed on her. But here, she could almost see something in the moist sky. Futures could be dreamed in that mist, worlds of possibility could be hiding there, just waiting for a sunny invite to life.

Blue
the sky was blue
sun shone bright and warm
with you
How I miss you
and wait for our next embrace

Glacier

Mia woke with her mind on the children, her mother and Javier, but a stirring deep inside brought her hands to stroke her belly and her mind shifted.

How I long for you
and wish you come
How I wait for your embrace
My heart aches with longing
to hear you
touch you
linger in your long looks
melting me
Glacier ice
streaming
catching us in the flow

A glimmer of bright sun was shining through the clouds outside. The house was quiet. A car on the street drove by. Mia turned with effort in the bed.

She got up and fixed coffee, decaf. The Christmas tree with ornaments and bright lights cheered the corner. Mia set down her cup, and went into the bedroom. Her hands picked through the rustling papers in the box. She carried a large white ornament to the tree and hung it on a middle branch. Stepping back to admire the addition, she sipped her coffee. "Oh, if I could make it so—just by wishing, just by hoping…"

The phone rang and she answered the call. "Hello?"

"I should be going now," Joyce said.

"Thank you for all your help, and for sharing the holidays with us, Joyce. It was so much fun."

"It was! Thank you for including Susan and I. Sorry I can't stay longer. Keep me posted on how you're doing. And call Susan if you need anything."

"I will."

"I mean it!"

"Yes, I will call if I need something, anything. That is one thing I've learned from all this. People genuinely want to help. It makes them feel good, too. You're a good teacher, Joyce."

"Awww, thanks."

"I love you."

"What was that?"

"I said, I love you, Joyce. You're a sister to me."

"I love you, too, little sis."

After their goodbyes, Mia was donning a hat and trench coat bought in Portland when she stalked the Tudor house where she'd lived with Tim. "I *thought* we loved there. I conceived and lost our babies where Tim and Valerie and *their* baby now live," she said with old hurt in her voice. She drew a cleansing breath and rubbed a spot on her abdomen where a foot was pushing. "Okay, little one. I know: I have to let all that go now. *You* are my love, my future." She finished buttoning the coat and went out. "We'll figure it out somehow. Together. With a little luck and a lot of prayer. None of us ever do it alone."

She walked down the block. Rain on the street swished under tires of passing cars. Houses with wide porches or small stoops watched with glassy windows like eyes. Mia studied the neighborhood: little picket fences, tall cedar privacy panels, evergreens, deciduous trees with bare winter branches, cats and dogs, a few kids bouncing balls to hoops. Not far away, the water of Green Lake reflected the grey sky.

Inside the local market, the extreme holiday hub bub was over, but decorations were still up and an air of festivity lingered. A year ago, Christmas went by with barely a notice as Mia had worked to finish the first draft of *Mending Stone* at the writer/artist retreat in the Piney Woods of NE Texas. Two years ago, she had been pregnant, and married. But that baby was lost, the husband, too. Back then, she suffered in seclusion. Now she was different. Her life was different. "Thankfully, different," Mia whispered. "I invite love and color and the sweetness of life into my heart." She drew a deep breath, and let it out with a smile.

Neat piles of colorful fruits attracted her to the produce section. She reached for a mango, brought it to her nose and smelled. "Mmmm. Sweetness."

When she opened her eyes, Mia caught a glimpse of a figure across the produce department.

Her breath stopped.

The man turned. He looked her way.

She tried to breathe.

His eyes drank her in.

Her face warmed.

He moved in Mia's direction, stopped on the other side of the display table.

She tried a smile.

His voice was deep and slow saying her name, "Mia."

Heat moved through her. She stumbled over words, "You're…here."

"Yep. Good to see y'."

She smiled more easily.

"Y' never called."

"I did! I left messages. When we got to the States, I went looking for you…and I saw…Charlotte is gone."

Gerald nodded. "After the stroke, every day she slipped away a little more. Gram didn't want to live that way—bound in a chair, unable to speak. She just let go."

Mia said softly, "Your houses looked so deserted. Where did you go?"

"Been teaching on reservation."

"Teaching what?"

"Art."

"Ohhh," she sighed. "That's good."

"Yep."

She looked down. "What brought you here to Phinney?"

"Checking out some galleries, old friends."

"Ohhh, galleries." She nodded. "I…I didn't know you had friends up here. I don't remember you ever mentioning having any."

"Y' never asked either."

"I'm sorry. I assumed too much."

He nodded ever so slightly.

"I thought you lived so rurally…" Discomfort showed on her face. "That it was all you wanted." She looked across into his dark brown eyes and whispered, "I'm sorry."

He nodded again. "Was just over at Francine Seders Gallery. Came in here to buy something fresh to eat."

Mia was glancing around at shoppers pushing by.

"Looked for y' last week."

Her face turned back to him. "Where?"

"Hospital wouldn't give any information."

Her brow furrowed. "How'd you know to go there?"

"Got ahold of Angelo. Didn't say much. Said y'r mother was here, too."

"She was." Then Mia asked quietly, "Why did you call Papa?"

"To find y' before missing y'r birthday."

"You remembered?" She tapped the bridge of her nose to stop a tear threatening to form.

"Didn't want y' to feel lost again at the holidays."

Her lips quivered with a smile. She glanced around, looked back to him. "It's strange seeing you here."

He was moving, coming around the display table.

She drew a breath.

He was near, his hand reaching out to her arm.

"Gerald, I…" Heat soaked into her.

His other hand reached for her.

She turned ever so slightly.

His eyes saw all of her.

"Ger…"

He didn't say anything, only drew her close, his arms gently wrapping around her.

"Come back to the house with me," she managed to say.

They moved toward the door.

Outside, he said, "Where's y'r car? I'll follow."

"Only if you drive really slow," Mia laughed. "I'm on two feet."

"Give y' a ride."

Mia smiled, "Bike or car?"

"Car. Old one from the yard."

"I did notice the vehicles were gone."

"Sold some for scrap, finished that one."

She looked where he pointed, and said, "OH, wow. What a color."

"Admiral blue."

"The whitewall tires really set off the shiny paint. I love the round headlights. Look at the doors. What car is this?"

"Ford. Lincoln. 1950." Gerald opened the door and helped her into the front.

"The seats are so springy," she giggled. "And the upholstery is stunning. This car looks like it just came from a showroom. You're not going to sell *it*, are you?"

He shrugged. "Might be hard to part with."

Mia directed him to the house; they went inside. She fixed cups of tea and a snack of cheese with sliced bread. They sat at the table, Gerald on the end, Mia on the side facing the living room. She got up and turned on the Christmas tree lights.

"That's pretty."

"I painted ornaments to give as gifts. And I copied the design for each person onto this one." She removed the largest ornament from the tree, and set it in his hands. She pointed to a design, "A pink rose for my mother, Rosalia, because she loves them. Texas petunia for Joyce. Sprig of herbs for Javier because he's a healer. Joyce's daughter, Susan, a book and certificate for her internship and another college degree she's earning. A star for Marisol, because she's such a bright light. And a smile for Benito."

"Y'r painting is good."

"This," she pointed to a blue flower, "is Mother's forget-me-not—like a pin I gave her on Mother's Day when I was little. The green, white, and red striped flag is for Papa Angelo. State bird of Idaho, a mountain bluebird, is for Maggie, his wife. The china cup is for Grandmother Angelina. I meant it also to represent ancestors: grandmothers, grandfathers."

"Nice." His eyes moved to her face.

"Thank you," Mia blushed under Gerald's look. "I painted another one." She went to the other room, brought out the box of tissues.

Gerald set down the large ball, and undid the wrapping on a gleaming ball painted with rainbows, and his name.

"I had been thinking so intently about you, when I saw you in the market, I thought you must be a vision I conjured."

He grinned. "Hang me."

She placed his ornament on a small branch near the top of the tree.

"Where's y'r ornament?"

"Here." Mia picked up the large white ball with all the designs. "This is me, surrounded with all the people I love. And this…" she pointed to a design on the metal top with the silver loop for hanging, "This rainbow I put above all others is you."

As she handed the ball to him, there was a tiny jingling.

His eyes settled on her face. He put the ball gently aside. His hands cupped her face, his lips kissing her as if she might break like fragile crystal. He pulled her onto his lap.

Her arms circled his neck. "Ger," she whispered, a tear wetting her lashes. "I thought I might not find you again."

"Thought I might not find *you*! Called Angelo for more information, but no answer."

"Papa is SO maddening!" Mia exclaimed. "He won't get a cell phone and has no answering machine. It didn't matter when he was with Mother: they were mostly at home or at Grandmother Angelina's. Now he and Maggie are gone so much. They're in Cabo for the holidays."

He nodded, "Explains it."

She picked up the ornament with all the designs again. "See, I'm the glass, you're the top—connecting me to the branch of the tree. The Christmas tree represents all of life to me." She shook the ball and there was a jingling. "Inside is a jingle baby—our baby."

"*Our* baby?"

"Yes," she whispered, nodding, her lips smiling. "Our baby."

"Figured someone else or y' would've let me know."

"I didn't know for months. I was so wrapped up in everything that happened with Mama, and then I had Marisol and Benito to care for."

"Who are they?"

She handed him the ornament, and pointed to their designs. "The children I hoped to adopt. We came to Seattle for Benito's surgery for cleft lip and palette."

"Where are they?" He hung the ball high on the tree.

"Mama and Javier took them back to Mexico." She looked up into his eyes that were looking back, and said softly, "I thought I could adopt them. Then I found I was pregnant. And I developed complications. And Marisol and Benito wanted to return to Mexico. I hoped I could make a new home for them in the U. S. But this is not their country. Their roots are strong and they love it there."

He nodded.

She sighed, her voice shaking a little. "They only left yesterday and I miss them already. Last night was about the longest and loneliest night of my life. I thought my heart was breaking."

"Making a space for me?"

"Yes," Mia whispered, "here." She opened her arms.

Wetlands

A fountain gurgled beside a bed of colorful stones and plantings. Lanterns hung from the wide porch.

They went up the brick walkway to the door. Their feet on the mat brought an audible, "Welcome!"

Mia laughed. "I've never seen such a thing!"

"Still haven't," Gerald quipped, smiling.

"True," she laughed, and pushed the bell.

Lonni answered with a quick opening of the door. "So delighted you could come, Mia!"

"Thank you for inviting me. This is Gerald."

"Pleasure," Lonnie cooed.

He smiled and nodded.

Lonni led them into the entrance hall. At the center, a round Tiger oak table with claw feet held a large plant with many vines spiraling out.

"How captivating!"

"It's from a fabulous nursery in Fremont: Urban Earth. I don't remember what the plant is called, but the owner—my friend, Susan over there—can fill you in if you're interested!" Lonni pointed.

"Oh, good. Thank you. It is an intriguing plant. Gerald is a great gardener. Especially growing vegetables."

"Terrific." Lonni led them to the open kitchen where people were snacking around an enormous island topped in sparkling granite and covered with overflowing serving dishes.

"Gerald, this is my friend, Deena, and her daughter is…"

"Mia!" Kelsey shrieked and ran over, hugging her with great enthusiasm. "I miss Marisol! I wish she could have stayed longer," Kelsey frowned momentarily, then returned her face to a smile. "But now she's my pen pal! Maybe we'll be lifelong friends and travel the world to exotic places!"

Laughing, Mia replied, "I hope so!"

"Will she be coming back for the birth? I'm sooo interested in babies and how they are made and…"

"Kels, Lonni needs help taking hor d'oeuvres around," Deena interrupted.

"Oh, sure! I'll go help her!" Kelsey said, and followed Lonni into the other room.

Deena served Mia and Gerald drinks, then said quietly, "I worked up my courage: told Kelsey the whole story. She shrugged and said, 'No big deal. My classmate's dad is trans.'"

"You told Kelsey Lonni was Lon, her father?"

"Yes. And she's cool with it. The biggest issue was how to address Lonni. So I let the two of them work it out. LonMom is what they came up with to acknowledge Lonni's role as both father and mother to Kelsey."

"What a relief for you, Deena," Mia smiled.

Deena nodded, eyes glistening. "Kids these days can help *us* learn new family dynamics."

Lonni called to Deena from the other room.

"We'll sample the eats," Gerald said.

"I'll be back in a bit." Deena patted Mia's shoulder and went off to welcome another guest.

They snacked and visited with others in the kitchen, then wandered to a window looking out over Puget Sound.

"Spectacular! I love the mountains in the background. Are those the Olympics?"

Gerald nodded. "Look down there. See the reddish building? That's the school."

"Oh, I didn't realize it's so close. I'm amazed you got the job so quickly."

He shrugged. "Had in mind what I wanted."

"Sounds like something Joyce would say," Mia laughed. "So strange to think you haven't met. She's like you in some ways—strong minded, funny, thoughtful, determined."

"Whoa!" He put up a hand.

Mia said softly, her hand grazing his smooth cheek. "Well deserved compliments."

Lonni brought over another guest. "This is my friend who owns Urban Earth."

They introduced themselves and chatted about the plant in the entrance.

"Gerald has a job at Adams Elementary in the integrated arts program. He's great with gardens. Wouldn't it be cool to include plants somehow?"

"Urban Earth is my business, but I like to think of myself as an artist whose medium is plants," Susan said. "Plants are nature's art."

"Yes," Mia sighed. "Such a creative way of looking at the world. We'd love to see your nursery sometime."

"Oh, my goodness!" Lonni said motioning to a guest who crossed the room to them. "I'd like to introduce Ira. He works at *The Review*, a quarterly community newspaper. I bet he'd like to write about Gerald joining the teaching community in our neighborhood!"

"Or Mia—she's an author with a debut novel coming out," Gerald offered.

She blushed.

"How great," the writer said eyeing them. "Interesting new couple in Ballard!"

Mia's brow furrowed.

"You *are* a couple aren't you?"

Gerald nodded.

But Mia said nothing, only took a drink from her glass.

Lonni showed them through the house and described additional projects not yet completed.

"I love the colors you've used. They have depth without being heavy or dark. The slate and wood of the fireplaces is grounding and rustic, also refined looking because of the splendid craftsmanship."

"Thank you, Mia, that's very kind of you to say. I've lost so much sleep over each choice! And choosing contractors! Oh, my! What a headache!" Lonni laughed. "Sounds as if you have some remodeling or decorating experience."

"I do. My former husband and I owned an old Tudor in Portland. I supervised the renovation, chose all the finishes, the features to enhance, re-designed the rooms for better flow. It was such a rewarding, but stressful, endeavor."

"I can imagine!" Lonni smiled.

"We had a very long time frame though. Which lessened the pressure probably. Still, it was quite aggravating. I thought it would never be finished."

"That would drive me mad!"

"It practically did," Mia groaned.

"Deena and I work quite well together. She's helping to expedite decisions. And she comes up with some amazing ideas. See the woven wood?" Lonni motioned toward two screens separating the room. Beyond the screens, a picture window framed woodland views illuminated by yard lights.

"How clever: the window beyond the panels looks like a painting. And I just did notice the piano to one side. What an amazing way to invite different uses for such a large room."

"You're a gem for saying so! Give Deena the credit!" Lonni beamed, then went to converse briefly with a handsome gentleman with greying hair and elegant dark shirt and slacks.

"I do love the woven wood," Mia said to Gerald. "So warm, and separates the room into elegant and casual sides without creating disharmony. The view out the window is enhanced like a frame enhances a painting."

Gerald smiled at her. "Perceptive."

"May I have your attention?" Lonni said, "This is Jerry Frank, accomplished pianist/composer. He will be playing for us an assortment of songs from his varied repertoire. I'm sure you will find a favorite! May you be captivated and transported!"

Jerry smiled and bowed.

"Oh, I forgot," Lonni said, "you can purchase his music online, and hear him again at local establishments! Lucky for us he's enjoyably hardworking and appears regularly! Check his website for scheduled appearances! Enjoy all!"

Jerry sat down at the ebony grand piano.

The group quietly conversed while Jerry played a dozen or more original songs.

"What a splendid renovation, and a lovely party," Mia said when it was quite late.

"I'm thrilled you could come!" Deena chimed. "Great to meet you, Gerald."

"Thanks. Good to meet y'."

"We rang in the new year in style!" Lonni gushed.

Smiles and hugs were traded, then Mia and Gerald departed.

The next morning, Gerald brought a plate of food and mug of coffee to Mia in the bedroom.

She opened her eyes and smiled, pushed back her wild hair. "Good morning."

He leaned down, but her arms went around his neck, pulling him close. "Happy new year!" he chuckled.

"2009," she sighed.

"Resolutions?"

"No resolutions," she whispered seriously, "but I do want to make plans."

"What?"

"I…I need everyone to meet you."

"Anticipate objections?"

Her eyes gleamed. Her mouth wore a tentative smile. "What *plans* would *you* like to make for the new year?"

"Plans for the future?"

She nodded.

"Sure?"

"I will be," Mia said softly, stroking his cheek. "The problem is: I can't fly right now. And I have only two weeks left in this rental. I have to find a cheaper place. I don't need this much room now that Marisol and Benito are not living with me. I had to make a good home. And I wanted them to see how it could be living with me in the U.S. I felt such a pull to this neighborhood. Thought I would have happiness here…" she smiled up at him. "Now I don't really know what the next step should be. And I'm running low on money."

"Thought y' had plenty."

Mia sighed, "I would have. But funds I was promised were lost. The investment firm is being investigated. I could sue, but recovery is probably unlikely." She placed a hand on her stomach. "Ehhh, I feel sick."

"Have a bite to eat." He handed her the plate of food.

She chewed a bit of cinnamon toast dunked in egg yolk, took a sip of the coffee. "Oh, my gosh! The baby just kicked sooo hard! Here feel." Mia placed his hand on her belly.

"Felt that!" Gerald smiled.

She took a bite, and sighed, "What if I'm too old to be a good parent? I'm forty-one! I feel tired already. How will I be when the baby is a toddler? A teenager?" She studied his face, crinkles at the corners of his eyes. "Do you feel old?"

"No."

"Not too old to have a baby?"

"Nope. Don't feel too old for anything. What difference does a few months or years make?"

"How old *are* you?" Mia whined, a sudden look of concern on her face. "I don't even know when you were born! I was so wrapped up in myself I haven't even asked. How can you stand me? What else don't I know about you?"

"April '66."

"What day?"

"Same as y'."

"Mine's December 23, 1967. Yours is April 23, 1966? That's two years exactly before the day Mother and Angelo married. Why didn't you tell me it was the 23rd?"

"Y' seemed to be bothered about odd coincidences."

"There have been a lot of them." She looked over at him. "Do you believe in coincidences? Or do you think everything is connected somehow?"

"No coincidences. Meaning is everything. Just have to look, see the patterns, be aware of what we're creating."

Mia's voice shook. "I feel like *everything* is strange. My life is strange. I don't recognize it, or myself. I'm old and fat and tired. My life events are too late." Mia glanced around for a view of the clock. "Eleven? I even slept late."

He brushed her cheek with his hand. "Like to go for a drive? Have a change of scene?"

"Yes! I would LOVE that!" She gulped down a drink of decaf, ate a few more bites, then got up and dressed.

Gerald drove around the Phinney Ridge neighborhood, went south by Woodland Park Zoo, over to Fremont and by the Urban Earth Nursery. "Have to check it out sometime."

Mia nodded.

Green Lake was passed.

"Doesn't really look all that green," she said sounding pouty.

"How long y' gonna be heavy with thought?"

"I don't know," she said quietly. "I don't know what to do to move forward."

"Maybe look at things differently."

Her eyes blazed at him, "WHY must you be so right?"

He only laughed.

Then she laughed. And her mood lifted.

Gerald drove in a loop over to the Ballard neighborhood west of Phinney Ridge. "There's my school," he said, passing Adams Elementary.

"Looks nice."

He looked over at her. "Just temporary. Filling in for a teacher out on maternity leave. Might open a door for something next year."

"You'd have to have a teaching certificate."

"Yep. Have one."

"When did you do that?"

"Years ago. Kept it up."

She stared at him. "We talked about college courses, but you never said you finished college."

"Y' never asked."

"What kind of degree?"

"Bachelors in History and Art. Dual Masters in Fine Art and Education."

"Why were you in RUFUS? Why did you work at an aluminum plant and do construction jobs and live in such a…"

"Gram was diagnosed with Diabetes around time of my divorce. When I was a kid, she gave me years of her life. Thought I'd do the same for her." He shrugged. "And, I didn't have anywhere else I really wanted to be."

Mia said quietly, "That's so generous."

He shrugged. "Had only her and Unc left."

"Oh, that's right; you said he lives at Wasco?"

Gerald shook his head. "They were close. Always in touch. Unc died day after Gram."

"How?"

"Heart attack."

"That's strange."

"Happens. Siblings that close…"

"Why did you leave your cabin?"

"Only renting. Son of the farmer up the road coming back. They want the place for him."

"I thought you owned it."

"Nope."

"What about your place here?"

"Been renting by the week."

She nodded ever so slightly, her eyes turned to the window.

The Ballard neighborhood was a showcase of old Craftsman and Tudor style homes and cottages with small yards. The quaint downtown area had abundant shopping on Market Street.

"This area is so hip!" Mia said. "It feels fun. Inviting."

After failed searches for a cheaper rental, Mia called Deena for help. They met at Cugini Café, in Ballard. "Nothing I've looked at seems right," Mia sighed stirring cream and sugar into a large cup of decaf. "*Too* small, too expensive, too scary of a neighborhood…" She sighed. "Then I wonder if I'm too picky."

Deena only shrugged. "If it's not a yes, it's a no."

"I only need one bedroom at this point. Maybe I'm being too restrictive. Hey! Is Lonni's basement apartment finished yet? Do you think she wants to rent it cheap?"

"Actually," Deena smiled, "Kelsey and I are moving in at the end of the month."

"Oh. That's terrific! So, you decided something? What did you decide?"

"Took my own advice. If it's not a yes…"

"It's a no? What did you say no to?"

"Yes to friendship. Yes to co-parenting. But I can't be in a romantic relationship with her. I loved Lon. I love Lonni in a different way. And I'm heterosexual," Deena shrugged with a smile.

"You do sound more sure of yourself."

"I am. I know my boundaries. Just had to let all the possibilities sift down. We can learn to love each other as friends, and as parents and work out a day-to-day relationship to raise Kelsey. Eventually, we'll have to learn to allow others into the mix as we develop new romantic relationships." Deena's eyes gleamed.

"*Is* there someone?" Mia asked suddenly.

"Maybe. At the party, I met an interesting guy," Deena smiled.

"OOOO, that's good! Who is he? Did I meet him?"

"The reporter, Ira. We've already been out a couple times. He's *fun*."

"Fun?"

"Yeah. So much FUN." Deena took a large bite of a sugary donut and smiled.

Mia grinned. "Good for you!"

Deena checked her phone. "Oh, sorry! I'd love to talk longer, but I'm pressed for time. I have to meet up with someone to turn over keys. Come with me. We can visit on the way." Deena stood up and started for the door.

"Ehhh, okay I guess," Mia tagged along behind.

Deena drove up to a house on 24th Street in Ballard, and parked at the curb.

"This looks nice."

"Come in with me."

"Is it okay?" Mia glanced uncertainly at the house.

"Sure. Sorry I rushed you. I hate to be late. I'd rather be early and wait around. Besides, it's a really cute house. You should see it!"

"Is it a rental?"

Deena glanced at Mia. "No, it was a short sale."

"Ohhh," Mia sighed. "Too bad. I like the neighborhood. And the house doesn't look too big; I might've been able to afford the rent."

They went up several steps from the street and followed the walk. Deena unlocked the door to an enclosed porch on the side of the house, and they stepped inside.

"I love this porch. It's perfect for the climate. You could take off your wet coat and boots. And you could sit out here in bad weather and just watch it rain. Or keep a bike or two out here, maybe have some plants…"

"Yeah. All good things."

"Ohhh," Mia cooed. "The kitchen is updated. Love the granite. Oh, my gosh, how pretty! Mind if I check out the other rooms?"

"Look around."

Mia wandered to the back of the house.

Footsteps were soon on the porch.

Mia rushed back toward the kitchen. "Oh, gosh. Sorry. Can I sneak out the front?"

"Too late." Deena turned and smiled at a man coming in the kitchen door.

Mia stared. She looked at Deena. Back at him.

"The new owner," Deena said.

"Gerald?" Mia gasped.

He smiled, face lighting like a lamp.

"How?"

"First time homebuyer loan for servicemen, years of living cheaply and saving."

Deena was laughing silently.

"Y' really like the house?"

"Yes," Mia smiled.

"Not far to Adams Elementary."

"That's good."

Gerald nodded.

"I need to run!" Deena said suddenly, and gave Mia a quick hug.

"Oh. I guess I can catch a ride with Gerald?"

He nodded, shook hands with Deena. "Thanks again."

"Like the house a lot?"

"This is so cute. Did it come with ppliances?"

"It did." Gerald went to the refrigerator, and brought out two iced coffees. They sat on stools at the bar, clinked the plastic cups together, smiled, and drank. Gerald pulled out his phone and glanced at it. "Got a message. Look at this." He thrust the phone toward her. "Push play."

Mia pushed the arrow.

Joyce was sitting and cross-stitching. Her head raised, eyes level with the camera. She held up the canvas. Words on it said, "YES. Most definitely, YES!"

"Watch the next video," Gerald said.

Mia watched: the clip was Marisol and Benito holding pictures with double rainbows over a house. Then one by one, family and friends in the marketplace in San Bartolome Quialana stepped up behind and nodded with smiles.

In another video: Rosalia and Javier were sitting on the hand carved bench on the upstairs deck of their house in Puerto Escondido. They smiled and said, "We say yes."

And in another, blue-green water like a jewel shined. The camera turned toward the deck of a boat, Angelo and Maggie looked at each other and said, "We say yes."

Next clip, Angelina's eyes stared coldly into the lens.

Mia's face clouded.

Gerald pointed and rolled his finger—motioning for her to keep watching.

Finally, Angelina spoke—her voice as cool as her look—"A woman must choose her life carefully."

"Ohhh, Grandmother," Mia groaned.

"A good man and a good woman can make a good life. YES?" Angelina's eyes softened with a smile, "I say, YES."

Mia stared at Gerald.

"Say y'll live here, love here with me, Mia."

She nodded. "I say yes, to whatever comes."

His hand opened—showing two bands with white gold on one side, yellow gold on the other, meeting in a gentle wave at center. The smallest band sparkled with diamonds along the wave. "Share the light with me, Mia? Marry me?"

She drew a long breath. And then words fell from her mouth, "I say yes. Yes to golden sun to warm us. Yes to silver moon to watch over our sleep." Mia opened her hands, "Yes to catching rain, and growing a life together."

After moving all weekend, Mia slept late on Martin Luther King Day. She wandered out to the living room strewn with boxes.

"Making progress," Gerald said looking up from unpacking.

"Ugh," she sighed. "I feel like a whale. No, worse! A barking sea lion. I'll look terrible."

His eyes were soft on her face, "No."

"Might take a while to get ready."

"We have time."

They had lunch out in Ballard, shopped for a few items needed for the house, then drove to Golden Gardens Park. They got out and walked a quarter mile on a trail from the parking area to the northern end of a loop at the wetlands.

"This is so pretty." Mia looked west to Puget Sound and the Olympic Mountains.

"Hoped y'd like it," he smiled.

A woman carrying an umbrella approached. "Gerald, Mia?"

"Leah?"

"Yes. Shall we chat about what you want to say?"

"Wrote something." Gerald handed her a paper.

"You did?"

He nodded to Mia. "Y' mind?"

"No," she said pulling paper from her pocket. "I wrote something, too."

"Want to read to each other, see how it sounds together? Gerald first, then Mia?"

"If you can coordinate, let's be surprised," he replied.

"Sure," Leah said, taking the papers to look over.

They waited at the water's edge. The sky was white and overcast, the water cool grey-blue.

A light breeze flapped at the edge of Mia's trench coat showing a peek of her new red dress. She looked down at her black rubber boots. "I'm not so fetching! But *you* look good. I love your hair down. The ethnic design on your coat suits you. And the colors are stunning."

"Old Pendleton Woolen Mill."

"I love your corduroys. And the red shirt is perfect."

"We match. How'd that happen?"

"Keen minds think alike," she chuckled. "OH! I almost forgot." Her hands sunk deep into her pocket and drew out two lengths of satiny fabric. "One gold, one silver," Mia said smiling, shaking the bell at the end of each as she tied the ribbons around their necks. "Little jinglings for music."

He smiled. "Brought y' something." He pulled a plastic bag from his pocket and gently removed a white bloom.

"White camellia," she breathed. "I saw some at the Quarryhill Botanical Garden in California where I took the children. We saw so many beautiful flowers there!"

He tucked the bloom into a narrow braid in her hair. "Bought a bush for the yard. Also bought a Himalayan blue poppy. Hard to raise, hope it does well."

"Oh," Mia sighed. "I saw those delicate blue flowers at Quarryhill also. How did you know?"

"Y' must've mentioned it."

"No, I'm sure I didn't." But she smiled up at him.

"Y' look perfect."

"I'm ready," Leah called, "if you are."

They stood on a damp beach. The sun was setting, turning the sky pink. Grasses waved in a breeze. Boats with colorful sails moved silently across the water.

"Only one problem," Leah said. "I was planning to begin with, 'By the water, with earth and sky as witness…'"

"Uh, oh!" They laughed. "We are a little early."

Passersby on the trail were enlisted to stand by.

Leah began, "Today, January 19, 2009 is a lucky day. January is the first month of our year. In Chinese culture, number one may represent a beginning, creation. The year is 2009. It is said of number two: good things come in pairs—like two of you.

Zero is associated with money. Maybe two zeroes will be double the money!"

They laughed.

"Nine has auspicious meaning: long lasting. It is often a number chosen for weddings. Gerald and Mia, you have chosen this one day, in all of time, to mark your commitment to each other. Interestingly, you are both dressed in red. Red is a color of joy. And it is with joy, I invite you to join hands."

Mia smiled up at Gerald and placed her hands in his.

His dark eyes looked down into her lighter brown eyes.

She smiled.

Leah said, "These are the words Gerald has written:

'I found you.
You are a gift.
You fell into my arms.
You rescued me from loneliness and solitary pursuits.
Your touch filled me with new energy.
Let me show thanks to you every day of our lives.
You have my heart.
Be my love forever, my wife, Mia.'"

Tears slid down Mia's cheeks.

"Mia, these are the words you have written for Gerald:

'You found me in the darkness.
You lit the way.
I found peace in your arms.
You shared your heart and home and all you had.
You filled me with new life.

Let me give thanks to you for all of our lives.
Let me show you what love we can grow.
Say you will be my honey man, today and every day.
Be my husband, my dear man, Gerald.'"

Gerald nodded, smiling, his eyes wet and soft on Mia's face.

Leah placed a ring in his hand.

He slipped it on Mia's finger and said, "I marry you. We grow together. We are united in joy."

Leah gave Mia a ring.

Mia slipped it onto Gerald's finger and said, "I marry you. We grow together. We are united in joy."

"By the power granted me by the State of Washington, I pronounce you married."

Gerald cupped Mia's face in his hands and kissed her gently. Then she wrapped her arms around his neck and kissed him with every passion.

Loud applause sounded.

They looked around to see a crowd of smiling faces had gathered. They laughed, kissed again, and signed their names to the documents.

Gerald held up the pen. "Witnesses?"

"ME!" Someone pushed through the crowd. "Didn't think you could get married without me, did you?" Deena smiled and signed.

A man stepped forward.

Gerald grinned and shook hands with him. "Mia, this is Leo, my coworker."

She held out her hand.

"Congratulations." He kissed her on the cheek. "Allow me the privilege of signing as witness."

More applause sounded.

Several individuals stepped forward to get contact information for sending video clips and photos of the ceremony they captured on their phones.

The crowd dispersed.

Leah refused the payment Mia and Gerald offered. "Truly my joy! Every day of your long marriage you will be doing me great honor, and honoring yourselves." She hugged each of them. "Congratulations!"

The sun was nearly down. The Olympic Mountains covered in snow stood like gleaming white wedding witnesses.

Gerald and Mia were alone by the water.

"Shall we go home, wife."

"Yes," she sighed, "There's no other place I'd rather be."

Two weeks later, Mia woke in a pool of sweat. As she sat up, her arm bumped Gerald.

He stirred awake.

"I was dreaming. Floating in a canoe. You were paddling. We were gliding over silken water…"

"Nice," he yawned.

"It was, until water was soaking our feet. I thought we were sinking. I said, "Gerald, paddle faster! I don't want to be wet and late.' Then I woke, and realized, I *am* wet! I think my water broke!"

"Okay." Gerald got out of bed, walked around, and helped her up. While Mia was in the bathroom changing, he made coffee, and turned the radio to an oldies station.

She joined him in the kitchen. Her hand skimmed the countertop as if feeling the coolness.

"Better make some calls."

Reaching her arms around his middle, she looked up at him and whispered, "We're having our baby."

He brushed her cheek with his hand.

Her head rested on his chest, her ear pressed against him. "I hear your heart. It calms me. You settle me. How do you do that?"

He smiled with his eyes—deep brown and warming.

"EHHH!" she gasped. "Oh, my GOSH! Was that a labor pain? THAT did not feel good!"

"Better make those calls."

A short time later, they went to the hospital. Labor continued through the night and into the morning. The baby arrived at 12:23 P.M.

Mia laughed, "Look at all the hair!"

Gerald kissed Mia's cheek, and the fat little hands of the baby. "Boy needs a name."

"His eyes are so dark. He looks wise. Kingly. The names we were considering don't seem to fit him."

"How about, Peyton? Means royal or regal."

"Peyton? Peyton Alexander?" Mia stared down at the little face, the dark eyes looking back. "Nooo," she sighed. "That's not his name."

Outside the hospital window, a brief clearing brought sun shining into the room.

"Peyton Alberto?" Gerald suggested.

"What does Albert mean?"

"Bright."

"That's our son, Peyton Alberto. The light of our lives."

Waterfall

A procession wove through the streets. They passed by the cathedral with flower window above heavy wooden doors. A priest in the open doorway nodded, and smiled.

Throughout San Bartolome Quialana, flowers were tied to posts and gates and sills. At each house, women and girls dressed in bright skirts and blouses, men and boys in colorful collared shirts joined the procession.

A mariachi band trailed and played their instruments with great enthusiasm.

Rosalia wore a dark pink *huipile*, a traditional dress covered in bright embroidery: fuchsia flowers, green vines, yellow canaries, small pink roses. Ribbons and flowers matching her dress were tied in her hair and on the straps of her sandals.

Abuelita Inez and Mia flanked Rosalia—Inez wearing a dress of brilliant blue with giant red flowers and exotic birds, Mia dressed in bright gold like the center of the flower pinned in her hair.

Gerald walked beside Mia. He wore a traditional styled shirt, *guayabera*, in crimson.

Javier's green *guayabera* was covered in trees and birds and other wildlife embroidered by Rosalia.

Baby Peyton was dressed in white.

Marisol wore a plaid dress with lace insets. Satin ribbons were woven into her braided hair.

Benito and other boys dressed in colorful shirts ran laughing alongside the group.

The gates of the family compound were thrown open. Bright paint coated the walls of the residences and pots of blooming flowers were in abundance. A waterfall constructed of tipping black pots transferred water from one pot to another with loud bubbling sounds.

The villagers squeezed into the courtyard where a large gazebo had been built of tree limbs from the old *ahuehuete*.

Javier and Rosalia, Gerald and Mia stood beneath the gazebo. Sitting in a chair at the side, *Abuelita* Inez cradled Peyton who slept in her arms.

The officiate conducted a brief ceremony with vows for each couple.

Marisol mounted a stool and draped a length of cording, *el lazo*, in figure eight wraps around the shoulders of each couple to symbolize their unity. Her proud smile brought tears to many eyes looking on.

The couples each lit a unity candle, and recited a prayer written on crisp paper to be framed later as reminders.

"Father sun, look down on us with favor.
Mother earth, nourish us so we may live in love
and do your good.

Sister Moon, shine softly on us so we may look at each other
with unfading appreciation.
Brother star, light our path so we may never lose our way.
Let the joy of this day rain down on us when we are parched,
soften our hard edges, melt us together as one.
Virgen, smile down on us with kindness
so our words will always be sweet."

At the close of the ceremony, guests on each side of Rosalia and Javier removed their lasso. As Rosalia turned to accept the lasso, she stared at the wrinkled faces of the couple, and gasped, "*AY, DIOS*!"

The old woman and man from San Bartolo Coyotepec, relatives of Mano, only smiled and shared a look with Mia who nodded with glistening eyes.

Another couple flanking Mia and Gerald stepped up to remove *el lazo* from their shoulders.

Mia turned and nearly yelled in surprise, "Papa! Maggie! Oh, my goodness! I am thrilled beyond belief. Gerald, did you do this?" She hugged each one and hugged Gerald and hugged her mother and Javier.

"Hold it!" A woman in the crowd stepped forward. "Didn't think you could get married a second time without me at the ceremony, did you?"

"JOYCE!" Mia laughed. "You came back to Mexico and to see San Bartolome Quialana! Look, I'm wearing the rainbow moonstones!"

"You do look glorious! But I must have a close look at your beautiful baby!"

Peyton was passed to Joyce's waiting arms.

"He's wearing the gown given to you by the couple in San Bartolo Coyotepec!"

"Yes! They're here, too! *Tia* Carlita and *Tio* Leon—aunt and uncle to my father, Mano. Isn't my life amazing?"

"Yes, most definitely, YES."

Mia looked around for the source of the voice.

The crowd parted.

"OH, MY GOSH! Grandmother Angelina!" Mia exclaimed. "This is the most wonderful day of my life! Thank you, *Virgen*! Everyone I love is here; I have a big family at last! I am so blessed. Thank you!"

Every dream is you
Every prayer is you
Every praise is you
My heart
My love
My miracle
My family

Attractions

Villas Carrizalillo
Avenue Carrizalillo NO125
Puerto Escondido, Oaxaca
52 552-789-5912

Bold Bodacious Jewelry
AnnaMariah Nau
703-763-1655
www.boldbodaciousjewelry.com

Manzanillo Beach
Playa Puerto Angelito
Puerto Escondido, Oaxaca

Mercado Benito Juarez
Puerto Escondido, Oaxaca

Bahias de Huatulco
50 miles East of Pochutla
Oaxaca, Mexico

Hospital General
Puerto Escondido, Oaxaca

Playa Zicatela
Puerto Escondido, Oaxaca

Catedral San Bartolo Coyotepec
Oaxaca, Mexico
Arbol de Santa Maria Del Tule
Federal Hwy 190 East of Oaxaca City

Las Mariposas B & B & Apts.
Pino Suarez, City Center
Oaxaca, Mexico
52 951-515-5854

Oaxaca City Cemetery
Panteon General
Oaxaca City, Oaxaca

Amate Books
Macedorio Alcala 307-2
Colonia Centro
Oaxaca, Oaxaca 68000
951-516-6960

Templo de Santo Domingo de Guzman
Alcala and Cinco de Mayo Streets
Oaxaca, Oaxaca

Monte Alban
Carretera Oaxaca-Monte Alban
Monte Alban, Oaxaca
52 951-516-1215

Doña Rosa
Benito Juarez #24
San Bartolo Coyotepec, Oaxaca
955-551-0011

Virgen de Asuncion
Tlacolula de Matomoros,
Oaxaca, Mexico
http://oaxaca-travel.com

San Bartolome Quialana
Oaxaca, Mexico

Hierve de Agua
80 KM from Oaxaca City
Off Hwy 179
www.visitmexico.com/en/waterfalls-and-ecotourism

Mitla
44 KM from Oaxaca City
Oaxaca, Mexico

Museo Textil de Oaxaca
Hidalgo 917
Centro Historico
68000 Oaxaca, Mexico
+52 951 501 1104
www.museotextiloaxaca.org.mx/

Clinica Hospital Carmen
Abasalo 215 (Oaxaca Centro)
Oaxaca de Juarez, Oaxaca
68000 Mexico

El Aldoquin
Puerto Escondido, Oaxaca

Pasteleria Reyzi
Hidalgo 71980
Puerto Escondido, Oaxaca
Facebook.com

Mario's Pizzaland
Avenida Gasga
Puerto Escondido, Oaxaca
(954)582-0570

Bay Landing Hotel
1550 Old Bayshore Hwy
Burlingame, CA 94010
650-259-9000
www.baylandinghotel.com

San Francisco Zoo
1 Zoo Road
San Francisco, CA 94132
415-753-9080
www.sfzoo.org

Golden Gate Bridge
San Francisco, CA 94129
415-921-5858
goldengatebridge.org

City of Petaluma, CA
cityofpetaluma.net

Bouverie Preserve
13935 Sonoma Hwy
Glen Ellen, CA 95442
www.egret.org

Quarryhill Botanical Garden
12841 Hwy 12
Glen Ellen, CA 95442
707-996-3166
quarryhillbg.org

Sorosis Park (North Wasco County Parks & Rec)
350 East Scenic Drive
The Dalles, OR 97058
(541-296-9533)

Elephant Bar and Grill
1600 Old Bayshore Hwy
Burlingame, CA 94010
650-259-9585
www.elephantbar.com

Port of Seattle
Sea-Tac Airport
Seattle, Washington
www.portseattle.org/sea-tac

Seattle Children's Hospital
4800 Sand Point Way NE
Seattle, Washington 98105
206 987-2000

Washington Park Arboretum
2300 Arboretum Dr. E.
Seattle, Washington 98112
(206)543-8800

MOHAI - Museum of History and Industry
860 Terry Avenue
Seattle, Washington 98109
206 324-1126

Spaceneedle
400 Broad Street
Seattle, WA 98109
206-905-2100
www.spaceneedle.com

Tower of the Americas
600 HemisFair Park
San Antonio, TX 78205
210-223-3101

Mukilteo Ferry
614 Front Street
Mukilteo, WA 98204
www.wsdot.wa.gov./ferries

Langley Chamber of Commerce—Whidbey Island
208 Anthes Avenue
Langley, WA 98260
360-221-6765
www.visitlangley.com

Star Store Grocery
201 1st Street
Langley, WA 98260
360-221-5222
www.starstorewhidbey.com

Prima Bistro
201 1/2 1st Street
Langley, WA 98260
360-221-4060
www.primabistro.com

Sassy Siren
109 Fist Street
Langley, WA 98260
360-221-7080

Langley Clock & Gallery
Down the Lane at 220 2nd Street
PO Box 888
Langley, WA 98260
360-221-3422

Pike Place Market
1st Ave & Pike Street
Seattle, WA 98101
www.pikestreetmarket.org

Steelhead Diner
95 Pine Street
Seattle, WA 98101
206-625-0129
www.steelheaddiner.com

The Moore Theater
1932 2nd Avenue
Seattle, Washington 98101
(206)467-5510
Stgpresents.org/moore/

Piroshky Piroshky
1908 Pike Place
Seattle, WA 98101
206-441-6068
www.piroshkybakery.com

Original Starbucks
Pike Place Market
1st & Pike Street
Seattle, WA 98101
www.starbucks.com

TM Dessert Works
6116 Phinney Avenue N
Phinney, WA 98103
206-789-5765
tmdessertworks.com

Marriott Residence Hotel Down town
800 Fairview Avenue N
Seattle, WA 98109
206-624-6000

Portland International Airport
7000 NE Airport Way
Portland, OR 97218
503-460-4234
www.pdx.com

Lillian Pitt
www.lillianpitt.com

City of Cascade Locks
140 SW WaNaPa
Cascade Locks, OR 97014
541-374-8484
www.cascade-locks.or.us

Columbia Gorge Sternwheeler
355 WaNaPa
Cascade Locks, OR 97014
541-374-8427
www.portlandspirit.com

Eastwind Drive In
395 WaNaPa
Cascade Locks, OR 97014
541 374 8380

Lorang Fine Art & Gorge-ous Gifts
360 SW WaNaPa
Cascade Locks, OR 97014
541-374-8007
www.lorangfineart.com

Multnomah Falls Lodge
50000 East Historic Columbia River Hwy
503-695-2376
www.multnomahfallslodge.com

Baldwin Saloon
205 Court Street
The Dalles, OR 97058
541-296-5666
www.baldwinsaloon.com

The Dalles Lock and Dam
US Army Corps of Engineers
541-506-7819
www.nwp.usace.army.mil/locations

Klindt's Booksellers
315 East 2nd Street
The Dalles, OR 97058
541-296-3355
www.klindtsbooks.com

Old St. Peter's Landmark
405 Lincoln
The Dalles, OR
541-296-5686
www.oldstpeterslandmark.com

Rufus Market
SE 1st
Rufus, OR 97050
Celilo Villge
I-84 Columbia River East of The Dalles

Sam Hill Memorial Bridge
US 97 & I-84 Biggs Junction
Columbia River near Maryhill

Stonehenge War Memorial
Maryhill, Washington
www.maryhillmuseum.org/stonehenge

Maryhill Museum of Art
35 Maryhill Museum Drive
Goldendale, WA 98620
509-773-3733
www.maryhillmuseum.org

City of Stevenson
7121 E. Loop Rd.
Stevenson, WA 98648
509-427-5970www.ci.stevenson.wa.us

Bridge of the Gods
Port of Cascade Locks
355 WaPaNa Street
Cascade Locks, OR 97014
541-374-8619
www.portofcascadelocks.org/bridge

Bonneville Lock and Dam
Columbia River
(E of Vancouver, WA)
OR 541-374-8820
WA 509-427-4281
www.nwpusace.army.mil/op/b/

Basilica Virgen de Guadalupe
Plaza de las Americas
Villa de Gusta
Gustano A. Madero
07050 Ciudad de Mexico
Distrito Federal, Mexico
+52 55 5118 0500
www.virgen deguadalupe.mx

Kens Market
7231 Greenwood Ave N
Seattle, WA 98103
206-784-3470
www.kensmarket.com

Francine Seders Gallery
6701 Greenwood Ave
Seattle, WA 98103
206-782-0355
www.sedersgallery.com

Urban Earth Nursery
1051 N. 35th
Seattle, WA 98103
206-632-1760
FB Urban Earth Nursery

Cuigini Café
5306 Ballard Ave NW
Seattle, WA 98107
206-784-2576

Golden Gardens Park
8498 Seaview PL NW
Seattle, WA 98117
206-684-4075
www.seattlegov/parks/park

Accuracy of information is attempted, not guaranteed

Visit these wonderful places

Follow a Mending Stone and
Catching Rain
Itinerary

Enjoy the adventure!

Discussion Questions

1. What part does intuition play in the plot?

2. Do you see growth in Mia?

3. How does the environment in Mexico influence Mia?

4. What do you find surprising or shocking?

5. Do you think Mia will continue writing? Or was it only part of her processing—a necessary step in her evolving thoughts and healing?

6. Did you enjoy the travel features?

7. What is your favorite part of the story?

8. Who do you think is the wisest character?

9. Who is your favorite character? Why?

10. Do you believe in fate? Divine intervention? Prayer?

Please visit

www.mendingstone.com

to leave comments and buy books!

About the Author

If I am not writing, you might find me walking my dogs, or with family and friends soaking in the beauty of nature. With wide spaces of time and landscape to explore, I am captivated by color and form. Natural elements inform my writing and varied creative endeavors!

Catching Rain is the sequel to ***Mending Stone***, my first novel. These stories came to me like a gift filling my life with interest and surprise. I hope you enjoyed the journey! Thank you for reading!

Sharon Duerst

If you like

Mending Stone

and

Catching Rain

Don't be shy

Share

your comments on Twitter, Facebook,
Goodreads, Google, Amazon

Follow

Mending Stone and Catching Rain

boards on Sharon Duerst Pinterest

Like the ***Mending Stone*** video on
Youtube

Snap photos of yourself reading

Mending Stone and Catching Rain

Include where you live and what you love about the stories!

Share with other fans on social media!

Ask your libraries and favorite bookstores to carry these books!

Great stories fill us with a sense of joy and wonder!

Spread the sweetness!

Read more from ***Sharon Duerst*** at

www.mendingstone.com

Mending Stone and Other Writing Wonders

Thank you for reading

Mending Stone

and

Catching Rain

www.ingramcontent.com/pod-product-compliance
Lightning Source LLC
LaVergne TN
LVHW010640110826
845149LV00014B/2896

9780985537821